OB[SCURE]

THE INFINITE SERIES: BOOK 2

NICOLE
CORINE DYER

MW00462234

Obscure
Copyright © 2016 by Nicole Corine Dyer.

Printed and bound in the United State of America

All rights reserved. Without limiting the rights under copyright reserved above, no part of this book may be reproduced or transmitted in any form or by any means, electronic or mechanical, including photocopying, recording, or by an information storage and retrieval system or otherwise without prior written permission of both the copyright owner and the above publisher of this book except in the case of brief quotations included in the case of reviews or other journalistic purposes.

All characters appearing in this adult fantasy are a work of fiction. Any references to historical events, real people, real places, characters, brands, media or incidents are either the product of the author's imagination or are used fictitiously. The author acknowledges the trademark status and trademark owners of various products referenced in the work of fiction, which have been used without permission. The publication/use of these trademarks is not authorized, associated with, or sponsored by the trademark owners.

Although the author has made every effort to ensure accuracy and completeness of information contained in this book, we assume no responsibility for errors, inaccuracies, omissions, or any inconstancy herein. Any slighting of people, places, or organizations is unintentional.

ISBN-10:0-9970212-2-5
ISBN-13:978-0-9970212-2-6

First Edition First Printing

Editing by Jennifer Tovar at Gypsy Heart Editing
Cover Design by Michelle Preast
Symbol Design by Adrian Aldaco
Formatting by Stacey Blake at Champagne Formats

DEDICATION

To the men and women that provide us with our freedom. I could never truly comprehend the hardships and danger you endure but without you, dreams such as mine would not be fulfilled.

PROLOGUE

RYAN KISSED JULIA PASSIONATELY as they laid in his bed. The cool ocean breeze tickled his bare skin and gave him chills up his spine. Julia shivered beneath him, but before he could offer her a blanket she moved her body closer to his.

He closed his eyes once more and when he opened them he stood in the middle of a throne room. Torches were the only source of light here and tapestries hung along the walls. A large table overflowing with food sat on a raised platform on the side of the room. Julia walked toward him dressed in a blue tunic and a lavishly bejeweled stola.

She walked up to him sensually and he almost fell to his knees to worship the goddess before him, but her hands did not reach out to him. It was as if she looked straight through him to someone else. Could she not see him? Was he invisible?

Ryan moved his mouth to speak and found he couldn't make a sound. Julia looked hungry, almost lustful and he felt his body grow hot at the thought of her against him.

She walked straight to him and he held out his hands to

her. She did not stop as she got closer though. She reached her hands out and they went directly through him.

Was he dead? A ghost that she could not see?

She walked right through him and he turned to find her embracing with Aden. He was dressed in a loose fitting white toga and sandals with a cocky glint in his eye. Ryan saw right through his façade. Not Julia though, she soaked up the attention. Aden pulled her into a tight embrace and they kissed.

Ryan wanted to scream yet his voice did not exist in this terrible daydream. He tried to escape this hellish reality, but the present still lingered in his brain and there was no blocking the truth.

Julia walked toward him with a dagger, which suddenly appeared in her hand. She thrust the dagger into his heart and twisted it all the while her eyes gleamed with excitement.

He snapped back to reality from his daydream, realizing the scene before him was just as worse. Julia was there, holding hands with Aden. His nightmare came true.

CHAPTER I

Ryan

THERE WAS A WAVE of anger that flushed over his body. Nothing could describe the intensity of his hatred toward Aden in that moment. Something was wrong, very wrong. Julia's hand in Aden's made his stomach churn. The very thought of that bastard's hands on her let alone having to see it outright made Ryan livid.

This was the last thing he expected to see when he got back from the Catacombs. The last he knew Julia had been missing and out of nowhere, here she was with Aden—kissing and acting as if she had never been held hostage.

It was wrong.

Ryan clenched his fists tightly. Any ounce of self-control he had was being used in this very moment. His eyes never once left Julia's. She looked hesitant and nervous. How could she do this to him?

After their conversation in the healer's quarters what he was witnessing made no sense. She loved him and he knew it. Never had she given any sign that she had any sort of infatuation with Aden. In fact, she seemed to hate him almost as much as he did.

Cato spoke and it pulled him out of his thoughts. The parlor room seemed to come back into focus around him and he was suddenly aware all eyes were on him. "How did you get away, Julia?" Cato asked.

She looked to her brother and smiled warmly. The tight bun in her hair was odd on her. She looked older and her demeanor was different. A warning went off in his head but how could he listen to that now? He wanted to kill Aden. The thought consumed him.

"Aden saved me." She smiled up at Aden and he kissed the top of her head.

"How?" Cato's voice was cautious and Ryan saw him glance in his direction.

Ryan studied her closer. She wore a tight black dress that hugged her curves and her heels were too high to be comfortable. She was sexy, but in a stripper sort of way. Everything about her attire was all wrong. *This is not Julia.*

"I went patrolling underground to find some clues about the Risen. I heard voices and followed them," Aden explained. "I saw them passing by with Julia and she looked so scared I could not help it, I had to save her."

Julia smiled up at Aden. "They tried to get me to join them. Fed me, bathed me, and dressed me. I refused and they started to bring me somewhere. Aden jumped out and fought three of them off. Then he threw me over his shoulder and

2

here we are."

"Okay am I the only one weirded out? Since when are you two all lovey-dovey?" Anna spoke up. She sounded puzzled and Ryan was happy she asked. He really wanted to know the answer as well.

"Just seeing him risk his life for me made me realize who truly cares about me. It put it in perspective that he would do anything for me." She smiled. "I owe my life to him."

Ryan was dumbfounded. Could this really be happening? Could she really feel this way toward him?

Maybe he ruined his chance with her. He never said how he felt and could he really expect her to wait for him? It just did not make sense that she would leave him high and dry so easily after everything they had been through.

His eyes left the lovesick face of Julia and drifted to Aden. He had the nerve to stare at Ryan with a smug look on his face. His heart seemed to jump out of his chest with adrenaline and his anger started to rise once more.

"Problem, Ryan?" Aden asked. He looked amused at Ryan's obvious frustration.

"Yes," he muttered, "you."

"What did he do?" Julia looked lost. "He saved me, Ryan."

"Let's just say I don't trust a damn thing he says."

Julia laughed. "Oh really? So does that mean I am lying as well?"

"I don't know what to think about you anymore, Julia." Ryan looked her up and down. "You seem pretty comfortable in that trashy attire though."

Aden let go of Julia, whose mouth had dropped, and lunged toward Ryan, his fist was balled. "What did you say?"

Ryan stood his ground. "I said it looks like your new little squeeze is comfortable looking like a hooker. You two make a perfect couple now. You're both trash."

Aden punched Ryan in the face. This is what he waited for. He wanted a reason to fight Aden. It was Julia's choice to be with Aden, how could he get mad about that? But getting punched in the face seemed as legitimate a reason to fight.

Ryan connected with the side of Aden's jaw and much to his amusement he fell to the ground. Ryan grabbed him by the shirt and pulled him back to standing. "Oh, I'm sorry. Let me help you up." Ryan slammed his fist into Aden's stomach and when he buckled over Ryan thrust his knee up into Aden's face.

Aden fell once more and scurried to get up. Fists were thrown back and forth. He did not care about anything in that moment. Adrenaline pumped so fast through him that he did not notice any pain. He wanted to see Aden's limp body lying facedown on the floor.

He was in one state of mind and that was to kill Aden. He hated him, despised him and was simultaneously jealous of him.

He felt someone hit him from behind and automatically swung his fist around to get them off. His heart dropped when he saw Julia fall to the floor and clutching her cheek. What did he just do?

Their fight immediately ended and Aden crawled over to Julia's side. Ryan reached out to help her. Hell, even just to sooth her, but what could he do? Never had he hated himself more than this moment.

"Don't touch me," she backed away from him. Tears wet

her face and Aden held her tightly to him.

"Julia." His voice cracked and he saw pure hatred in her eyes. "I'm sor—"

"Don't fucking talk to her Ryan," Aden spat.

He was in disbelief at what he had done. He'd hit her with his full force, holding nothing back.

Cato grabbed Ryan's vest and shoved him toward the men's dormitories. "Get the hell out of here Ryan before I kill you myself."

"I-I didn't know," Ryan fumbled with his words. "I didn't know."

"Get out of here!" Cato yelled at him.

Ryan glanced around the room and no one would look at him. The air was heavy and he never felt more alone. This was unforgiveable. Not even Damian caught his eye.

He turned and dejectedly walked to his room. Every step felt heavy and his body started to grow weak from the mental strain. Nothing felt right anymore. He had just hit someone he loves, and she hated him for it. He hated himself for it.

Ryan reached his room and did not even bother to close the door. He looked at all of his belongings and the urge to destroy it all came over him. He flipped his desk over and the sounds of breaking objects filled the room. The wooden chair was next as he smashed it against his tall mirror causing shattered pieces to trickle to the ground.

He broke anything he could get his hands on. Things were thrown around and he made holes in the walls. Everything in his path needed to be destroyed. He hated it all. His life. This life. It was all pointless.

After awhile his adrenaline died down and he stopped

his rampage. His heart began to even its pace and his knuckles throbbed in pain. He deserved it. He deserved even more though.

Much more.

In his state of mind there was only one solution and he grabbed a gun off of his wall. Smith and Wesson, model 29. This would undeniably get the job done.

He found one bullet and slipped it into the chamber. His heart did not race. He was not frightened. Death seemed a viable punishment.

There was no way he could live with what he just did to Julia nor did he want to. He sat on the edge of his bed and looked out the window.

His grip on the pistol was loose as he closed his eyes and he listened to the waves crash against the shore in the early morning light. A gentle breeze blew through the open window and danced across his skin. It was a peaceful moment, a perfect moment.

Ryan exhaled and placed the barrel against his temple. "I'm sorry." It was a plea to all those he had ever wronged.

CHAPTER II

Anna

J UST AS RYAN LEFT the room, Anna turned to glance up at
Damian. He looked shocked and disgusted. His helmet remained on and she tried to quietly take hers off. It did not
seem she would need it for awhile given what just happened
and she had no idea what to do with herself.

Cato pushed Aden out of the way, picked up his sister
and gently set her on the couch. A bruise was already forming
on her cheek and Anna could not help but stare at her. She
seemed so different. Anna felt like she had no idea who this
person was even though she barely knew her.

Cato delicately grabbed Julia's chin and tilted her face up
to analyze her cheek. He shook his head and Anna felt an instant disgust for Ryan. He'd hit her. He really hit her and left
without a word. *What a jerk.*

She wondered over and sat down on the couch opposite

of Julia. As she looked her up and down she was amazed how fine she looked besides the obvious mark on her face. Part of her was glad she'd come back from the Risen untouched, but the other part was suspicious. Why was she so unharmed when Ryan and Damian were mauled to the brink of death?

Julia's tears ceased and Cato looked on the verge of ripping someone apart. She had never seen him so enraged and it was pretty damn scary. Thankfully Mr. Silent stayed silent.

Damian joined her on the couch and put his hand on her knee. She looked up into his eyes and he gazed back at her this time. There was nothing to say, and even if there were it would be awkward after what had just happened.

"I'm going to kill him," Aden muttered.

Anna watched the scene unfold. Cato stood up and pushed Aden against the bookshelves causing a few to tumble to the floor with a soft thud. "Don't fucking touch him, Aden."

"Seriously? You're sticking up for the man who just assaulted your sister?" Aden was up and in Cato's face at this point. *Holy shit.*

"If anyone deserves to do something to Ryan it is me or Julia," Cato started. "I don't condone what he did, but I know he had no idea it was her."

"You've got to be kidding? You're not going to do anything?" Aden was shocked, quite frankly so was Anna.

"You saw the look on his face after he did it. He didn't mean to and I can guarantee he is going to punish himself for it," Cato said.

Julia sighed. "Agreed."

Aden's head almost snapped off his neck. "Julia, he struck you."

"I'm fully aware of that," she grumbled. "I know him and he would never do it on purpose. It was an accident."

"I cannot believe what I am hearing."

"Believe it and trust me, I will have a lot more than words to say to him," Cato added.

Anna had to admit, Ryan had looked like his childhood dog died or something. She suddenly felt worried about him. Ryan was never the sad or guilty type, at least from what she'd gathered about him.

"I'm going to go check on Ryan," she whispered to Damian. His eyes looked glazed over and when she spoke he seemed to snap back to reality.

"Okay, I'll come with you."

As they set out toward the male dormitories Cato called to them, "Where are you going?"

"To check on Ryan," Damian muttered.

"Are all of you insane?" Aden looked furious. "He just hit Julia and you are worrying about him?"

"If I know Ryan he is not in a good state of mind about it," Julia reasoned. "Please go check on him. I know he didn't mean to."

Anna nodded and felt like Julia was herself once again. Though part of her was surprised Julia was not going to talk to him herself. Not to mention what the hell she was doing with Aden? Anna did not know her well, but even she knew their relationship was odd.

Damian grabbed Anna's hand and they proceeded to Ryan's room slowly. "Why are you so upset with Ryan?"

Before they came back from the Catacombs, she could sense the tension between the two men. Something happened when she was trapped within the bone walls and it was not good. Damian seemed to hate Ryan and Ryan seemed depressed.

"I'm done with him," he said simply.

"Why?"

"He almost got you killed, Anna. Don't say it wasn't his fault. He had you come with us when I knew you shouldn't have."

Anna looked straight ahead and her annoyance built. "First off, I wanted to go. You are not my boss—you are my boyfriend. Second, he saved me down there and you should be thankful. He needs you, Damian."

He shook his head sadly. "He has never needed me. He has made that perfectly clear on many occasions."

"Are you kidding?" She laughed. "You are basically brothers. Please don't stay mad at him."

Damian groaned. "I love him, but I can't deal with it anymore. I feel like I am his father, constantly making sure he stays in line and doesn't make poor decisions. He no longer cares what he does or how dreadful it makes him look. I can't deal with it anymore."

"Then don't. Just be there for him." She understood Damian's point, but Ryan was pure good. He may mess up from time to time, but he didn't deserve to be depressed and alone. She could not explain why but she felt anxious to check on him. He'd looked worn and beaten down when he left.

"I'll try," Damian muttered.

Ahead of them loud crashes could be heard and she looked to Damian. All he managed to do was sigh and shrug. "I had a feeling he would destroy something."

He did not seem in a hurry, which made Anna nervous. *This cannot be normal. Why was he taking his time getting to Ryan?*

"He'll be fine," he assured her as if he'd read her mind. "He isn't going to do anything stupid."

They got to his open door and she looked inside. Ryan was on his bed, facing the window. She felt relieved that he had calmed down and Damian rolled his eyes. His room was absolutely destroyed.

Damian let go of her hand. "I'll go talk to him," he whispered and kissed her forehead.

She stayed standing in the doorway as Damian slowly made his way over to Ryan. He did not seem to notice they were there and sat still on the bed until he finally moved. He brought a gun up to his head and time seemed to slow down.

Damian ran toward the bed, Ryan's finger was on the trigger and Anna stood there in shock.

"I'm sorry," Ryan's voice was barely a whisper.

Damian grabbed Ryan's arm and a shot went off. Her hands bolted to her mouth and she stifled a scream.

"What the hell do you think you are doing?" Damian yelled, and smacked Ryan in the face. Anna felt relieved he'd made it in time, but grew nervous at Damian's reaction. Damian was always calm and now he was beyond any anger she had ever seen from him.

Ryan sat there, as if nothing had happened. He did not move or even look up at Damian. This day was by far the weirdest and most drama filled day in her life. Sleep was indeed needed.

Damian looked over to her and she cautiously made her

way over to the two. Ryan was like a statue and her concern for him only grew. The guy was seriously out of it.

She had to step over a large number of broken things lying all over the floor. Lamps, books and glass had fell victim to his wrath. It was like a tornado had passed through here.

Coming around to the other side of the room, she was able to see Ryan's face. He looked like he'd aged twenty years and had a blank stare that went nowhere. This guy was definitely checked out.

His hands rested on his thighs, the gun hung from Damian's hand and Anna felt sick. He really was about to kill himself. Legitimately almost committed suicide and they were milliseconds from being too late.

"Ryan." Damian glared at him but Ryan did not move an inch. "Ryan!"

Damian looked to Anna, his eyes were lost and helpless. She felt the urge to hug him and to reassure him Ryan would be fine but she really had no idea. This was not normal to her and she'd never had to deal with something like this.

"Ryan," she said softly. "Ryan, Julia is fine. She isn't mad at you. She knew it was an accident. I think it just freaked her out."

His mouth twitched when she said Julia's name. The mental stability of the man in front of her seemed shaky and she did not want to be here.

"Ryan," Damian tried again. His voice was softer yet still forceful this time and Ryan finally looked at him. Damian held up the gun. "Why would you do this?"

"I do nothing but ruin everyone around me," he mumbled. She felt a stabbing pain in her heart for Ryan. She could only imagine how Damian felt. It was sad and so unlike Ryan's personality to be this way.

"That's not true," Damian muttered. "Don't you think this is being a little overdramatic?"

"It's true, you said it yourself in the Catacombs." Ryan closed his eyes. "I hit Julia, Damian. I don't care what anyone says. That is not okay. It is not right and I should in no way, shape or form, be forgiven for it."

Damian tossed the gun to Anna and she fumbled to catch it. He crouched down to Ryan's eye level and stared at his best friend. Anna glanced down at the gun and shamefully found herself impressed with Ryan's choice of weapon. It was gorgeous and very powerful looking. Just like a gun in an old western movie but polished and shiny.

"Ryan." Damian gripped Ryan's arms. "Stop beating yourself up about everything. We all need you. The world literally depends on you and if you haven't noticed, I think Julia does too."

"Why?"

"She is obviously involved with Aden right now, which concerns me." Damian huffed. "Something is not right about that guy. After the conversation we heard him having with Caleb and Jesse ending up a traitor, it doesn't sit well with me. I don't care if Jesse said he isn't involved."

"Agreed, but that is her choice, Damian." Ryan opened his eyes and looked to Anna. She fidgeted with the gun nervously and his eyes moved to the sleek object. Was he thinking about shooting himself again?

"I can teach you to beat the Brahmastra, Damian," Ryan muttered, never taking his eyes off the gun. "Then I will do what I need to in order to protect you all."

"Stop," Damian growled.

"No, you stop," Ryan looked deep into Damian's eyes. "You are right. I ruined you. I ruin everything and I know this. I hurt women without care. I think about only myself and now I need to do what's best for everyone and cease to exist. I don't want to hurt any of you anymore."

Damian's grip on Ryan's arms seemed to tighten. Anna really did not want to be here right now. Not one bit. "I think I should go."

Neither one of them said a word so she set the gun on his bedside table and left the room. She was so glad to be out of that conversation. This new world of hers was suffocating her with constant thoughts of death.

She reached for the door handle to close it but was stopped by a hand pushing it back open. Julia looked up at her bashfully and put her finger to her lips. "I want to listen."

Anna gapped at her. Julia's face was swollen and bruised. "Are you okay?"

To her surprise Julia laughed. "Not the first time I have been punched in the face and it won't be the last."

"What are you doing here?"

"I wanted to check on Ryan." She shrugged. "Aden is furious of course and I know how this may look to you all."

"Yeah, it looks pretty damn shady, Julia—I'm not going to lie."

"I get it, but he saved me from the Risen, Anna. I can't explain it, but I feel as if he would do anything for me." Anna could see she truly believed this. "Ryan has always pushed me away and I can't wait for him anymore. I won't. It hurts to much."

Anna sighed. She completely understood even if she still hated the whole thing. Aden was a dick. "I guess. Just be careful with him. They don't trust him and neither do I."

"I can handle myself, believe me." She smiled. "Is he okay?"

Awkward. Should she tell her? "Well, no."

Julia's face fell. "What happened?"

"He umm," Anna shifted from side to side. This was not good. "He almost shot himself. Damian barely managed to get the gun in time."

Shock and worry raced across Julia's face. "I heard a noise but I didn't think it was a…"

Anna bit her lip and patted Julia awkwardly on the back. "Yeah."

"Excuse me," Julia groaned and pushed her way into Ryan's room.

Oh shit.

"This is certainly my cue to leave," Anna mumbled and made her way to her room, away from the drama.

Julia

"What in the hell do you think you are doing?" Julia screamed as she barged into Ryan's room.

She'd had enough of his drama and infantile behavior. His behavior was ridiculous and she could not stand it anymore.

15

Ryan quickly turned around on his bed gapping at her. It gave her satisfaction to see him look so guilty. Damian stood up with an uncomfortable look on his face that gave her an odd sense of pleasure.

"Should I leave?" Damian asked.

"Yes!" she answered.

"No," Ryan pleaded to Damian.

She glared at Damian, daring him to defy her. Her anger level was at a pinnacle and Ryan was going to get a piece of her mind whether he liked it or not.

"Yeah, sorry Ryan, but she's scaring the hell out of me." Damian shuffled around Julia and toward the door. "Don't kill each other."

"Not funny," she growled.

"Wasn't a joke," Damian mumbled as he closed the door gently behind him.

Julia turned her attention back to an awestruck Ryan, his gun on the table next to his bed. She crossed her arm and planted her feet. She meant business.

"What in the hell were you thinking?"

"I—"

"Don't interrupt me," she snapped. "How could you do that? Do you not realize how it would effect the people who love you?"

"That's—"

"I am not done! That is the most single handedly selfish thing anyone could do. Why the hell would you do this?" She felt her pulse quicken and her cheeks flushed when he said nothing. "Well, answer me!"

"Are you going to interrupt me again?" he grumbled.

She glared. "Answer me. Now."

"That is exactly why I tried to do this, Julia. To save the people I love from me."

Julia rolled her eyes and sat on his bed by him. "Why would we need to be saved from you, Ryan?"

"Besides what I just did to you?" He looked at her cheek and she flushed. "Damian is sick of me, I hurt women continuously. I think my existence has run its course."

"I am fine. It's not like I haven't been hit before and killing yourself over it is a little extreme. As far as Damian is concerned, well, that man needs you like he needs air to breath." She sighed and picked the gun up off of his side table. As she opened the barrel she noticed no bullets inside.

Ryan took the gun from her—his fingers brushed her hand and her stomach flipped at his touch. How could he still do this to her?

"I will never forgive myself for hitting you and I hope you will never forgive it." He looked so desolate, so unlike Ryan. She pitied him. "I'm in love with you Julia."

Her world stopped in an instant. He loved her. This should make her feel happy. Why didn't she feel happy? This was what she wanted from him.

Aden. Aden was hers now. However, something inside of her felt wrong about it. Her head started to hurt.

"I don't know what to say."

"You don't need to say anything." Ryan croaked. His hands gripped the gun tightly and she saw his knuckles turn white. "I messed up with you. I should have told you how I felt earlier. I ruined my chances of ever calling you mine."

She wanted to tell him she felt the same. She loved him

with all her heart. *No.* She loved Aden. Just Aden.

"Look," she started. "I know we had a little fling, but that's all it was. I don't think you really love me, Ryan. I think you are just used to getting easy girls and I was a challenge. That's all."

To her surprise, he smirked and dropped the gun to the floor. She longed to reach out and make him feel better. His short hair needed her hands to touch it yet she could not do it.

"I am one hundred percent in love with you. Challenge or no challenge, it doesn't change that fact."

Her heart flipped. "I don't love you, Ryan."

Why did she say that? She loves him. Loved him. Loves Aden. What was going on with her?

"I see that now," he grumbled and put his head in his hands. "I know this sounds idiotic given what just happened, but if he hurts you in anyway, I will kill him."

"I know."

Ryan looked up into her eyes. He hesitantly reached out to her cheek and gently ran his fingers along her face. "I'm so sorry," he whispered.

Her eyes fluttered. She wanted to lean into his touch. "I know."

"I wish I could kiss you, Julia."

"I know."

She felt the bed shift under her and his lips found hers. For a split second she leaned into him until her mind flared in warning. She pulled away and grasped her head as her brain throbbed in pain. "I can't."

"Julia, please." He sounded so heartbroken.

"No." She glared at him. He looked like he was in so much

pain but she could not help her words. "I don't love you, Ryan. I love Aden and I am with him. Please stop or I will tell him what you just did."

He looked defeated. He lay back on his bed and covered his face with his hands. Ryan was the biggest ticking time bomb she knew and part of her felt nervous being around him right now.

"That's truly how you feel?" Ryan asked. "You have no feelings for me at all and only want Aden now? You want me to leave you alone?"

Although he could not see her through his bloodied hands, she nodded. "Yes."

"Okay." He uttered.

He pushed himself up from his bed making his way out to the balcony and leaned over the railing. Part of her was worried he would jump over the railing while the other part of her was complimenting him on how handsome he looked in his gear, until it hit her. "Why are you in your gear?"

He didn't turn to face her, merely said, "We went to Germany to see if we could help out some of the civilians there. It's been in a panic since they denounced all religion."

Her eyebrows scrunched up. "Really?"

"Yes," he said shortly.

"Why did Anna go?"

"She wanted to." He turned toward her and leaned his back against the wall of the balcony. "Please leave."

"Why?"

"I can't be around you right now, Julia."

"Did I do something?" Her heart hurt, not only for him but also for herself. Why were her feelings being torn like this?

Shouldn't she be perfectly fine leaving him alone?

"No." He snapped. "I really want to make love to you right now and I can't. I want to be as close as I can to you. Part of me thought you were dead when they took you. I feared they were hurting you like they did me and now here you are, alive and well and I can't even touch you."

What could she possibly say to that? He was worried about her but went on a mission. Yet here he was, opening up to her like she always wanted and she felt nothing.

Why did she feel nothing?

"I'm sorry, Ryan," it was all she could say at this point.

"Don't be. I ruined my chance with you. I will never stop loving you, Julia, but I can't be around you. You have no idea how much I want to be close to you right now." He looked at his feet and closed his eyes. "I *need* to be close to you and I can't. I don't know how to handle that."

For the first time in her life she felt torn between two men. This was not right, something felt wrong, but what could it be? Could she love two people at the same time?

"I'm apprehensive to leave you alone right now. Given your recent interest in blowing your brains out."

Ryan laughed. "I really need you to leave."

"Why?"

"Because I will do something else to you and I will hate myself for it if you don't leave," he growled.

"Such as?"

"Dammit, Julia!" His fist hit the windows on the French doors shattering them. She jumped out of shock but remained sitting on his bed. "I know part of you wants me and I will do everything in my power to make you want me back."

That statement admittedly baffled her. "You'd force yourself on me?"

At that, he actually laughed out loud. "Do you think that little of me? No, I would never do that to a woman. But I know how to make you want me. Even for just a little while."

"How?" Why was she curious about this? There was a small part of her wanting him. Could she really cheat on Aden?

"You need to leave."

"No, tell me, because I am very confused."

Ryan prowled up to her and unstrapped his protective vest. He tossed it to the ground and began to undress right in front of her, his eyes never once leaving hers. Her breath caught in her lungs as she took in the sight of him. He was downright gorgeous.

"You really need to go now," he groaned.

As much as her mind told her to get up and walk away, she couldn't. "I'm curious as to how you would make me cheat on someone. And why you would want to?"

He pulled his shirt off and leaned over her, forcing her to lay back on his bed as he maneuvered himself between her legs. The black dress rode up her thighs and she immediately grew self-conscious. *This is wrong.*

"I need you," he whispered in her ear and her stomach fluttered. "Just let me have you one time. I promise to leave you alone. Just give me this, please."

His hips moved against hers and she gasped at the feeling it gave her. "I can't."

Her words came out weak, which did not seem to bother him in the least. He pressed himself into her again and gently kissed her neck. This was a new side of Ryan. He was gentle and she craved more.

"Please baby," he groaned. "You are my only reason for living."

His lips brushed against hers and her eyes fluttered closed. Her mind screamed at her that this was wrong. He was the enemy. Yet here he is, seducing her. Wanting to love her and she could not resist it.

"Is this what you meant, by making me want you?" she muttered.

His hand ran up her thighs and pushed her dress up further. Her body craved his touch and she willingly let him explore her. He kissed her up jaw and to her temple. "Maybe, but it is backfiring horribly." She could feel what he meant when he rocked his hips against hers and felt him straining in his pants.

She heard his boots fall to the floor, one after the other as he kicked them off and her eyes opened quickly. This cannot happen. She pushed against his chest and felt the scars that lay under her fingertips.

The Risen did this to him. It was terrible, but necessary.

Did she really believe that?

"Oh my," she gasped and ran her fingers along the scars. His body tensed under her touch. "They've faded."

"Thanks to some cream from the healers." He smirked. "It's worked like a charm actually."

His attention veered back to making her sexually frustrated and it worked very well. He sat up and pushed her dress up further, revealing her underwear and stomach. The look in his eyes was full of lust and sadness. He really did love her.

"I can't do this, Ryan," she managed to say more firmly. "I cannot do that to Aden."

His eyes closed and he gripped her bare thighs. He looked just as frustrated as she was, if not more. "Please, just this once. No one will ever need to know. I just need this Julia. I need you at least once."

How did this go from him hitting her, trying to commit suicide, and then to him trying to have sex with her? It was an odd turn of events to say the least.

Ryan picked up each of her legs and slipped her heels off. They each landed on the floor with a small thud. Not one bit of him was being rough with her, not like the last time they were in bed like this. She was thankful they were interrupted before but had to wonder why. Most of all, she wanted to know why she wasn't making more of an attempt to stop him.

"Ryan," she groaned. "Please stop."

Ignoring her plea, he leaned down and kissed her neck, before trailing kisses down to her stomach. Each kiss was so gentle and sensual her body could not help but crave him. Her eyes closed as his hands tugged down her underwear and she felt exposed to him.

"Are you sure you want me to stop?" he whispered as he kissed her inner thighs.

"No," she moaned. "I mean yes."

"Tell me, love." His mouth trailed up her stomach and chest. He looked into her eyes, while his own blazed with desire. "Please."

"I want to say yes to you, but I can't and I don't know why." What was wrong with her?

His mouth hovered over hers and his hips pressed into her

body, forcing her to feel how much she affected him. "Don't think about it. Just let me love you—that's all I'm asking."

Her head ached. She could not do this but he made it so tempting she could not help it. For some reason she needed him right now. Every touch and kiss of his set her on edge. "Okay."

A broad smile appeared on his face and he seemed to light up like she had given him the world. After the way he looked before, it warmed her heart. "Thank you."

Her lips crushed into his and she heard him undoing his pants. Never had her heart raced this hard. She felt him lift her up gently and put her down correctly on the bed. With one effortless motion he pulled her dress up over her head then dropped it to the floor.

Her hands made their way over his chest and felt every dip of his abs. This man in front of her was the epitome of what a man should look like, and he wanted her.

"You're beautiful, Julia," he said as he caressed her face. She almost flinched when he touched her swollen cheek.

"Not too bad yourself." She grinned.

That smile of his was back and his lips crushed down on hers once more. He removed the rest of her clothes and she pushed his pants, along with his briefs, down with her feet. She could feel how ready he was for her and her body was more than ready for him.

"You're still a virgin, right?" He broke contact with her mouth.

She looked up at him with annoyance but he seemed legitimately worried about that. "Why?" She noticed her breathing was heavy.

"I just..." He shook his head and cleared his throat. "I want to make sure this is what you want and if you are still a virgin I sort of need to know."

Her eyebrows raised and she cocked her head to the side. What possible reason required him to know that bit of information? He towered over her and she wrapped her legs around his body. "Yes, I am and yes, I do."

"Okay," he kissed her lips gently as he continued to look into her eyes. "I'll go easy then."

"As opposed to what?"

"Giving it all I've got."

Those few words rendered her speechless.

This was it. After hundreds of years of saving herself she was going to give herself completely to Ryan. Her heart felt like it was going to jump out of her chest. And what did he mean by going easy?

He reached down below himself and her eyes followed. Against her control, her mouth dropped and her eyes widened. "This isn't going to work."

He looked down at himself and back to her shocked face. "What?"

"That can't possibly... fit." She felt her cheeks redden.

She witnessed Ryan's ego inflate right before her eyes. "I'll be gentle, love."

Julia wasn't so sure, but before she could protest she felt him slid gently into her. She winced at the new feeling and her eyes closed from the pinching pain of her body being invaded. This was not what she thought it would be like at all.

"Look at me, love," he groaned.

She looked up into his sad eyes as he slowly moved inside

25

of her. The pain started to subside and became more tolerable. What in the world was so appealing about this? "Ugh."

"Are you okay?" He looked worried. His thrusts remained slow as her body tried to get used to being invaded. She concentrated on his muscles flexing in his arms as he remained above her.

She nodded and realized her breathing increased, as did the feeling of pleasure that radiated throughout her body. A groan escaped her lips and that little smirk of his was back. His thrusts grew faster and she suddenly realized why people loved sex so much. This was incredible.

"Oh Ryan," she moaned and she gripped his hips with her legs and he moved against her.

"Look at me," he ordered once again, but this time his fist gripped her hair tightly. She was shocked to realize she liked it. "You're so beautiful."

Her eyes struggled to remain open. Ryan's eyes never left hers as he continued thrusting into her body.

There was no controlling the moans that escaped her lips. This feeling was pure ecstasy. Why did she wait so long for this?

No wonder women threw themselves at him. He was well endowed for sure and she could tell he knew how to use it to his advantage. With desperation, she tried to remove the thought of all the other females that had experienced this with him.

Ryan's mouth found hers and kissed her with such intensity that she could feel his need in every movement. It was exquisite and she lost control of her senses.

Anything in her mind that warned her against having

sex with him was gone and all her thoughts scurried to Ryan. His body moving against her, his lips and hands caressing her. Nothing else mattered.

"You feel so fucking good," he groaned against her lips. Why did that make her more excited?

"The feeling is mutual," she panted.

As inappropriate as she felt it was, he chuckled. "Are you okay?"

"More than okay, why?" she asked after he bit her lip playfully.

"If it gets to be too much, tell me." He kissed her forehead. She was curious how this would go.

"Okay."

He sat up on his knees, his thrusts grew more intense and quite honestly it sent her on edge. Her body tensed and she felt like she was going to explode from how astonishing it felt. Her insides shattered in the most wonderful feeling of ecstasy. It was like she was on cloud nine and the high from it made her dizzy.

Finally coming back to the ground, she looked at Ryan who smirked in amusement. Could men tell when that happened? How embarrassing.

His hands grasped her breasts and he thrust deeper into her. His abs stood out so prominently in this position and she was glad he was above her—he was a sight to behold.

Continuous moans escaped her lips as his thrusts grew faster, more urgent. His breathing grew heavy and he closed his eyes for the first time. The feeling was so unexplainably mind-blowing that she felt her body ready to burst again.

His hands moved to grip her hips, pulling her harder

against him. To her surprise it did not hurt, if anything she wanted more of it. She felt his body tense up. His grip tightened on her and a low groan escaped his lips. "Fuck," he muttered.

"Not yet," she urged.

Ryan slowed his thrusts, looking at her obviously confused. Even more so when she pushed him down on the bed and climbed on top of him. He was about to speak, but she silenced him with her lips pressing against his softly.

"Not yet. I don't want to forget this." Taking his earlobe between her teeth she felt his body shudder. She took that as a good sign.

"I promise you, I will never forget this for as long as I live," his voice growled.

Without really knowing what to do, she moved her hips on top of him. After a moment of uncertainty, he gave pity on her and his large hands guided her hips.

"I'm sorry. I am terrible at this." She was embarrassed at how awful she was in bed.

Ryan stopped moving her hips with his hands and pulled her face down to his by the back of her neck. His blue eyes sparked as he gave her a weak smile. "Julia, being with you like this is everything I have ever wanted and more. If I ever find myself consumed by darkness all I will have to do is think of this moment and I will be delivered back into the light. This isn't terrible for me. This is perfect."

The insecurities she felt were chiseled away by Ryan's words. She started to move against him again. He must have sensed her hesitation at her movements. Flipping her on her back once again, his body towered over hers.

"Let me love you." His eyes pleaded with her.

As soon as she nodded, his body worked against hers tirelessly. His arm was wrapped around her back, pulling her closer against him while the other held her head up. Every movement he made was filled with such intensity it almost felt as if he were saying goodbye.

He whimpered. It was a sound she'd never heard from him and it was almost sad. A word escaped his lips that she could barely hear, "Please…"

Julia felt his body tense along with her own until he fell down beside her as they both tried desperately to catch their breaths. Her heart leapt. Ryan had just made love to her. Remarkable, unbelievably great, to die for, love to her for the first time in her life and it was heaven.

He propped himself up over her and kissed her lips gently. "Thank you."

She almost wanted to laugh. Thank you? That was all he had to say after sex? She felt cheap. Then she remembered she was with Aden and guilt swept over her. Ryan seemed to realize what she was thinking and climbed off of her.

As he sat on the side of his bed, he ran his hand along his short hair and sighed. Ryan stood up, totally unashamed of his body, making his way over to his armoire. He slid into a fresh pair of briefs and pulled on a pair of sweat pants.

"Are you okay?" Sadness adorned his face. He was a sad shadow of the man who'd just turned her world upside down in a fit of happy kisses and moaning.

How could she answer that? She just cheated on the man she loved with someone she may have to kill in the future. What was she thinking? What would the General think?

Chapter III

Ryan

"So why aren't we telling Julia about our plans?" Grace asked, obviously frustrated and torn.

Ryan sat down on his bed and flushed when he thought of what he and Julia did this morning. "Something is off with her. The fact she is with Aden is just wrong and I just want to be cautious."

"You don't trust her?" Colette asked.

"Not at the moment," Ryan admitted. "She was captured and came back unharmed. Let's just keep this between us for now."

Cato rolled his eyes. "I guess it's not that big of a deal keeping her in the dark. It's not like she would be coming with us anyways."

Damian was looking at his and Anna's entwined fingers as they sat on Ryan's couch. It almost irked Ryan at how happy they were. He really was a selfish person. No doubt about that.

"I will agree and say she is different," Grace added. "So we will keep it to ourselves, but how will you explain your being gone to her?"

Ryan wondered the same thing. Julia was not an idiot and would realize they would be gone for long periods of time. "We could just say what I already told her—that we are going to the mortal world to help out civilians."

"Should work. Might want to actually send out some others groups as well to make it more believable," Cato added.

"How about we go as well? Keep her busy or something?" Grace offered.

"Yeah, get her away from that asshole she's with now." Cato smirked when he looked at Ryan.

He was glad Cato hated her being with Aden as much as he did. He realized it had more to do with the fact they did not trust Aden and less to do with the fact that he was a douche.

"So when should we get going to the next fun obstacle?" Damian asked.

"I think we should wait a week," Ryan answered. "Get our strength up and be less suspicious."

"Do you think Ahmose has that long? They are probably beating the hell out of him." Cato was rightfully concerned.

Ryan felt the same way, but part of him knew better. "He can hold out. I know he can. We are no use to anyone if we run into trouble half-cocked. In the meantime we need to train up, help Urbs out before we go, and get prepared. The Sirens will not be as easy on us as the Catacombs were."

Anna's eyes seemed to widen and he could not blame her. She was probably going to experience posttraumatic stress disorder after the whole ordeal. Damian squeezed her hand and whispered something into her ear.

Once everyone seemed to agree with the plan, Grace and Colette took their leave. In an obviously agitated mood Cato asked, "Can we trust them not to tell her?"

"If anyone knows Julia, they do. They admitted the situation is off. Even if Julia was kept in the dark it doesn't matter anyway. She isn't part of the plan."

Damian sighed. "Why can't we just go back to the way things were? It was easy then."

Ryan disagreed. He had not felt this important in a long time. Part of what the Risen believed was right. The Immortals were becoming obsolete in a world without belief and it scared him. Would there be a day when they were completely unneeded? What would become of them?

Anna

"Holy shit," Anna gasped as Ryan body slammed Cato into the mat. "The guy is a beast."

Damian sat next to her on the couch. She had never been in this part of the Domus. It was a gym for boxing, wrestling, and apparently mixed martial arts.

"I don't even bother trying to fight him. He's got too much pent up anger." Damian didn't seem the least bit jealous of her statement and it made her happy inside. "Cato is crazy."

"He would have to be," Anna agreed. Cato was taller than

Ryan but Ryan was ripped. Like super built. MMA fighter built and she hardly noticed it until now. The guy was all muscle; there must not be an ounce of fat on him.

They sat on the couch just outside of the matted area. She was glad the couch was there, she didn't want to sit on the ground or in metal chairs.

Ryan and Cato were in the middle of the mats dancing around one another until Ryan grabbed Cato's leg with both hands and drove him to the mat. He then proceeded to lock his legs around Cato's neck and arm.

"Whoa," she muttered.

"It's called a triangle choke," Damian informed her.

Anna's eyes widened. "Shouldn't he let go?"

"He needs to tap out first," Damian sounded bored, while she panicked for Cato's life. After a few seconds Cato tapped on Ryan's leg and he was released.

"This is intense."

"It's fun," he laughed. "When it's not against Ryan."

"I'm surprised Cato isn't laying into him after what happened with Julia," she muttered.

"It's the way these two work things out," Damian answered.

They were standing up again and started to throw jabs at each other. Cato landed a few good hits, but Ryan looked unfazed. Ryan's fist thrust up underneath Cato's chin and connected. "Damn. Nice uppercut."

Damian grinned. "So you know a bit about fighting?"

Anna rolled her eyes at the stupid question. "You do realize I was in the Marines, right?"

Damian draped his arm around her shoulders and pulled

her in close. She enjoyed the feeling of his body against hers but was somewhat irritated at the notion that she had no idea how to fight. Was he being sexist?

"Sorry, my love. I think it slipped my mind." He kissed her hand. He was so old school it was funny.

A loud grunt came from the mats. Ryan had Cato in a bear hug and he slammed him back down into the mats. To her surprise, Cato scrambled around to stand but Ryan had already jumped onto Cato's torso and straddled him.

"This is sort of sexual," she observed.

Damian squeezed her against him. "It's called the mount position. It's a dominant position and he can control Cato easier like this."

"Pretty sure he is just dominating him anyways." Anna laughed. "Seriously, Ryan is insane."

"Well, he enjoys to fight and Cato is less experienced than him. They don't know the meaning of taking it easy. They full out brawl and I think there is a bit of pent up frustration on both of their parts." Damian kissed her head.

"That's stupid. They could get hurt before we leave."

"Oh well, they can suck it up." Damian's shoulders lifted with a shrug.

It was idiotic to her. She didn't get it but whatever. If they broke a leg then no big deal, right? It's only the fate of the entire world that rests on their shoulders—nothing to worry about.

There were plenty more groans, grunts, and the sounds of flesh being beat on. Cato was undeniably not up to par with Ryan. She could not understand why the man just took the beating, but thankfully there was no blood to be seen. Just red, raw flesh, and sweaty bodies.

Part of her wished it was Damian rolling around getting all hot and what not. It would be one hell of a sight. "Are you next?" She grinned just thinking about his muscles flexing in a fight.

Damian looked down at his attire. He was in jeans and a black cotton t-shirt. "I don't think so."

"You could always wear your boxers." She grinned mischievously and winked at him.

Damian glanced back at Ryan and Cato wrestling on the ground, then back to her. He looked so amused it was cute. She wanted to kiss him. "Are you getting all hot and bothered by this display of testosterone?"

"One, Ryan and Cato don't turn me on. Two, women can do this too," she countered. "I just want to see you get all sexy and stuff."

"Dammit, I give up!" Cato yelled.

Anna refocused on Ryan and Cato, who was on his back once again with Ryan's legs twisted around Cato's arm. Ryan hyper-extended Cato's elbow who was tapping furiously on the ground with his other hand.

Damian ran over and pulled them apart. "Dammit, Ryan, don't break his arm."

Anna was sitting on the edge of the couch in anticipation for another brawl. Ryan seemed out of it as he stood up, his eyes a little crazed. "I was trying to tell him how to get out of an arm-bar, but he wouldn't stop whining like a baby."

"You did it full force, you jackass. There was no getting out of that." Cato rubbed his arm.

Damian checked out Cato to see if he was fine. He seemed

to be the unofficial parent of the group. Next he checked out Cato's face, probably making sure nothing was broken, bleeding, or worse.

"He is fully intact, I promise," Ryan grumbled. "I wasn't being that rough on him."

Sure looked like he was beating the hell out of Cato to me.

While Damian looked Cato over some more, who stood there patiently as he did, Ryan made his way over by Anna where his work out bag was. He pulled a bottle of water out and chugged it. Anna wasn't checking him out, but she was studying his half naked form.

Ryan was ripped. Guys like that were in movies, not in real life. Damian had more of a lithe build like a runner or swimmer.

"What?" Ryan grinned when he finished off his water.

Her cheeks turned red. "Nothing." She was busted ogling him. Anna hoped he didn't think she was checking him out. Damian would be so mad.

"Are you okay?" His grin got bigger. *The cocky bastard.*

"Just admiring how much you guys take care of yourselves." It was the truth. "Don't be so full of yourself."

"Thanks."

"No problem."

Ryan pulled out a towel to wipe his head. A bottle of pills launched toward her when he pulled up the towel. His face froze when she picked it up. It was pain medication. She looked at him perplexed with her arm extended to give it back. He snatched it up quickly and turned to see if the other two men witnessed the exchange.

"Don't tell them," he said lowly.

"Are you in pain?" she whispered.

"Not at the moment thanks to these," he grumbled and stuffed his belongings back into his bag.

"Why are you fighting with Cato if you are in pain?" Anna didn't like it. If he was in pain he should be resting.

Ryan scoffed. "I've had enough of these to numb pretty much everything and it's a good way to make them believe I'm fine. I can't have them worrying about me while we are on our mission."

Judging by how Damian jumped into mama bear-mode with Cato, she knew he was right. Hell, Damian would probably lock Ryan up and not let him leave his room if he knew Ryan was in pain. Still, they had a right to know and pills were hardly the solution.

"What happens when your body just gives out?" She eyed him.

"I guess we will worry about that when it happens. It's not terrible pain, but it's there. Don't worry about it." He zipped up his bag and tossed it back to the ground.

"How long have you been taking them?"

"Just the past few days." His answer was short due to Cato and Damian walking up. Cato's face was still red and slightly puffy. She knew just by looking at him that Ryan was right— he wasn't very hurt and would be fine. Still, it looked damn rough.

"You okay, skipper?" She forced a smile up at Cato.

He shook his head as he rolled his eyes. "One day Anna, I will grasp your concept of linguistics."

"Don't hold your breath. I have an entire bag full of whimsical words." She winked.

"You okay?" Damian asked Ryan.

Ryan merely nodded. He looked tired and upset. *That man is exasperating and I'm not even with him.*

"You ruined my plan to beat your ass for hitting my sister this morning," Cato grumbled.

"Sorry to ruin your plan." Ryan looked almost as disappointed at Cato.

"You two just go get some rest. After getting back just this morning you shouldn't be doing this anyways. Get out of here," Damian commanded. Anna was somewhat shocked he was giving orders to Ryan.

"Okay," Ryan mumbled.

"Yeah," Cato followed.

Damian seemed fine with their answers and held out his hand to Anna. "Come on. Let's go watch that flick you wanted to show me."

"I don't understand what you made me just watch." Damian sat back on her couch as stared at the ending credits.

Anna had managed to finagle a television and DVD player into her room to watch movies, but Damian seemed more or less uninterested in cinematic adventures.

"What do you mean? You didn't like it?" She tossed some popcorn in her mouth.

"Why would you like watching this? A literal boat-load of people died." He seemed actually shocked with her and she tried her hardest not to laugh.

"It's just a movie, Damian."

He eyed her warily. "Yes, a movie showing hundreds of people dying as a boat sank. And those people just trudged around filming it instead of helping them?"

"It wasn't real life, it was actors and special effects." He seemed confused still. "You know, you guys had plays back in your day I'm sure, it's like that but filmed."

"So that didn't really happen?" Relief washed over his face.

How in the world am I going to explain this? "Well, yeah it did happen, but it's just for entertainment. Have you seriously never watched movies?"

"A few, but I've been busy. I still can't get past the fact you find people dying entertaining." The smallest hint of a grin tugged on his lips. "Are you a sadist?"

"It's a classic movie!" she protested.

"I don't get why you like this. So many people die and as soon as the two lovers finally fall for each other, the man is left for dead by the woman he loves." Damian took a drink of his beer. "This is depressing, not entertainment."

"She didn't leave him for dead." Anna groaned into her hands as she covered her face.

"There was enough room on that door for them both. She practically killed him herself." Damian's voice was amused at this point, she could tell.

He is so enjoying getting a rise out of me.

Anna bit her lip. "I don't think that was the point the director was trying to make."

Damian raised his eyebrow. "Then he should have made it a smaller door."

"It's a love story! Quit begin all technical." She had to admit the door was pretty big, but she didn't want to let him win.

"A love story would be them both dying because they could not live without each other. She didn't even argue. She just let him freeze to death." That amused tone of his still hung in the air and she wanted to slap him for being so cocky, but at the same time she was amused herself.

"You are unbelievable," she finally said. "I can't believe you didn't know this actually happened."

"We were sort of occupied at the time I suppose. You said this happened in 1912 right?" he asked and Anna nodded. "We were busy with the Italo-Turkish War. Then a few years later World War I."

Anna's jaw dropped, but she closed it quickly. It still was so odd to realize how old they were when physically they looked so young. "I guess you get a pass seeing as you were risking your life and all."

Damian grinned, pulling her into his lap and kissed her nose. She loved the little adoring things he did to her. "I've never seen this side of you." He smirked.

"What side?"

"Your romantic side." That amused tone was back and she could not help but roll her eyes.

"I'm not romantic."

"I beg to differ since you think that a death filled movie was a love story." Damian's brown eyes seemed to penetrate hers with such a loving gaze she kissed him, sending a currant throughout her body. He groaned into her mouth when she bit his lip. "You are a vixen."

"Who even says that anymore?" Anna laughed and interrupted him before he could answer, "Oh yeah, the super old dude with a hot body."

Damian's brows knit together. "That sounds revolting."

"Well, it is what it is." She smirked. "You old man."

"I've never been old," he countered. "Always young with a 'hot body,'" he mused.

"Yeah well your soul is old as shit." She kissed his lips gently and straddled him.

Damian kept his eyes closed when he spoke, "My mind is mature and wise, but my body is young and ready whenever you need it."

"Whenever I need it?" Her eyebrows rose. Damian grabbed her hips, pressing himself against her and she felt the need he was talking about. "Yeah that's a good thing."

He grinned wickedly, looking up at her. "I don't think I will ever get enough of you and your zealous attitude, Anna."

"I know this is a random thought and totally not what we are talking about, but do you think Ryan is okay?" Anna asked.

Damian inhaled deeply. "I can't be sure but maybe I should check in on him."

"It's late so hopefully he's sleeping." Anna doubted Ryan would be able to sleep after everything that had happened lately. The last thing she wanted was for Damian to leave her right now, however Ryan's life was much more important then her lustful wishing. "If you want to go check on him you should go."

Damian shook his head. "I bet Julia laid into him enough this morning to make him see how his actions were idiotic."

Anna silently disagreed. She would never be able to handle all the things Ryan had gone through and come out living.

Anna's cat Calypso jumped up on the couch where Anna was sitting before and curled up. She stared at Anna and Damian, her white fur started to get longer as she grew more into a cat than a kitten. Her black feet seemed to disappear against her dark leather couch.

"I feel like she is judging us," Damian stared at Calypso who stared back. The only movement she made was a repetitive swish of her tail. "You are in a compromising position."

"She'll get over it," Anna murmured.

Damian affectionately rubbed her thighs. "I'm glad you are worried about Ryan. I really thought you hated him."

"He is important to you and I think I am starting to see the real him underneath the asshole exterior. He is a good person." She bit her lip. "Now, romance me, you old man."

CHAPTER IV

Ryan

H E MADE HIS WAY into the dress store. Julia stood at the counter, her gaze fixated on what she wrote. The blue dress she wore was modest as always. This day and age was so prudish it annoyed him. An over abundance of layers in the long gown and large cuffs, with the only possible sight of her figure being the fitted waist.

He wore a simple black doublet with white breeches, which he always felt more than uncomfortable in. "Hello." His voice was calm and even.

Julia looked up at him, her blue eyes always mesmerized him, but he knew better than to think anything of her in such a manner.

"How are you?" she asked brightly.

Her mood was obviously fair. Regretfully the news he had to bring was anything but. As he made his way to the counter *he saw her face contort as if she knew something were wrong.* "I have news."

She stepped around the counter to meet him and he could not help but stare at her hair in ringlets that framed her face. "Has something happened?" He nodded. "What is it?"

"I regret to inform you that your father has perished." Her hand went to her mouth as he expected it would and still he went on. "I know this is beyond tragic given your mother was taken not too long ago. Which is why I wanted to be the one to tell you."

"How?" Julia clutched the counter behind her.

"We were near Armagh when we came upon an ambush. The Irish took out at least nine hundred of our men. You father was shot," he said plainly, trying his hardest to keep his voice even for her sake.

He'd told Cato who'd insisted on leaving his team for theirs. Julia, on the other hand, was in the middle of being a Warrior as well as a dress shop worker. She had minimal experience.

"Explain it to me," she muttered. Her response took him by surprise.

"I do not believe that is wise, Julia." He placed a hand over hers.

"Now," she growled in a very unladylike manner.

He took a deep breath. "He was shot. I then returned fire to his killer and held your father until the light in his eyes extinguished. His blood drenched the ground, as did many others. That is all I will say." He made sure to leave out the promises he'd made. They were for no one's ears but himself. He still could not shake the memory of the other man's blood all over his own body.

"Does my brother know?" she asked quietly.

He nodded. "Yes."

"And?"

"Needless to say, he has been very adamant about transferring to our team." They were now down one companion and he could think of no one better to fill that void, than the man's son.

"Thank you." Her eyes welled up but she held it back like the proper woman she was. Deep inside he wished to comfort her, to pull her close in an embrace meant only for man and wife, but he had to push the thought from his mind. This woman was unobtainable. Too pure to tarnish just for his enjoyment. She was utter perfection.

Ryan woke, almost jumping out of his bed from the memory. Alone in his room, he lay back down in the comfort of his bed, tossing his arm over his eyes. "You are a fool, Ryan," he spoke softly to himself. "She has even claimed your dreams."

It had only been a day since Ryan and Julia had slept together and she acted as if nothing had even happened between the two of them. It frustrated him deeply and he could not get his mind off of it.

It had been years since he felt that close to someone. He had many sexual conquests over the years, but this was different. It was not an insane or wild encounter and yet it was one of his favorite memories of being with someone.

Gentle, sweet, lovemaking that gave him goose bumps when he thought about it.

He had no idea how to get past the feeling, especially as her and Aden sat at a table together in the parlor room laughing and showing too much public displays of affection.

With copious amounts of effort, he remained calm and continued his discussion with Cato and Damian. Although, it became very clear that Aden was making him mad on purpose since he kept stealing glances at him.

Ryan sat alone on one couch and faced Cato and Damian. A large map of Europe spread across the coffee table between them.

"I want to throw up," Cato mumbled.

"You're not that only one." Ryan grit his teeth. They now kissed and stared into each other's eyes. Ryan looked back to Cato. "How can you watch your sister get molested in front of you?"

He shrugged. "She's an adult. Believe me though, I want to bash his brains in."

"At least she is back and safe—that is all that matters." Damian was back to being the optimistic one of the group. Ryan was relieved something was back to normal.

"Shoot me now." Ryan cringed when they started to make out heavily.

"That's not funny." Cato glared. "I am still pissed you tried to shoot yourself, you moron."

"Can we focus?" Damian shifted on the couch. "We need to figure out how to get to Anthemoessa."

"We won't be able to transport there. The Siren's island is pretty much blocked off from mystical transportation." Ryan hummed in obvious thought. "The only way there is the old fashioned way. Let's hope we don't get killed."

"Should we really be discussing this while Julia and Aden are over there?" Damian glanced behind him.

"They can't hear us, even if they ask what we are doing we will just say we are figuring out where to send help for the mortals." Ryan was really not looking forward to the Island of the Sirens. They were merciless creatures and quite frankly he was terrified of them. They worked in odd ways.

Some stories said they lured men in by showing them their deepest desires in song. He could only imagine what he would see and hear if he allowed himself to. He already felt on the brink of madness as it was.

"Okay, so we get to Naples and get on a boat. Sail out to the Capri and Ischia islands." Ryan pointed off the coast of Italy.

"It's not between Ischia and Procida?" Cato inquired.

"I don't think so. It's hard to say. Everyone has a different view where they are and this is the most common belief."

"Not to mention little miss Indian queen told you?" Cato smirked.

Ryan cleared his throat. "Uh, yeah."

"You don't want to go from Sicily? We could cover more area heading toward the islands from there instead of Naples," Damian suggested.

He may have a point. Ryan knew it was in that area and it may be better to be out further and head into Naples than wondering across the sea. "Okay, we can do that."

This was going to be difficult. He had not sailed in quite some time and really preferred to be on foot. He heard Julia chuckle and his eyes met hers briefly. She did not look bothered in the least by his presence. Was it that easy to get over him? Was he terrible in bed yesterday?

"Okay, call the nearest port. Buy a boat and make sure it is ready in five days." Ryan looked back to Julia while Aden looked directly at him with a smirk on his lips.

"I'll look in Palermo. Should only take eight hours to get there." Damian nodded. "Must we take Anna?"

Ryan was getting sick of this conversation but could he really blame Damian after what happened? Part of him wanted to leave her behind and bring Julia, but that was a ridiculous idea. He couldn't trust Julia at all right now. "Yes, I really don't see any other option at this point."

Damian rolled up the map and as he tucked it under his arm, he and Cato stood up ready to leave. "We will get the boat ready. You make a list of supplies we may need. I doubt this will be a one night mission."

Ryan nodded. "Will do. I will consult some people on the legends of the creatures and see what might be useful."

Damian looked back at Aden and Julia. "Be good."

"I always am."

Just then, Zyanya, a fellow Warrior walked through the door. Her long black hair was parted in the middle and fanned out over her back. She immediately went to a bookshelf and stood on her toes to reach a book. He watched with increased interest, as her shirt rose up in her effort and he could see her tanned skin.

They had always exchanged pleasantries to one another but in all honesty he never thought much of her. She was good looking and sported a slender body, but what really caught his attention were her light eyes though. Not many Native American's had them and it made her stand out.

She pulled down a book and scanned through the pages. He watched her crinkle her nose and pull her hair to one side. She must have realized she was being watched and looked around until they made eye contact.

Ryan heard Julia giggle again and his heart dropped. He had to get over her and fast—Zyanya may be a needed pawn in that effort.

He casually waved her over to him. For a second he thought she would deny the invitation. She did not disappoint though as she slowly sashayed over to him with a friendly smile on her lips.

"Hello Ryan." She smiled. She really was a lovely woman.

"Hello." He returned the smile. She looked comfortable with him. Not nervous or smitten like most women by his reputation. It was nice.

"What's up?"

"Just realized we have lived together for years and never really conversed." He offered a seat next to him. "Thought we could change that. I really need a distraction."

As if knowing what he meant, her eyes jerked toward Julia and Aden then back to him. Was everyone aware of their situation? *How annoying.*

She sat down next to him and looked as comfortable as could be. "Why do I have a feeling talking is the last thing on your mind?"

He felt a surge of nerves crawl in his stomach. Did he really just get called out? This was new.

"I do believe you're blushing." She grinned and patted his knee.

"Hardly." He smirked. "But an honest conversation would

be nice right about now."

She glanced back at Julia and scoffed. "Yeah, I heard she was with the creeper. How are you holding up?"

"What do you mean?"

She rolled her green eyes and laughed. "Everyone knows that you two had some sort of thing going on. Aden was boasting about how he beat you at your own game or something."

Deep inside, Ryan was pleased because he in fact, had beat Aden to the punch. However, he did not see it that way. If anything he regrets it. It was so much harder to stay away from Julia now that he'd experienced her in the most intimate way possible.

"I am perfectly fine." Which was not true, but Zyanya seemed to believe him. "What are you up to anyways?"

She held up the book and revealed it was about Japan. "Going on a mission there to help the mortals tomorrow. Don't have a damn clue about that place."

"Who assigned you?"

"No one. They are having a lot of problems there though and my team decided it was worth our time to help instead of sitting around here."

He instantly had respect for this woman. How did he overlook someone like her all these years? "I can't believe you never been there, especially during the World Wars."

She rubbed the back of her neck. "Well, I was pregnant when it started and of course the council didn't want me to fight until my daughter reached her Immortal age. So my husband went instead."

Sadness washed over her and he knew what must have happened. They lost a good number of people during those years. "I'm sorry."

"He was a good man and died fighting for what he believed in."

He knew all too well about losing his loved ones, even a wife. "Then he died well. How did your daughter take it?"

"She decided the Immortal life wasn't for her." Zyanya looked distraught, but managed to force a small smile. "She died a few years ago. Cancer."

At first, Ryan saw her as a sexual partner to drown his sorrows in for an hour or so. However, actually talking made those thoughts seem wrong. He did not talk much with the women he had sex with and it made him realize how terrible he had been. They could have been going through something terrible personally and he just used them like it was nothing. Because to him it was nothing, it was just physical.

He decided to change the subject. "Japan can be a lovely place."

"Yeah, just never had any interest going there. Water makes me nervous and it is surrounded by it."

"You're afraid of water?" He tried not to laugh.

She acted offended and punched his arm. "Shut up. You have no idea what is under there and it scares me. I hate not knowing things."

"As do I."

"So what? Are you wanting to sleep with me now or something?" She smirked.

Ryan raised his eyebrows in surprise from her being so forward. He rested his ankle on his knee and leaned back against the couch. "To be honest, that was my first intention, but now..."

"What?" She really was a no nonsense type of girl.

"I find myself actually intrigued by you. It's a rarity."

Her eyes rolled and he could not help but smile. She reminded him of someone, but he could not put his finger on it. "Sorry Ryan, but regardless of your outstanding reputation, I am not the type to sleep around."

"I never said you were, Zyanya."

"Call me Zee. It is so much easier to say." She smiled slowly. "I do think very highly of you Ryan. But as far as anything physical goes, it's pretty much out of the question."

Amusement filled his entire body. This was one stubborn woman.

"Zee, I have no intention of doing that with you. I find myself respecting you a little too much at this point." A very true statement. "And if I must be honest again, I would actually like to get to know you. If that is okay?"

She looked hesitant, as was he, but he needed to move on from the pain he felt. Julia did not wait for him and he must get past it. Sure, it had only been a day since she showed up with Aden, but it was clear from their present encounters that they were crazy for one another.

If she was happy, then that is all that matters. Even though he desperately hated it being with Aden. He did not trust him and would keep watch on him. Julia may not be Ryan's, but he'd be damned if something would happen to her.

Zee looked over at Julia. "I would like that, but I'm not an idiot. You must really like her and I doubt you would have room to get to know me fully."

"We can start as friends." He felt an odd connection to her, yet he felt like he was betraying someone. "Again, if you want to. I don't want you to think I am some crazy man with an agenda to seduce you."

Her chuckled was like music to his ears and she became gorgeous to him in an instant. It was then that he studied her features. Her striking oval green eyes and full red pouting lips did not match her tanned skin and black hair. Mixed raced women had such beautifully combined features that stuck out as exotic and he had to admit, she was breathtaking.

"What?" she asked.

He must have been starring. "Just baffled as to why you haven't caught my attention before this."

"Well, I used to be a guy." She laughed at his shocked expression. "Just kidding. I don't know. I was married for a very long time and kind of keep to myself I guess."

"That would do it." He smirked.

"Julia is glaring at me." She cringed. "I am undoubtedly uncomfortable now."

"Don't be. She made her choice and I accept it." He tried to convince himself. Zee was much too intelligent for her own good. "You read people well."

"It's a curse."

Ryan sat up and put his hand on her knee. She did not flinch, didn't even stiffen but looked at ease. It warmed his heart for some reason. "Have dinner with me?"

She shook her head. "I don't think that is a good idea."

"Why not?"

"I've heard how you are, Ryan."

He groaned and rubbed his hand along his short hair. "This is exasperating."

"What is?"

"The fact I cannot get rid of my reputation is ridiculous, but I suppose I have done it to myself."

She bit her lip and he felt a surge in his body to kiss her. What was going on with him? "Okay fine, dinner."

Ryan grinned and squeezed her hand gently. "Be at my room at eight. Don't worry, we are going out, not staying in."

"Sounds good. They better have beer where we're going though."

Chapter V

Anna

"Should we really be doing this?" Anna asked.

Damian smirked and tightened her vest before patting her on the helmet. She pulled goggles on over her eyes and gulped. This may or may not be fun—she had yet to decide that one.

"We need to blow off some steam," he answered.

"I could think of other ways to blow off steam," she muttered.

Damian smirked and handed her the paintball gun. "Pretty sure twice by mid afternoon is sufficient."

"Hey, a girl has needs." She pouted.

"Not that I am complaining," he grinned, "but let's do something besides stay in bed all day."

"What kind of guy are you?" She was finding it harder and harder to keep her hands off Damian. It may have only been a short period of time but she had grown very fond of him.

Nathan remained in her mind everyday, but mourning forever was unhealthy and Damian made it easier. He made her happy.

Today he got a hair cut, sort of. The sides of his head were buzzed down and the top of his head still had longer hair that was slicked back. It looked pretty damn hot actually. He absolutely rocked the prohibition haircut.

Damian put on his helmet and goggles then held up his gun, ready for battle. "Let's do this."

"Who are we shooting again?" She laughed.

"Ryan and Zee." He smirked.

Anna nodded. She had only met Zee this once and she had no idea who she was besides some American Indian chick with a too perfect complexion. It could not be natural. Actually, two things bothered her about Zee.

One, she was not Julia and Ryan seemed a little too fond of her. Two, she looked a great deal like Anna, except her green eyes. What sort of Indian had green eyes? Her mom probably hooked up with a white guy or something.

I'm going to hell for that comment.

She felt guilty being around Zee. Julia liked Ryan and now he was with someone else. But she was with Aden now. Their bizarre love triangle gave her a headache. She was glad it was just her and Damian. No questions. No drama. Just him and her and no one bothered them.

"Are you sure we should be having fun while the world is being destroyed?"

"Anna." He caressed her face causing hers eyes to flutter

closed. "We have to do something while we wait to leave for Italy. Sitting around sulking would probably make us worry and anxious. And when you are worried and anxious you mess up."

"I guess, it just feels wrong to have fun while others are suffering."

"We are going to help everyone. Just enjoy one day before we throw ourselves into hell, okay?"

Ryan and Zee marched up to them and Ryan slung his arm over Damian's shoulders. Zee smiled warmly at Anna and she forced a smile back. This was awkward for her and it shouldn't be. She felt like she was betraying Julia for some reason.

"You love birds ready or what?" Ryan grinned.

"Ready when you are." Damian pointed his gun at Ryan's head, which he promptly swat away and laughed.

"You're going down."

"Hold on," Zee spoke up. "Let's do boys against girls."

Anna screamed inside. That was like committing suicide, paintball suicide.

Ryan and Damian exchanged looks and shrugged. Ryan had a big stupid grin on his face. "Fine by me."

He winked at Zee who seemed to blush. Guilt flooded her once again. Would Julia be mad at her? She really hoped not.

"Come on Anna. Let's whip these boys butts."

Anna wanted to smack her right then and there. Did she not realize that they were tortured? Judging by her regret-filled face, Zee must have realized what she said and they scurried away from a laughing Damian and Ryan. Well, if they could laugh about it then it was okay.

They walked in silence far away from the guys and waited until the horn went off signaling the start.

The paintball area was in a football-sized field with various trees and obstacles set up. They could climb ropes onto perches or duck in trenches. It reminded her of boot camp except there was a large pond in the middle for God knows why.

"So, you don't seem to like me very much," Zee said.

Balls.

Anna shrugged. "I don't know you enough to not like you."

It was an honest statement but not the entire truth.

"Is it because you were close to Julia?"

Mother cracker, how did she know?

"I feel guilty I guess. But she's with Aden so I don't know," she admitted.

"Must be confusing," Zee replied. Her tone was understanding instead of rude. It really did take her by surprise.

They scaled down into a small trench that led to a shed. Zee headed toward it and Anna followed along. "It's just weird. One minute they were all over each other and the next she is with Aden and Ryan is with you."

"Whoa," Zee laughed. "We had dinner last night and are playing paintball today. Not sure I would classify that as being together. No offense."

A sigh of relief escaped her. "Well now I don't feel so bad." She grinned.

Zee smiled back—her teeth were annoyingly perfect. "You shouldn't. I know Ryan's reputation and unless he shows some sort of change, he isn't getting near this." She pointed up and down her body.

Anna started to like her and relaxed a little more. They needed to have fun today, especially before the next mission to an island full of crazy bird ladies.

"So how old are you?" Anna blurted out.

Zee laughed out loud and continued on her path. "Well, aren't you blunt?"

"What can I say? I'm curious." Anna picked at her pant pockets. "It's like living around a bunch of celebrities. Except these celebrities are actually important."

"Well, I am positively not as old as Ryan and Damian. I'd say I am about five hundred give or take."

That was odd. She seemed so much older for some reason. Then again five hundred was pretty dang old. "Who were you?"

Zee laughed again. "No one really. My teammates took the led on most missions. I was usually their maid or servant or something. I'm not a fan of being the center of attention."

"Then how were you chosen?"

Another laugh. "Reborns do exist, Anna."

Now she felt like an idiot. "Oh yeah. So your parents were chosen?"

"They sure were. My mother was a Zapotec Indian. She didn't play by their standards of what a woman should do so she was banished and somehow was chosen. Don't really remember much about it actually."

"And your dad?"

"My mom said he was killed in a mission when I was six. I don't remember him much," she answered.

"Was he white?"

Zee stopped in her tracks and looked stunned but amused.

"You are so odd. Yes, he was white." She laughed.

Anna's eyebrows knit together. "Just wondering where you got colored eyes."

Zee rolled her eyes and started to walk toward a few trees next to the shed. She sat down in the dirt. "You have so many questions. Did you ask Ryan about his eyes too?"

"Nope, he won't tell me anything anyways. Still trying to figure out who they were as mortals." It was frustrating not knowing who your boyfriend was. It was annoying how his best friend had him so controlled that he would not tell her.

"Hold on." Zee propped her arms on her knees. "You don't know who they are?"

"Nope."

She shook her head. "Damn girl. You are constantly in the presence of one of the most celebrated military commanders in the history of the world and you are clueless to it."

"What?" This was news to her. If anything it made her nervous about who they were. "Who are they?"

A loud horn went off and Anna cringed at the sound. It was overly loud and annoying, like a car horn.

"Alright, these guys are the best of the best. So let's come up with a plan. They will most likely split up," Zee declared. "So let's stay together."

"Are you sure? One can take us out at once."

"Yeah, pretty sure. We will set little traps, but stay together." She grinned. "No mercy."

Anna shivered. Even though it was not bullets, she did not relish in the thought of getting shot by two skilled men.

"Okay."

"You perch up in those trees." She pointed to the trees by

the shack. "I will be up on the hill across from you. Once one of them comes into view, let em' rip."

Simple enough.

Zee jogged up to the hill and Anna had to admit, Zee scared her. She was a tough woman with a no bullshit attitude that reminded her a lot of Ryan. Julia too.

Anna sighed and threw her gun strap over her head and climbed up the tree. She perched herself fifteen feet off the ground and waited. Zee had disappeared and she felt like a sitting duck.

The tree was full of leaves, which provided good camouflage, but she still did not like it. She was not the sniper type at all. Somehow she was able to find a decent seat on the branches and kicked her feet up on another. Her gun lay in her lap and she waited for signs of movement.

Why their idea of fun was to shoot each other was beyond her. Playing with guns was an everyday thing for them. She went along with it and had a suspecting feeling she would get a paintball smashed on her somewhere.

It did not take long for Damian to come into the clearing. She smirked—he was like a sitting duck. Anna brought her gun up and aimed for his chest. He moved slowly and it wasn't too hard to hit him. The paint splattered over his chest and she realized Zee had shot him too.

That was way too easy. Anna looked around nervously for Ryan but there was no sign of him anywhere. She felt something smack against her chest and looked down. Blue paint was splatted over her chest protector and she looked around in utter confusion.

Where the hell did that come from?

Damian remained standing in the open and his gun hung to his side. It obviously hadn't come from him then. Anna climbed down the tree and jogged up to Damian. His helmet was propped up on his head and his goggles hung from his neck. He looked sexy.

"What's up buttercup?" He grinned.

"Did you do this?" She pointed at her chest.

"No ma'am." He grinned again.

Zee came running into view and Anna opened her mouth to talk.

"How the hell?" Zee panted as she ran past them. Anna shut her mouth again and stood in bewilderment.

Ryan came running past them now and he was laughing to himself. He was seriously chasing her. "What is happening?"

"Looks like she is trying to avoid getting shot." Damian laughed.

"How did I get shot?" Zee ran behind large tires that were planted randomly in the area. Ryan ran behind them and they chased each other like kids playing tag.

"I was bait. You guys took it and both shot me." He shrugged. "Ryan was watching to see which directions the shots came from and determined where you were that way."

"What the hell is he? A mathematician or something?"

"Well, he was taught by a pretty smart guy when he was mortal." Damian gave her a one-armed hug and led her toward Ryan and Anna.

She heard shots go off and saw a painted Zee tackle Ryan to the ground. "You cheater!"

He laughed and got on top of her. He pinned her arms to

the ground and she tried to buck him off her. This was weird. That seemed like a personal moment between them and Damian just led her casually over to them.

"I didn't cheat, you sore loser," she heard Ryan laugh again.

"You tripped me," she growled.

If Zee wasn't smiling, Anna would of thought she was actually mad. It was nice to see Ryan enjoy himself. She never really saw that side of him much. Julia popped in her mind again and she groaned. Why did she feel like this was wrong?

"Easy there kids, we won fair and square." Damian laughed and pulled Ryan off Zee.

She stood up and brushed the dirt off of her clothes. "I thought you guys would split up."

Ryan smirked. "Why must you underestimate me?"

"Because it's probably all just hype." She stuck her tongue out and Ryan shook his head.

They were sort of cute to watch argue. They were purely playful, like puppy love. Anna realized she was smiling and turned to Damian. "Do we act like that?"

"No." He beamed. "At least I don't think so."

He kissed her gently on the lips and she felt warm and fuzzy inside. She really did love him at this point. It happened quickly but she felt it. He was everything she needed in this life and according to Zee, him and Ryan were the cream of the crop.

"That wasn't too difficult," Ryan boasted and pulled Zee against him.

She looked uncomfortable and it surprised Anna. Women did not do that with Ryan. He seemed to sense her awkwardness and let go of her.

"You are too smart for your own good you know that?" she groaned.

"Yes, I know."

"All right ladies," Damian spoke up, but Ryan and Zee's eyes never left each other. There had to be something there. "Let's go get some food before tonight."

"What's tonight?" Anna asked.

"Funerals for the Warriors that died when we went looking for Julia and her team." Ryan's mood changed in an instant and Zee looked at her feet. "Let's eat."

CHAPTER VI

Anna

THEY WERE DRESSED IN their white ceremonial gear and Anna had to admit, being here was uncomfortable. She barely knew the people that were killed and honestly, a few she had never met.

Five people in total died the night they marched through the city looking for the Risen and Julia. Ryan's guilt seemed nonexistent as he looked at the funeral pyres.

They were on the edge of the city, facing the ocean in an area that seemed made for funerals. It was actually very beautiful. Opposite of the ocean was a large garden with flowers of every color with stone benches for viewers to sit. There were ten spots in the sand that were made for the pyres. It was sad how they all looked very used from the scorch marks on the slabs below.

It was night and torches were sticking out of the sand surrounding the area. Behind her she heard fountains trickling and in front of her waves calmly slid their way up along the edge. It was a send off that would make anyone proud—gorgeous and beautifully sad to witness.

They stood on the edge of the sand, a respectable distance away from the families that were busy at work with the bodies. The last rites of their religions were being performed and Anna found it interesting. Some walked around the pyres with the body, others wailed in distress, which was very uncomfortable. One person had bagpipes being played by their body.

Anna looked down at her feet, half in the grass and half in sand. It was such an awkward and gloomy end to a good day.

Ryan and Damian stood by one another and Damian grabbed her hand, unwilling to let go of her. Zee stood by Ryan and whispered in his ear. If things were not already uncomfortable, Julia was next to Zee with Aden among many other Warriors.

Julia looked sullen, but worst of all was Damian. His eyes welled and he squeezed her hand tightly. Ryan had pulled her aside and told her that Aja, a Warrior that had been killed, and Damian had been involved.

If anyone knew how he felt it was her, which Ryan made sure to point that out. She would never get used to his blunt personality. She was at the point where she had to keep reminding herself that he does not realize how much of an ass he makes himself sound like. Must be natural.

Against some of their religious beliefs, the fallen Warriors were dressed in their fighting gear instead of their religions traditional funeral clothes. Apparently Hinduism was very particular in what you wear and Aja was Indian.

"What if they don't accept her?" Damian muttered.

"You know perfectly well that she will find her way, Damian," Ryan muttered. "Every Warrior is burned in their gear."

"I'm just saying," Damian fretted. "What if the Gods don't care for it? What if they deny her?"

"They won't. She died for them."

"She died for your ambition to get Julia back, Ryan," Damian spat.

Ryan stood still and looked straight ahead. How did he have so much restraint? It was not something he was known for.

Damian let go of her hand and ventured slowly over to Aja's body on the pyre. Her family stepped aside as he came up to her body. They did not look pleased, but no one refused his advance. What Zee told her came back to mind—they were the cream of the crop. No one would refuse him or Ryan.

Damian climbed the pyre and kissed Aja's forehead. She was pretty even in death with long black hair and a perfectly symmetrical face. Anna was not jealous even if it was awkward seeing how much he cared for her. They must have been important to one another.

He pressed his cheek against hers and he must have been saying something.

"They were very good friends," Ryan muttered.

Anna did not bother to look at him. She was expecting a smartass remark and she was not in the mood for it. "I can tell."

"What I mean to say is, that they realized they no longer had romantic feelings for one another. They saw each other as family. She was there for him when I was too selfish to be." He actually sounded sad, but his face was still set in stone. "He told her he had feelings for you and she pushed him to talk to you."

A sting in her heart made her wince. She somehow felt she lost someone as well. This woman made Damian and her come together and she would never be able to thank her. Death was dumb.

Damian came back over to her and took his place in-between her and Ryan. She grabbed his hand and saw his cheeks were stained with tears. The overwhelming need to embrace him almost took over until she saw the pyres were being lit.

Her heart dropped. She had never actually witnessed cremation. It was actually gruesome to watch.

Lifeless bodies burning, making it clear there was no soul in there to scream in pain from the flames. The fire danced all around their bodies and engulfed them beyond recognition. The smell made her sick to her stomach as she watched Aja's hair burn away.

Her beauty was gone and replaced with a grotesque figure. Anna hated this. She wanted to leave. How could people stand and watch the bodies of their loved ones become disfigured?

She looked down the row of Warriors. They stood still and silent. No one looked bothered by what was happening in front of them except Damian.

She adverted her eyes. It was hard to see him like this and looked back to the blackened bodies. Something odd happened to them. A thick white smoke started to come out of their mouths and reach toward the sky.

No one seemed surprised by this except her. The white snakelike smoke escaped the bodies and floated up into the air. They raced higher until they disappeared, leaving new stars in the sky.

She cocked her head to the side and looked at the newest additions to space. "What happened?"

"They were accepted by their Gods into the heavens," Damian whispered and his eyes finally met hers. He looked more relaxed now. "Whatever heaven they believed in."

"What did Aja believe in?"

"She will reach the heaven of warriors in her faith and if she wishes, will be reincarnated." Damian sighed and looked back up to the sky. He pulled Anna to him and kissed the top of her head. "Don't ever leave this world, Anna."

Ryan

They made their way back to the Domus and Ryan had a terrible feeling in his gut. Those deaths were because of him. They would never have been killed if he thought about a course of action instead of plunging out into the city to look for Julia and the cretins that harbored her.

Damian's words stung when he blamed Aja's death on him. It was the truth and he could not deny it. All of this was his fault—at least it felt that way.

Damian walked ahead with Anna, his arm around her waist and Zee followed next to Ryan. He felt comforted by her presence, especially with Julia and Aden holding hands behind him. He would never be able to accept their relationship. He loved her with all his being and it would never go away.

Zee made it easier though. She was in many ways like Julia. Expect she was not what you would call a proper woman. She was rough and did not particularly care for feminine things. It was odd, but he found it refreshing.

"You're quiet." Zee brought his mind back to reality.

"It is my fault they're dead," he muttered. He saw Damian's shoulders tense when he spoke but remained facing forward. "I feel like my presence insulted their memory."

To his surprise Zee slipped her hand in his. He didn't pull away. "You are only a man. People make mistakes. You made a judgment call and we all took the risk knowing what could happen. Don't blame yourself for the choices other people make."

Only a man? He really had never thought of himself that way. All his life he was told he was meant for great things. He was told that a regular life was impossible for him and as true as Zee's statement was, he did not feel like he was only a man.

People expect so much out of him that failure is impossible. Their blood is on his hands, even if what Zee said was true. They followed him because they thought he knew what he was doing when in reality, it was a hasty decision and he should have thought it through.

"What are you thinking so hard about?" she asked.

"I rather not talk about it," he muttered. Ryan looked around the city. Symbols of the Risen were painted everywhere. He grit his teeth at the thought of those traitors taking over the city.

"Guilt setting in?" Aden spoke up from behind him.

Ryan stopped and faced Aden's smug face. Even after the funeral of their brethren he looked amused at Ryan's expense. He caught Julia starring at his hands entwined with Zee's and he let go.

"This is not the time to get into it, nor the place, Aden," Ryan growled. The families of the deceased walked among them and the last thing he wanted was to make it worse for them.

"Don't you think their families deserve to know who killed them?" Aden looked like he was trying to suppress a grin. "Maybe not by your hand physically, but technically it is your fault."

"Enough, Aden." Damian apparently had stopped as well. His cheeks were flushed and his new haircut made him look intimidating. "If you start anything while the families are still here, I will kill you. Laws be damned."

Anna's eyes went wide and Ryan, for the first time, stayed out of it. No part of him wanted to cross Damian's wrath to-day—even if he relished in Aden's shocked face. Julia looked between the two men squaring off and never made a glance to Ryan. It stung.

Something was off about her. Was she was wearing eye-liner? It was dark too and he hated it. She was so naturally beautiful that it did not look like her at all. It looked good, but it was not Julia, not the woman he knew.

"Damian, you of all people should be pissed at Ryan. You and Aja were like family and here he is, spitting in the face of her friends and family by showing up," Aden continued on.

A few select families of the fallen Warriors stopped to watch the confrontation. Ryan closed his eyes and tried to remain calm for their sake. He would not fight Aden. Not now with despair hanging in the air.

Aja's family stood nearby and watched them like hawks. Her two sons glared at Ryan and it looked as if they blamed him as well. How much more stress could his body take at this point?

"You know who is to blame?" Damian's face just inches from Aden's, who looked ready to fight. "The Risen. All this is their fault. They are pathetic, childish, and selfish people who are throwing a tantrum because they cannot get their way. They are murderers and nothing more."

"Damian—" Aden started.

"No, Aden," he laughed. "Do not start with me. When I see your little friend Jesse, I will kill him slowly and enjoy every ounce of pain I cause him. He deserves nothing but suffering for his betrayal. All of those bastards deserve it."

Aden smirked causing blood to rush through Ryan's veins and he knew right then and there that Aden was a traitor. He had to be, but he couldn't prove it. Deep down he knew it with all his heart. However to accuse him of it would be a death sentence for Aden, even if it were not true.

Ryan looked at Julia, whose head was down trying not look at any of them. What was going on with her?

"And I will be right there with you, Damian. I promise," Aden answered.

"But on who's side?" Damian asked. A hint of maliciousness in his voice brought Ryan's attention back to them.

Did he really just ask that?

"How dare you." Julia shoved Damian, who was now the shocked one.

In all his life he had never seen Julia speak to Damian like that. They never fought, never said unkind things to one another, and it worried Ryan. This was his limit. Something is without a doubt wrong with Julia.

Ryan stood in-between the two and glared down her. He studied those black-rimmed eyes with the smoky eye shadow that made them stand out gorgeously. His instinct to kiss her faded when he saw how furious her eyes were.

"I advise you to leave right now, Julia." Ryan's voice was barely a whisper. He did not want to upset the families anymore than they had. Especially seeing the Warriors divided like this. "You are the ones that are unwelcome."

"Ryan, because you foolishly wanted to save me, people died. This is on you. You presence here is an insult." Julia's face was only inches away. "Maybe if you would have died when you were tortured, they would still be here. I wish they were."

His heart beat so fast he thought he was having a panic attack. How could things change this much between them so quickly?

"If you people intend on fighting, take it somewhere else." One of Aja's sons came up to their group with a scowl on his face.

He looked a lot like her. Same dark hair and round brown eyes that made you melt but he was tall like Cato. Ryan felt a mix of emotions come over him, guilt set in and they were obviously being too loud.

Damian pulled him over into a brick-walled alley that was moderately lit in the darkness of the night and their little group actually followed. Cato, Zee, and Anna leaned against a wall a few feet away. Meanwhile, Damian and Ryan stared at

Julia and Aden.

Julia shoved him against the wall and he could not help but laugh. "Do you really think that hurts?"

"No, but I can make it hurt," she spat.

Caleb marched up to them and looked at the scene. He seemed puzzled and stood away from the obvious hostility. This poor kid could not catch a break with the people around him.

"Try it." Ryan pressed his body into hers. "I dare you."

"My pleasure." She jabbed him in the side with her fist. "You deserve to die after what you did to them."

Again, his heart began to race from her words. It was a pain he never wished on anyone. It felt as if his heart was literally breaking. Part of him wanted to let her beat the hell out of him.

He grabbed the bun in her hair and yanked it down, her head tilt back and she glared up at him. "Oh, so this doesn't turn you on anymore?"

"What are you talking about?"

He pulled on the bun again and raised his voice. "I mean you liked it a few days ago when I deflowered you. Wonder how your new boyfriend feels about that?"

Sharp intakes of breath filled the alleyway, but his eyes never left Julia's. There was pure hatred in those baby blues and he felt himself returning the feeling. She hated him with every fiber of her being and he knew it. Part of him had begun to hate her as well.

A shock spread through his entire body and he doubled over in pain. His stomach hurt so much it made him nauseated and groaned when Julia placed her foot back on the ground. Why did she have to knee him there?

His knee dropped to the ground and he instinctively grabbed his privates. The need to throw up was overwhelming, but he took deep breaths to keep the bile from rising. He did not have time to recuperate before her knee connected with his forehead and he saw black spots cloud his vision.

Things began to clear up and he realized he lay on the ground with Zee between him and Julia. Both women looked furious.

"What the hell is your problem?" Julia asked, her lip was bloody, small amounts of blood dotted her white ceremonial gear and she wiped it away. *Did Zee hit her?*

"My problem?" Zee laughed. "That was a low blow, no pun intended. You don't hit a guy in his junk. I don't care if he banged your mom or your sister, you just don't do that."

Julia glared, it was a spin-chilling, murderous glare that was foreign on her face. "He deserved it and you know it."

"So he took your virginity." Zee crossed her arms. "Get over it. Looks to me like you should be worried about your little boyfriend over there. He looks pretty pissed."

Aden did look furious. In fact, he glared at Julia and part of Ryan was worried for her. Would he hurt her? He would not put it past him.

"I want to kill him." Julia looked at Aden. Her voice was low, but not low enough. He understood she was mad but wanting to kill him? That was a little much. She was becoming increasingly violent since he last saw her.

"You know Julia, I used to have a lot of respect for you. You always seemed so dignified and classy, now all I see is a heartless bitch." Zee looked her up and down with disgust.

"This is a funeral for Warriors who died looking for you. How dare you act this way."

Ryan sat up and Julia's eyes were squeezed shut. Her head started to make small twitching movements and everyone looked perplexed. Was she having a mental breakdown?

Aden saw her and immediately grabbed her arm and roughly yanked her away from the group.

Cato started to go after him but Damian held him back. "She's made her decision."

"That little prick almost pulled her arm out of the socket," Cato hissed.

"She's a big girl," Damian reasoned. "She could easily kick his ass and yet she is choosing not to."

Ryan leaned his head against the wall, sat back on his knees and placed his hands on his thighs. The pain from being struck was not going anywhere and he tried his best to breathe through it. He hated when women did this. It had to be worse than childbirth.

Cato turned on Ryan and hit him in the jaw. At this rate he was going to need to see a Healer. Damian did not hold him back. Ryan did not blame him. He knew Cato would be pissed when he found out about them and expected nothing less.

"You slept with my sister? When?"

Ryan moved his jaw around. "When we got back from the catacombs."

"After you hit her?" Damian looked surprised.

"Yeah," he groaned.

He was hit on the other side of his jaw and he fell forward. His hands held him up before he hit the ground and he slowly pushed himself back up into a sitting position. Part of him was glad he was being hurt. After the days events he needed it, wanted to be punished for all the mistakes he made as of recently. He was going to have to scrub off blood and dirt from his ceremonial gear.

"You crossed the line, Ryan," Cato spat on the ground by him. "After this mission I am done with you. I'm transferring to another team."

With that being said, he stormed away from the group and left Ryan at the mercy of two women and a furious friend. He could not bring himself to look at anyone, he just concentrated on the aches all over his body instead.

"Why did you do that?" Damian asked. "Seriously, Ryan."

"I don't know. I asked her to leave and she wouldn't and it just happened." The memory of her body under his gave him chills all over. It was torturous knowing it would never happen again.

"I don't know why you all are surprised," Zee spoke up. "It's Ryan—he does that. Everyone knows he is head over heels for the girl."

He did not want Zee knowing all this. There was a connection there that he could not explain and he felt like it was ruined now. 'It's Ryan—he does that'. *Great*.

"You don't sleep with your friends sister, especially after you accidentally hit her," Damian added.

"I get it. I really do. You can't help who you love though. It'd be like someone telling you to stay away from Anna." He was amazed at how she knew the full extent of Damian's feelings for Anna. Word spread like wild fire around the Domus.

Zee crouched down by Ryan and gently placed her hand

along his jaw, her touch was soothing. He hated the pity in her eyes. For the first time since Julia had come back, he felt relaxed.

"I should have told you," he whispered. Thankfully Damian and Anna were talking amongst themselves.

"Why would you need to? Are you okay? She got you pretty good."

The nauseous feeling did not want to go away but he managed to push himself up to standing. "Yeah, pretty sure the boys just got murdered."

Zee chuckled. "I'd offer to make it better for you, but we aren't that close yet."

"Yet?" He smirked.

She blushed and it made him smile. "Yeah, maybe we should go." The other two faced them now and Damian nodded.

They made their way out of the alley and he could see the pyres still burning. His heart felt heavy. The only thing comforting him was that they were accepted into the heavens and it was just their vessels that were disappearing, not their souls.

"Hey!" Cato came running back to them, his face flushed. "Come to the temple."

"Why?" Damian asked.

"Not sure." He grimaced. "I was told to come get you."

Despite his aching groin, they all ran toward the temple. It was not too far away thankfully and they reached it in just ten minutes. A small crowd of people had gathered in front of the closed doors and seemed to be looking at something.

They ran up the stairs, Ryan reached the group first and they parted out of the way. There were members of the Council of Command at the front of the group and their faces looked sickly pale.

Ryan's heart dropped when he saw a message written on the door in blood. Damian ran up beside him and he felt that familiar weight of burden on his shoulders. Zee's hand somehow slipped into his and he gripped it tightly.

AHMOSE HAS JOINED US.
THE PEOPLE OF URBS HAVE UNTIL THE NEW YEAR TO FOLLOW SUIT.
IF YOU REFUSE, YOU WILL ALL DIE.
MAKE THE RIGHT DECISION.
⫟THE GENERAL

CHAPTER VII

Ryan

RYAN TOOK ATHOS OUT of the stables and after he was saddled and bridled he mounted the beast. He got light in the saddle and squeezed his legs as he leaned forward. Making clicking noises with his tongue he shortened the reins. Athos grunted, but listened to his command to go quicker.

Ryan pushed the white stallion as fast as Athos could gallop around the track. It was lit only by torches, which set off an eerie glow in the arena.

The reins rubbed his hands raw, but his mind wasn't on the pain in his hands. Just the feeling of the powerful beast below him was enough to rock his senses out of the hell his mind was in. It was an ecstasy his body craved, freeing up his thoughts of the altercation at Aja's funeral only hours ago.

The dry earth below them was being kicked up by Athos' hooves and added to the ghostly scene he'd created for himself.

He grimaced when he saw Damian out of the corner of his eye. He was on his own black stallion and galloping right along with Athos. "Ryan!" he yelled.

Ryan ignored him and made another clicking sound with his tongue. Athos got the message and lurched forward to pass Damian's horse. He'd come to free his mind and Damian came to interrupt. Why couldn't anyone leave him alone?

Athos started to breath heavily and Ryan felt guilt surge through him. He didn't want to push his horse in to the ground and it seemed to be just what he was doing. Damian caught up to him with ease as he pulled gently on the reins to let Athos know to slow down. He sat back in the saddle and stopped gripping the horse's sides with his knees.

Athos proceeded steadily from a trot to a walking pace as Ryan meant to cool him down before he fully let him rest. Damian was right next to him. "What are you doing?" His voice was full of agitation. Ryan merely looked forward without an answer. "Are you trying to kill Athos?"

"No," he spit out.

"Looked like it to me," Damian growled. "Don't take your shit out on the horse."

"I was unaware of my action and quickly corrected myself." Ryan was trying to keep his cool but Damian wasn't helping. "Athos is fine."

"What are you even doing out here?" Damian asked.

"Trying to clear my head, but you interrupted that. How did you even know I was here?" Ryan decided to look at his friend now but his eyes were anything but friendly.

"I followed you. So sue me." Athos' breathing steadied.

"After you got kicked in the goods and Cato's murderous looks I thought perhaps you needed to talk to someone."

"You thought wrong," Ryan grumbled. The look on Damian's face was a mixture of hurt and agitation. "I'm sorry I am being so cold. Thank you for looking out for me. There are a lot of things I am trying to process right now and everything seems to be mixing together. I can't think straight."

"I get that," Damian said quietly as the horses came to a stop.

Ryan dismounted Athos and pressed his hands against the stallion—Athos wasn't hot enough to worry. "I can't focus on anything but Julia," he admitted.

"For now I think you need to push her out of your mind, Ryan. I know it won't be easy since you slept with her, but the world needs you focused. We can't do any of this without you. I don't mean to add more weight on your shoulders, but I have to speak frankly."

"I understand." Ryan nodded. "I just love that woman more than life itself."

"I know the feeling," Damian muttered.

"Do you think Cato was serious about leaving the team?"

Damian shook his head. "After a long talk with him he calmed down. He isn't happy about it, nor do I blame him, but he's even more unhappy about her choice in Aden."

"As we all are." Ryan grimaced.

"Zee is a lovely person, always has been, pursue her and keep your mind off of Julia for now. If it is meant to be, it will be." Damian patted him on the back. "Now quit with the women and concentrate on the Staff of Brahma."

"Tomorrow I will get back on track. I have to."

Damian grinned. "Pun intended?"

Ryan looked around the track and rolled his eyes. "You are really idiotic sometimes."

Damian shrugged and they both led their horses in the direction of the stalls. "Just trying to lighten your mood."

Ryan snorted. "Do you think I can make this mess of a life I have into something worth while or am I destined to live as I always have—carefree, single, and an empty shell?"

"You have the ability. It was who you were when you were mortal. I think you've just lost your way during the years trying to distance yourself from who you were born as. To be honest, I miss that man." Damian put a firm hand on his shoulder.

"You really are the only person that understands me." Ryan laughed.

"Yeah, I've been around your dumb ass for far too long."

Chapter VIII

Julia

"WHERE THE HELL DO you think you are going?" Cato asked.

After the events at the funeral yesterday, Cato took it upon himself to talk to her about Ryan. Julia was not in the mood for it, especially when it came to the sex talk. He had no right to judge her on the subject.

"I am not going to stand here and let you treat me like a child," she groaned and opened her door.

He pushed his hand against the door and slammed it back shut. She was trapped with an irate brother and wanted nothing more than to find Aden. Lately, he had been her only saving grace.

"You are being a child," he growled. "You slept with Ryan of all people. And you're dating that prick? What is wrong with you?"

"Nothing is wrong with me," she screamed. "I am a damn adult I can do what I please."

Cato grabbed her arm, bringing her to her couch and sitting her down. She was sick of being treated like this by him. They were hundreds of years old and it was about time she dipped her foot into the promiscuous ring anyways. Her virginity lasted longer than anyone alive.

"Have you slept with Aden?" He crossed his arms and looked down on her. He was so much like their father when he was fuming that it was terrifying. They both towered over everyone and their sharp features made them intimidating.

"That is none of your business," she groaned and leaned back against the couch.

This conversation was already tiring. Although she had to agree sleeping with Ryan was wrong. Why did she do such a wonderful thing with such a disgusting excuse for a man?

She loved him once. She knew it, but that was over. Her feelings were gone for him and all she had left for him was distain. It dripped from her very being and she could not wait till the Earth consumed him. Why she felt so strongly about that? She had no idea, but the feeling was deeply embedded in her.

"Answer me right now."

"Yes," she snarled.

Cato looked on the verge of exploding. The long scar along his face seemed even more menacing with the look he gave her. He was disappointed and angry, and it terrified her in a way she never felt before with her brother. He'd always showed affection, always kept calm with her and made her feel safe, but not now.

He rubbed his face with both hands and he turned away

from her. Now she did feel like a child.

"Let me get this straight," he started. "My sister, who valued her virginity so much that she held on to it for hundreds of years, slept with two different men in the same week?"

"Yes," she said quietly. It was very unlike her, she had to admit.

With Ryan it felt, real. Like part of her was finally getting what she wanted. But afterwards, it felt so wrong it made her sick to her stomach. With Aden it felt forced. She had no enjoyment out of the experience. She felt like she had to do it and that made it right for her. Maybe it was the odd tasting drink she had before hand that made her mind fuzzy. Aden did say she seemed out of it.

Cato punched her mirror causing shards to fall to the floor. She was glad he wore his gear—gloves included. Otherwise he may be bloody. He turned toward her and screamed, "What is wrong with you?"

"Nothing," she said.

"You are not my sister." His voice cracked. "My sister has class. She stands up for herself and would never let a man hurt her physically like Aden did."

"He didn't hurt me." That was a lie. Her arm had a bruise around it from were Aden had pulled on her. "He was just upset I never told him about Ryan."

She stood up and approached her brother. His usual high and tight haircut must have taken the back burner as his hair was grown out more than she was used to. She placed her hand on his shoulder and he pulled her into a bear hug. They could never stand being upset with one another.

She hoped with her whole being he would realize the error of his way and join the ranks. She could not bear for him to be killed. Her heart hurt just thinking about it.

"If something was wrong you would tell me wouldn't you?" he mumbled against her neck. His grip around her did not loosen. He held onto her like she was going to disappear at any moment.

Desperately wanting to tell him the truth, she could only say, "Yes, I would tell you."

The words would not form. Something in her mind kept her from exposing the truth to her flesh and blood. He was a traitor—brother or not. Right?

She felt her head twitch from the back and forth game it played with itself. Nothing was black and white anymore. It was a mix of colors that she could not fully understand.

"I hate him," Cato spoke into her neck. He relaxed his hug enough to be able to look at her and tucked some hair behind her ear. This is the brother she loved.

"I know you do, but he saved me. I love him and he loves me. There are no complications between him and I. Plus it's better than me being with Ryan." She tried to make it sound optimistic but knew her brother's feelings for Aden would never change. Then again his feelings for Ryan were obviously less than optimistic, either way she must be driving him nuts.

He sighed. "In all honesty, I'd much rather it be Ryan you were with."

She eyes him up and down knowing her face looked utterly perplexed. "Why?"

"He has his faults, but he is a good man. If anyone could protect you it would be him," he explained. "If he weren't such a whore he would be the ideal man I would pick for you. Don't tell him I said that. I am still pissed at him."

Her stomach fluttered for some unknown reason. After all the hell she had been through to be with Ryan her brother suddenly approved of him when she moved on. She did not need his approval though. It was her life, not his and she wanted Aden.

"I highly doubt we will ever talk again." She kissed his cheek. "Besides, he seems to have moved on anyways."

"In all honesty, I think Ryan loves you so much it scares him Julia. I think he brought Zee in the picture to help himself move on."

"It doesn't matter." She shook her head. "Enough of that topic—where are you heading to again?"

"The Unites States. Some of the government officials are demanding religious changes in their states and causing riots. A great deal of the military personnel are turning on the government to protect the people. Brave bunch of men and women, if you ask me."

Julia smirked. "There isn't much you can do about it, Cato."

"Helping the citizens under arrest for not cooperating seems like a better use of my time Julia, as it should be for everyone. Especially when all of this is our people's fault." Cato gave her a disapproving look.

There was something in his look that made her uneasy. She had to play nice with the Warriors. They could not suspect her. It was becoming difficult pretending to be the sweet sensitive Julia they all knew when she wanted to be oh so bad.

"I don't think leaving Urbs right now is a good idea. The people are turning on us." She tried to turn her obvious disgust for his plan into something else. After all, she wasn't wrong.

Word had gotten around that the leader of the Warriors was now affiliated with the Risen and it made people nervous. Most believed the Warriors were now corrupt and either followed them or hated them for dispelling the Gods. Either way, it made life as a Warrior unpredictable. Just a day after the news, citizens had become intolerant of Warriors and shunned them from the city.

A civil war had begun and it'd happened so easily too.

"They locked the gates to the Domus and we aren't going to sit here and do nothing. There are innocents dying and we have to help in anyway we can." Cato hugged her again but this time it was so long she grew impatient. It felt like a goodbye. "Be careful while I am gone."

"How long will you be away?" If Ryan and his team were gone, they could do some serious converting of the Immortals.

"Not sure," he answered and headed toward her door. He turned back to look at her before he walked out. "If something happens to me, know that I love you and I hope your life is everything you ever dreamed it would be."

He made it seem like this mission was highly dangerous and it made her weary. It didn't sound like a difficult mission. Hell, it sounded just like they were going to help calm things down. The fact he believed his life was in danger gave her the chills. He never did this, not ever. "I love you too, Cato."

Ryan

"Do you need help?" Zee asked him. She set down the book she was looking through and eyed him up and down. He tried to ignore how her mouth hung slightly open as she stared at his bare chest. Nevertheless, he couldn't help but relish in the effect his body had on her.

He found it difficult to get his gear on by himself. After everything his body had been through it was becoming increasingly difficult to hide how weak he really was at this point. No one would be in top shape after the continuous beatings their body endured, not even a Warrior

Ryan caught the look on her face. He hated seeing her pity him while he struggled to put his clothing on.

He tucked his trousers into his boots and started to lace them up. His chest felt sore to the touch so he waited to put his shirt on. He felt self-conscious around her now. Scars still littered his chest and back, making him feel like damaged goods. Never in his life had he hated his body more than he did now.

"I'm good." He forced a smile. He wanted to see her before he left and to his surprise, she agreed. There was something about this woman that he could not get enough of. She made the ache in his heart easier to bear. "Do me a favor though?"

"What's that?"

Ryan leaned over her body to grab a jar of ointment off his side table. He heard her sharp intake of breath and couldn't help but smile. Maybe he just thought he looked terrible. She did not seem to mind. Just his close proximity seemed to get her going.

"Will you put this on me? I can't reach my back." He

handed her the jar of ointment the healers had given him. It made the scars gradually disappear along with a little something to make his body numb as well. His body was healed even though the pain remained. Part of him wondered if the discomfort was all in his mind.

Usually he had Damian do it for him, but he started to ask why it made his hands feel numb afterward. Last thing he needed was for people to know he could not take the agony he constantly felt. Damian would probably not let him go anywhere. They were on a time limit, pity and caution was the last thing he needed from others.

She took the jar from him and opened it. Just like a woman would, she smelled it and grinned. "No wonder you smell so good."

"Thanks darling." He stood up straight, ready for her small hands to caress his body. Oddly enough, he felt nervous to have her touch him.

"I cannot believe that in a month Urbs may cease to exist." He had a feeling this would be the talk coming out of almost everyone's mouth until the New Year.

"Hopefully it will be," it was all he would say and she seemed to have taken the hint that he did not want to talk about it any further. If anything, he just wanted to concentrate on the task at hand. In particular, her hands on him.

She stood in front of him and they stared at each other for a moment. Her green cat-like eyes studied him so fiercely that he started to feel a longing to touch her. There was something about her that was intoxicating, but he could not get Julia off of his mind. He loved her, more than he ever thought possible again in a lifetime. He needed to move on and Zee was someone special, he could tell already.

"Chest too?" Her voice was seductively low as she dipped her fingers into the jar again. *Why is she teasing me?*

He nodded as she set the jar down on the side table, rubbed her hands together and touched him gently on his chest. Their eye contact broke when she seemed rather intrigued with her hands at work on him. He saw a hint of pity on her face as she went over the various scars that plagued his body. Again an instant feeling of self-consciousness washed over him.

Her touch was tender, almost soothing and he closed his eyes. It was an intimacy he had missed for a long time. Nothing sexual, just sensual and he relished in it. She moved her hands lower over his abs and felt her pause. His eyes opened to see Zee looking on the brink of tears.

"What's wrong?" He felt insecure again.

Zee shook her head. "I heard what happened, but I never imagined it was this ruthless. The fact that these scars are faded is even more troubling." She sniffled. "The rumors were terrible and most of Urbs saw you both strung up, yet I never thought it was like this. I have no idea how you even survived."

"I'm not much to look at anymore." He knew he was being pathetic, but he couldn't help confirming what he thought of himself. "I know, sorry."

She laughed and her eyes met his again. "You are very fun to look at. Trust me." She bit her lip. "You have the most prominent V leading down stairs that I have ever seen."

Goose bumps raced down his arms. He wanted to bite that lip of hers and taste her mouth against his so badly in that moment. It was shocking given Julia was still floating around his mind. *Self control Ryan.*

"Huge arms." She got more ointment and worked on his arms. "Wide, washboard abs." That lip was stuck between her teeth again. Zee seemed to be taking her time rubbing in the ointment. *What is going through her mind?*

A sharp intake of breath happened once again when she came upon his back. Her hands stilled against his skin. His shoulders tensed just imagining the pity in her eyes once more. His back had gotten the worst of it when he was tortured and it almost looked as if he were a burn victim or mauled by a tiger.

"If you don't want to do this you don't have to." His voice quiet and reserved. He hated feeling disgusted with his body when he'd always been proud of it. Zee came into his life when he looked his worst.

Her hands started to move over him once more. "How are you even alive, Ryan?" She ignored his comment, and it made him feel better.

"That is a very good question." He honestly had no idea how he could survive what he'd been through. Most people would be dead.

"Does it still hurt?"

"Honestly?" he asked.

"Yes." She got more ointment. The numbing agent started to kick in on his chest and he relaxed.

"It's an odd feeling," he admitted. "It hurts even though the wounds are gone. My guess is that it messed up the nerves in my body or something. Besides that, I haven't really given myself time to properly rest and heal. I think it's all in my head. Sort of messed up, aren't I?"

"Maybe you shouldn't go on your mission then." She wrapped her arms around him from behind and he felt her face pressed against his back. To his surprise she kissed him between his shoulder blades. He froze in place.

Why did this feel wrong? And why did he want it so badly?

He answered after a long pause, "I have to. People are depending on me." Her contact made the blood rush in his veins. Ryan clenched his fists trying to control his urges.

Her hands skimmed over his chest making his eyes close. "People always depend on you, Ryan. Maybe you should think about yourself for once."

He laughed and turned to face her. Tears silently rolled down her cheeks making him panic. "Whoa, what's wrong?" He grabbed her hands, holding them in his. The last thing he wanted was to make more women cry on his account.

"It's just terrible. Ahmose told everyone you were in bad shape. That it looked worse than it actually was. He obviously lied to us." She shook her head. "Most of the Domus was in an uproar when we found out what happened. You have no idea how much we all care about you, do you?"

"Not a clue. Why would they care about me so much?" He laughed and wiped away her tears. She closed her eyes at his touch.

"We see you as a leader, Ryan. You are the best of the best and everyone looks up to you. You and your team are the people we all aspire to be like. We know very well that you would die for any one of us. You cannot buy that sort of respect, Ryan."

Ryan knew he was seen as a leader but to be respected

like that? He figured everyone viewed him as nothing but a womanizer that could care less about self-preservation. She was right about one thing—he would gladly give his life to save another Warrior. It may be a fault of his, but he could not help it.

"I'm not someone to look up to." He ran his hand along her hair and tugged on a strand gently. His self-control was losing this battle. He was so desperate to touch this angel in front of him. "Nor am I someone you should want." He might as well be honest about it.

"You really think so little of yourself don't you? It's very annoying." She smirked. "I think you push people away so you don't get hurt. But guess what? I am not going anywhere unless you tell me to. So suck up the self-loathing, pity party and enjoy the ride, you sexy animal."

She kissed the corner of his mouth and he felt a surge of energy rush through his body. There was a hunger buried in him that he had no idea was so intense until she kissed him.

He gripped her upper arms and a look of panic washed over her face. He must have grabbed her too hard but he could not let go. He was starting to feel animalistic with her. Just that one simple act of her lips near his made him lose his mind.

Without thinking, he led her back toward his bed when she stopped him. "What are you doing?"

"Sorry," he groaned and let go of her arms. What came over him, he did not know. One thing he was sure of, he felt an ache from frustration now and barely managed to avoid adjusting himself in front of her.

"I like you, Ryan," she admitted. "I just know you're not over Julia and I don't want to complicate your life. Honestly, I don't want you to hurt me either. I'm sorry I kissed you, but I couldn't help it. Maybe with time and after you heal we can try something? If you are even interested in a relationship."

There's his reputation coming back to bite him in the ass once again. "I don't know why, but I feel drawn to you and I would really like to get closer to you."

"You've barely even noticed me until recently. Chill out, Romeo." Her smile was contagious. He still felt that ache in his groin that he desperately wanted to go away. Women had no idea how terrible the feeling was.

"I like you Zyanya and I can't explain it but I find myself..." he paused.

"What?"

"I don't know. I am oddly drawn to you and I do still have feelings for Julia, but it is obvious there will never be anything between us again." It hurt to say it, even if it was true. He loved Julia, with every fiber of his being. He loved her and it would never go away. He had to move on though. He needed to because it hurt too much to wallow in misery over her.

Zee was a wonderful girl. He liked her but it still felt wrong. What would come of it? He did not know. But he would not wait for a woman that hated him.

"I think you need to take some time to yourself and figure out what you want," she seemed to force herself to say this. "I still can't believe you took her virginity though. She seems to hate your guts and it's weird that she would let you do that."

"Agreed." It was a thought he had repeatedly. "I honestly felt like we were together. But then she showed up all in love with Aden and well, you know. I must not be as desirable as I thought."

"Yeah right." She smiled. "At least you got to her first though. I bet no one can live up to your obvious talents. Well, from what I hear anyways."

He had to laugh when she winked at him. Ryan had honestly never thought about it. He did not do anything crazy with Julia, he didn't want to hurt her but she certainly seemed to have enjoyed herself.

"Enough of Julia." He grabbed her waist and gently pulled her into him. "Julia and I are over. And I know this is fast between us, but I really would like it if you gave me a shot. Forget about my reputation." It was as if he were trying to convince himself of this.

"Ryan, how do I know this isn't some sort of trick you pull on women?" She was teasing him but he could tell it was a serious question. "Is this a suspiciously good line of yours?"

"I don't tell women lines," he said firmly. "If anything I tell the women I want to sleep with it means nothing to me. For some reason they still agree to it. Some get feelings, but I am very upfront about it not going any further than sex for me."

"Wow." Her eyes widened. "I would say that you're an ass, but then again you are honest with them. Most of the women I hear talking about you made you seem like a jerk that uses them."

He shook his head. "In a way I did, but they knew it and kept coming back for more."

She was making this difficult, and it was starting to get annoying. If this was too much for her he would just forget it. No matter how much he wanted to see where things could go with Zee, it was not worth trying to continuously convince someone of his feelings. It was tiring.

"I just don't get why me?" She placed her hands on his chest. "I'm not really high up in the ranks as far as Warriors go. I have nothing to offer."

"Please quit arguing with me. I am telling you how I feel. Take it as you will, Zee. The fact you are a Warrior makes no difference to me. I like you, but if you want friendship that's fine. If you want to just hook up then that's okay too, but know I am willing to try for more. For the first time in my life I am letting the woman decide as to how we end up."

"My hands are numb," she blurted out.

He raised his eyebrow. "I'll take that as you avoiding an answer." He laughed. Ryan moved past her, grabbed his black shirt and pulled it over his head.

She watched him and bit her lip in the process. Reluctantly, he put on his flak jacket and avoided eye contact with her. This was frustrating and he really had to get a move on. They were going to leave through the portal in thirty minutes and there was no time to argue with her.

"I'm making you mad aren't I?" Her voice was almost a whisper.

"Your are frustrating the hell out of me, but I understand your hesitation." He strapped his tactical vest on and wondered around his room to gather what he needed. He propped his favorite pair of sunglasses up on his head.

"No helmet?" she asked.

"I have a feeling it will just get in the way." He slung his M4 Carbine around his shoulder and holstered a M9 Beretta Pistol on his leg along with a SIG-Sauer P226 on his chest rig.

Ryan took a few of his pain pills with Zee behind his back before he slid the pill bottle into a pouch.

He sat down on his couch and strapped on his kneepads. Sadly, she was letting him get dressed even though he half expected it. They had just met and he was pretty sure she wasn't the type to just sleep with a man. *Or I'm just losing my touch with women.*

"You're damn good looking you know that?" She sighed as she sat on his bed.

He leaned his elbows on his knees and watched her cross her legs. She wore gray sweat pants and a tight tank top. Something about a woman in sweats was sexy. Her hair was pulled back into a high ponytail and he felt the ache come back in his groin.

"Can I be honest?" He grunted.

She pulled out her ponytail and let her hair fall down over her chest. "Yes."

What the hell is she doing?

"I want you right now," he rasped.

Was that a smirk on her face? This woman was playing a game with him and he did not like it at all. Okay, maybe he did a little bit. *Such a complicated creature in such a small body.*

"Oh really?" She climbed up further on his bed and lay on her stomach facing him. Her arms propped up her head, but the look in her eyes was anything but innocent. "You want me?"

"Yes." He did not like her right now. Actually, he liked her a little too much and that was the problem. She let him get fully dressed and now she was playing with him. He was dealing with the ultimate tease right now.

"Come here," she said softly.

It took effort to look as if her sudden interest did not

bother him but he managed. He casually made his way over to her and stood at the foot of his bed with his arms crossed. The best way to frustrate a woman was to look indifferent to her advances. She looked up at him with those damn green eyes and his frustration kicked in full force.

"What can I do for you, ma'am?"

She sat up, grabbed his vest and yanked him toward her. "I like you Ryan. For now, we can be friends but with some benefits involved. If that's okay with you."

It was not what he expected from her, but he would take it. "If that is what you want than okay." He smirked.

Zee leaned up and kissed his lips, gently at first but then a hunger seemed to develop in her. She bit his lip roughly, making him grin against her lips. "What?" she groaned.

"You just had to let me get dressed didn't you?" Ryan grumbled.

Zee bit her lip seductively. "I knew I'd take it further if you weren't ready to go."

"Why would that be a problem?" He laughed.

"I don't want to just jump all the way into it, Ryan. I'm not the type. Could we just work up to it or something?" She pulled back to look at him with a worried look in her eyes.

What the hell sort of benefit is that?

Ryan took the M4 off and set it down on the floor. He pushed her down on the bed with his body pressed against hers and she looked up at him nervously. Women always assumed the worst of men. She looked like he was going to try to have sex with her against her wishes. No part of him had ever been interested in taking that choice from someone.

He climbed on top of her then brushed her hair behind

her ear before he placed a gentle kiss on her lips. He didn't want to scare her with being too passionate. "If that is what you want then okay. Just so you know, I'm going to be hurting later because of your sexy ass and I am not too happy about that."

Zee laughed and covered her mouth quickly. "Sorry."

"Yeah, I'm sure." He kissed her again. "You seemed to make up your mind rather quickly. I thought you would need days to decide what we will be."

"Yeah, well, you look pretty damn good right now. I couldn't help it." Her attitude was so nonchalant.

Her arms wrapped around his neck and she ran her hand up along the back of his head. Ryan felt his eyes grow heavy at her touch. He loved when women did this but his vest was definitely in the way of him taking it any further with her, which caused more frustration on his part.

"I like your hair like this," she groaned as he kissed her neck. He nipped it gently and she let out soft moans. "You look much more intimidating and manly."

Ryan laughed. "Yeah, I guess."

Her hands took him by surprise when she grabbed his backside and he involuntarily thrust his hips against hers. She burst out laughing. "Did I really just make *the* Ryan jump in shock?"

"You sure did." He grabbed her hands and placed them back around his shoulders. "Don't get any ideas Miss, I am a gentleman and I expect to be treated as more than a piece of meat."

"You may be a gentlemen, but I hardly believe that is the case in bed." She wrapped her legs around him and pulled him against her again. This woman was insatiable.

"Why do you have to do this to me now?" He closed his eyes trying to contain himself.

"Because it's fun seeing you squirm. I don't think you're used to it." She kissed his lips again and he bit hers gently. Her groans made him feel somewhat satisfied but the ache he felt was becoming unbearable.

"I can easily get undressed," he grumbled when she thrust her hips against his.

His hands ventured up her thighs, along her stomach, and under her shirt. She instinctively arched her back making him thrust his hips against hers again. There was no way she could deny him much longer. He could feel her body begin to give in to his touch. The hesitation in her waned, her hand made that apparent when she grabbed his erection.

"You are not being fair," he moaned when she did not answer. Her eyes met his and they blazed with desire.

"Get undressed," she said finally.

"Thank the gods," he mumbled and kissed her roughly. He started to take off his vest.

"Really, Ryan?" He heard Damian groan from across the room. He must have been too involved with Zee to hear the door open.

He looked down at Zee, who was trying to hide her smile. "Glad this amuses you," he said coarsely.

"Sort of." She giggled.

"Damian, I'm begging you. Give me fifteen minutes." Ryan glanced toward his friend. Anna stood there sheepishly next to Cato who rolled his eyes. Cato was one of the last people he wanted to see him in this position.

Damian adjusted his duffel bag. "As hard as you would try, we both know that's not enough time. Get your ass up and grab your stuff. We need to head out."

Chapter IX

Anna

"So Colette and Grace are going to keep watch over everything, right?" Damian asked Ryan.

Anna stood back and felt unimportant to the group. The three men all had their gear decked out with weapons and gadgets and all she'd managed to find was a rifle, pistol, some grenades and an emergency kit.

How do you prepare for a place you know nothing about?

"Yeah, Grace will keep us informed of what is going on here. Tomorrow or the next day they are going to take Julia into to the mortal world for a bit while we are gone to keep her busy." He slid a very sharp looking sword into his back scabbard. "The civilians are starting to get more restless, which makes her nervous but so far the doors are holding up against them. She doesn't want to be away for too long."

"What are they doing?" Anna was afraid of the answer,

but since they lived in a city with professionally trained killers, she felt she had a right to feel scared.

"Rioting outside the Domus. It hasn't gotten too out of hand, yet," Cato said. "Some of them are demanding our blood. We've become the enemy to both the Risen and the God's followers."

This was a perfect time for me to join, she thought sarcastically to herself. It felt like ever since see came into the picture, everything went to hell. "Well, that's peachy keen."

Damian smirked and slung his duffle bag over his shoulder. "You guys ready? Or do you have anyone else to sleep with before we go?" He turned to Ryan. That was a bit harsh when he was doing nothing but standing there.

He rolled his eyes. "Fairly certain you interrupted me so I don't see that as a valid question."

"I hope you have blue balls," Cato seethed.

"That I do." Anna looked away when he readjusted his business. She really needed to meet more women in this place. Boys are so disgusting.

"Alright ladies and gents', ready?" Damian took a deep breath. It worried her that they looked nervous. They never looked nervous and she felt herself becoming very uneasy.

Ryan took his little black pouch out of a vest pocket then tossed a small crystal up in the air. "Palermo, Sicily."

An oceanic scene burst into life right before her eyes. It was a beautiful morning and the beach looked empty. Why did she feel so excited about this now? Her brain was going to have a field day with her mood swings. Nervous, uneasy, excited. She made no sense, not even to herself.

They marched through the portal and her boots sunk

down into the golden white sand. The view was breathtaking and she could not help but stare at her surroundings. She was in love with this place in an instant.

A tall mountain was to her left and loomed over them with contrasting dark hues of rocks at the edge of the gulf. The seafront was a combination of blue and green and the city behind her flourished with vegetation. The air was hot and dry—her gear made it even worse. She wished she could put on a tank top and shorts. However, the view she had made her not care about the heat.

The red-roofed city behind her was bustling to life and the welcomed smells of spices and citrus filled the air. It made her hungry even though she had already eaten this morning. It was an intriguing fusion of ingredients meeting her nostrils and brought her to a mouth-watering orgasm.

She could see there were many different types of architectural styles throughout the city. Some things looked ancient and some modern. It was like a melting pot of history in one place.

She turned back toward the sea and saw a small, motorized boat floating on the shoreline. She raised an eyebrow. Were they really going to travel eight hours in that thing? Anna knew the Immortals couldn't be made of money, but this seemed downright stingy.

"You were able to get the boat early, right?" Ryan eyed Damian warily, obviously thinking the same thing.

"Yes." He pointed out toward the sea. "It's out there. Someone is going to bring us out to it."

Anna looked around and saw a short, petite woman make her way toward them. She had long brown curly hair and light skin. She was pretty and looked a lot better than Anna did as she sashayed toward them wearing a cute blue sundress. The light breeze tossed her hair gently around. Anna looked at Damian to make sure his jaw was not hitting the ground.

To her surprise he looked unaffected. She really needed to get over her self-conscious jealousy. Damian had been nothing but faithful to her. Not that she had ever been cheated on—she just felt unworthy. It was probably from being a foster kid and no one actually ever wanting her, but hey, what did she know?

"Hello," the woman called over to them and smiled brightly. Of course her teeth were white and her green eyes were outlined with perfect wings at the corners. "My name is Ayde, I will be the one taking you out to the yacht."

A yacht! Oh hell yeah!

Ayde seemed confused by their attire but Ryan was the master of making women swoon it seemed. He was the first to receive her. "We are going hunting on an island off of the coast," he explained. "I would ask you to join us, but you look too exquisite to be getting dirty." He flashed her that ornery smile Anna was becoming accustomed to.

She blushed red, a smile plastered on her face. "Thank you. If you all will come with me I will bring you out."

They piled into the small motorboat and Damian wrapped his arm around Anna's waist as they sat on the small boards. Ryan sat by himself in the middle and Cato sat next to Ayde. He seemed interested in the girl and Anna could have sworn her cheeks still looked red.

The little boat was off, heading toward the enormous white vessel sitting alone in the sea. Cato and Ayde talked with one another quietly. Cato threw out his bright smile, making her giggle. They were going to crash if he laid his charm on any thicker. Two out of three men had given her attention and they were all damn good looking. Could Anna really blame her for being distracted?

As they got closer to the vessel, she felt Damian push her mouth back up. It had literally dropped from the size of the boat.

"It's so big," she breathed. "Shut up, Ryan." She watched him open his mouth and close it with huge grin on his face.

"What?" He smiled wickedly. "You set yourself up."

She ignored him. "It's like eighty feet long."

"About one hundred actually." Ayde smiled at Anna. "The Azimut 98 Leonardo was a very good choice."

"Couldn't just get a speed boat or something?" Anna laughed.

"We need to travel in comfort." It seemed perfectly clear to him. "Yacht's are much better."

Anna rolled her eyes as they neared the large yacht. It was gorgeous and she would have rather been lounging on it than running off to get killed by mythical creatures.

Damian and the other two must be loaded to be able to afford something like this. It made her feel insignificant. She had no money. Everything was provided for her at the Domus and she never needed money.

They pulled up to the back of the boat and Ryan grabbed the railing. After everyone jumped on board, Ryan kicked the small motorboat away from the yacht. Ayde smiled and waved at them as she drove away from the vessel, making Anna feel a little more at ease. The green-eyed monster seemed to shrink back down into her stomach to take a nap for now.

They proceeded up the two small stairways on each side of the yacht and up under the overhang. This thing was for rich people and she felt uncomfortable being here. Under the overhang there was a circular glass table with a bar on the left behind it.

She needed to utilize the bar as soon as possible. Her nerves started to get the best of her just being in a rich place that she could never afford herself. Not to mention whatever beasts were waiting to maul her to death.

Damian and Cato dumped the duffel bags on the floor and fell onto the leather couches opposite of the bar. Ryan ran up some stairs to the top deck and after a minute she felt the yacht come to life. She was somewhat relieved Ryan was being kept busy. His smart-ass comments were not what she needed right now. Her brain was a jumbled mess of anything and everything.

Damian looked up to her with a small smile on his lips and patted the seat next to him. She trailed over and dropped down. The couch was so comfortable that her eyes grew heavy. It was early morning and she had no reason to be tired yet she was. Stress was taking a toll. She snuggled up to Damian as best she could in her gear. It was awkward with her bulky gear on, but she craved his touch too much to care.

He wrapped on arm around her as she studied her surroundings. *Who rents something like this for a mission? Seriously.* This yacht was meant for vacationing, not to transport gung-ho Immortals to a death trap of an island.

"I need a drink." Cato got up and went around the bar. There were a lot of clinking noises being made and Cato swore. "Where the hell is the whiskey?"

"Don't get drunk, Cato," Damian said nonchalantly, entwining his fingers with hers. He studied Anna's hands, seemingly entranced with her nails. He was so odd the way he studied every inch of her.

"Aha!" Cato held up a bottle in triumph. "I'm not going to get drunk. We have like eight hours to kill, probably less with Ryan driving."

Ryan would be a speed demon wouldn't he?

"Just take it easy."

"Yes, sir." Cato saluted him and twist the bottle open. "Anna?"

She looked at Damian who gave her a halfhearted salute. Good, she can drink. "Yes, please."

"That 'a girl." Cato grinned and brought her a glass. "Damian is a little stiff, but I for one think we need to have a little fun before we probably die."

"What a comforting thought." Damian rolled his eyes. "I just prefer to be at my best."

"Yeah, well, me at my best is not stressing over what's to come." Cato had a good philosophy on life. When she first met him he seemed like a really cranky guy. He seemed to be letting loose now though. Maybe he was just getting used to her.

Anna downed the whiskey and stuck out her tongue in disgust. "Yuck!"

"Easy killer." Cato snickered and casually drank his own. How anyone could enjoy sipping that crap was beyond her. "So, what are your opinions on this Ryan, Julia, Aden, Zee situation we have going on?"

Anna looked to Damian who seemed as if he wished to

talk about anything else. "I have no idea," he admitted.

"Give me some sort of opinion because I am going insane over her." Cato sank back down on the couch after he filled her glass again.

"I know for a fact both Ryan and Julia had very strong feelings for one another. It makes no sense that she is with Aden, none at all and it concerns me. Especially when she seems to have conflicting feelings. She isn't acting like herself," Damian replied.

"Like when she was twitching after she hit Ryan?" Anna mentioned.

Damian nodded. "That was unusual."

"Maybe she is doing drugs?" Cato mused. "I know she hates the stuff, but after everything going on, maybe she finally snapped."

"Julia, do drugs?" Damian laughed at the thought.

Cato shrugged and took another drink. "I don't know what it is but it bothers me. She seems a lot more hostile. She has been nothing but sweet her entire life unless she's in battle. I don't think she's ever hit a guy in the nuts either."

"Just don't mention her in front of Ryan. It bothers him and I can tell," Damian replied.

"Looks like he's moved on quickly enough to me," Cato fumed.

"What other choice does he have?" Damian asked plainly. "Julia made it clear she doesn't like him. He has to move on and Zee is a good woman. Ryan has never been good with things like this. Why do you think he sleeps around? He can't stand being heartbroken."

Cato went back to the bar and refilled his now empty

glass. His anger level seemed to be rising as the conversation progressed. Suddenly, she realized she never really thought about what went on in Cato's life. Was he with someone? Cato was a mystery to her, whereas Ryan was an open book. She certainly needed to get to know him better.

"So you were reborn right?" she asked Cato. He looked up at her with a surprised look on his face. "Were you ever someone famous?"

He looked to Damian and back to Anna. She did not know what his buttons were but she felt as if she'd pushed one. They had hours to kill and she wanted to know once and for all who these guys were.

"Not really," he answered. "Ryan's always been the lead on missions."

"That's not really fair."

Damian smirked. "It's not his fault he was made to be a leader. Even as a child he was a leader not a follower. Just his nature."

"That's got to be frustrating for you guys though," she insisted.

Cato shook his head. "Given his history I knew I would never outrank the guy when I joined the team. Even when my father was on the team, Ryan was the leader."

"Ryan's always been in charge since the day I met him. I don't know any different," Damian added.

They both seemed perfectly fine with this, but it had to be frustrating. They probably convinced themselves a long time ago to not get upset. She would be annoyed. Actually, no, she would not like to be in the spotlight on a mission. Too much pressure.

"Okay, so are you going to tell me your real name yet?" She grinned. Damian's smile faded and an annoyance filled inside of her. "We are dating, I'd like to know who you are, Damian."

"I can't say," he grumbled.

"Just tell her." Cato downed another glass of whiskey. "She will find out and you know it. Better she hear it from you then someone else."

Damian rolled his eyes. "Ask Ryan. I'm not going to get yelled at about it."

Well that was the end of that conversation. Anna huffed and took another sip of her drink. She would never get used to the taste. Whiskey was disgusting.

"Well, I'll tell you one of the men Ryan was." Cato winked at her. She loved him for giving her information. "Not his original self, but one of many."

She grew excited while Damian tensed beside her. "Who?"

"He was a gladiator. Rome hated him with a passion and they believed they killed him in battle. No one ever found the body so of course he wasn't actually dead." Cato looked out the boat window and laughed. "I mean honestly, he was the most hated slave in the republic and no one bothered to recover his body? Get real."

Anna waited patiently for a name. None of this was ringing a bell for her. Damian gripped her hand tightly and she took another drink. She looked at Cato blankly. "Okay?"

Cato rolled his eyes at her. "He was Spartacus. It was his first big mission after he'd joined the Immortals."

Spartacus. That sounded familiar. She would have to research this guy. Or, research Ryan. *So weird.*

"Were you with him?" she asked Damian.

He nodded and closed his eyes. "Of course."

Guilt rose in her stomach just by looking at him but she had to know more. "Just the two of you?" she asked.

Damian shook his head. "No, our other team member was killed. We were all gladiators and he was killed in the final war. It was the first time Ryan ever lost a battle and it didn't sit well with him. He got a large number of people killed when he had the chance to get them to freedom. Instead, he chose to fight like he was trained to, but they were just untrained slaves instead of soldiers. Cato's dad replaced our fallen Warrior after that on our team."

It was disheartening but death came with the territory it seemed. "So why did the Romans hate him so much?"

"Do you not know the story?" Cato almost choked on his drink. "Spartacus is one of the most famous slaves in history. He almost defeated the Roman Empire."

"Sort of," Damian added.

"Pretty damn close in my opinion." Cato laughed. "He shook the Roman's up like he was supposed to."

"So he was just sent to piss them off?" she asked. "Seems like a stupid reason to risk your life."

Damian scratched his cheek. "In a way. I wasn't told much, but I know that some slaves ended up freed because of it and some slave owners treated their slaves better in fear of another revolt."

"Did he have a wife?" Anna continued to bombard them with questions.

"Ryan has had many wives throughout his life." Damian seemed to be getting tired of this conversation.

"Who were you during this whole thing?" She kept on. It was the most she ever knew about them.

Damian laughed. "Just another slave Anna, no one important. I suppose the other slaves thought I was his right hand man, but that was about it. The name I went by isn't even in the history books." He started to look exasperated.

"I bet you were more important than you think," she grumbled. "Where were you during all this?"

Cato smirked. "Still living separately inside my parents reproductive organs."

That was a gross image.

"Spartacus." She rolled the name around in her mind for any recollection of it.

"At your service."

The three of them looked up at the stairs that Ryan stood on. His arms were crossed over his chest and his face was expressionless. Lack of emotion was a cause for concern in her opinion. There was no way of telling what he was thinking and she hoped she did not cross a line with him. With Ryan, everything was like walking on glass or in a smart-ass bubble.

"Shit," Damian said under his breath.

"Telling stories are we?" Ryan descended down the rest of the stairs.

Anna never realized how terrifying Ryan's presence was until now. He seemed older and wiser, not the carefree young man he always was. As he got closer, she could see the anger in his eyes. She wanted to sink into the couch and hide.

"Just the one." Cato would not look at him. Instead, he kept his eyes downcast, as did Damian. Feeling left out, Anna's gaze found the floor. They were children about to get yelled at by their parent.

"I see," his voice was cold.

"I just wanted to know more about you guys," Anna spoke up when she caught sight of Ryan firmly placing his hand on Damian's shoulder. "It's my fault."

Ryan towered over Damian and squeezed his hand tight. Damian winced at the contact. "The past doesn't matter. It's the man I am now that is only important. Those were roles I played and nothing more." Damian did not move an inch. It made her extremely heated at the way Ryan was treating him.

"I'm sorry," Damian muttered finally after much awkward silence.

"I'm sure," Ryan sneered.

Anna stood up and looked Ryan straight in the eyes. She had no idea what come over her or how she got so brave. She hated this situation. She hated that Damian could not even look at Ryan because he was somehow trained to lower his head in his presence. "What's the big deal? So dreadful things happened to you. Get over it and move on. Who cares if people know?"

Ryan's gaze was without a doubt, scary. He now looked like a killer to her. His entire being was a deadly weapon, ready to fight without a second thought. This was the man people looked to for leadership and guidance. A man people respected and feared. The look in his eyes made her instinctively want to cower, but she amazingly held her ground.

"I care," he answered. "I do not want to be defined by my past. If you wish to know then perhaps one day I will tell you, Anna. Until then, back the fuck off."

Ryan

Ryan sat in one of the overly comfortable white leather chairs on the bridge and stared at all the dials in front of him. It was a simple set up and he was thankful for that. Water was not his forte, but he did like driving big things. It had a lot of power to it, which made him feel tough. Man complex he supposed.

There was plenty to think about while being alone up here. He'd briefly managed to block it all from his mind. It was a gorgeous day out and he would not waste it on unnecessary drama in his life. Julia hated him, fine. Zee obviously likes him. He'd see where that went, if anywhere. Regardless of his feelings for Julia, he would not wallow in pity about her.

His responsibilities tried to push their way into his mind but he quickly subdued them. The world may be coming to an end, and he would do what he could to save it. If he could not save it than he couldn't. There was no use obsessing on things he could not fix.

"Pouting are we?" Cato asked.

Ryan did not bother to look at the other man. After much consideration he had decided not to give a damn about much. Cato hated him, he had a feeling of it anyways and he was tired of worrying about others' feelings. He was no longer the little boy Ryan taught to become a Warrior.

"Just maintaining our course and keeping an eye out for the island, Cato." He kicked his feet up on the dash. "Besides, I think my presence causes enough staleness in the air as it is."

"You're not wrong there," Cato muttered and took the seat next to him.

"What do you want?"

"First, I am sorry about what happened down there." He heard Cato sigh. "Mostly, I just wanted to ask you why you did that to my sister."

Ryan rolled his eyes. He was sick of this conversation. It'd become overly tedious and he wanted to forget about it. Ryan knew that eventually Cato would come to him about this. "I love your sister and after I hit her I didn't know what to do. So I tried to kill myself, but Damian stopped me." It was simple.

"So your first thought was to sleep with her to make up for it?" Cato cringed.

"Like I said, I love her. Seeing her with Aden just made me see red and she came to see if I was okay." This was sickening to talk about. Flashes of what transpired between the two kept popping up in his mind. "I wanted to be as close as I could with her at least once because I knew it was all I'd ever get. I don't expect you to forgive me."

They sat in silence for a few minutes. He half expected Cato to get up and attack him or leave without at word. He was unpredictable in that sense. Nevertheless, he told Cato the truth and that was all he could do.

A beer flew in the air toward him and he caught it. Apparently, Cato brought some for the both of them. "I'm really mad at you." Cato cracked open his beer.

"I bet."

"I still want to trade teams."

"I don't blame you." Ryan opened his beer.

"I hope I change my mind though."

Ryan finally looked at Cato and realized how little they actually spoke to one another once Cato got older. It was always Ryan and Damian. Cato must feel left out sometimes. "I do too."

"Look, I get you love my sister and I understand the need to be close to someone you love." Cato turned toward him and they stared at one another. "Just don't give up on her. Aden is a disease to this world and I can see he is changing her and not for the better. I'd take you over him any day."

Ryan felt like this was some sort of setup. "Uhh."

"I'm serious," Cato grumbled as he sat back in his seat once more. "Anyways, can I ask you something that has been bothering me for years? It's pretty much a change of subject. I don't really like discussing my sister's sex life."

Great. "Sure."

"Are you bisexual?"

Ryan spit out his beer and choked. "What?"

"Well, when I did research on you and Damian when I was a young kid, it suggested you've slept with men, though people aren't sure if that's true." Cato shrugged. "Not judging, but I have never seen that side of you before. You've only been with women since I've known you."

Ryan rubbed his face with his free hand. This was really not the conversation he thought would ever come up in his life. "Why are you asking me this?"

"Just curious and honestly I feel the need to know seeing as we are around each other a great deal." He was so nonchalant about it that Ryan felt disgruntled.

"Back then we did not define it as homosexual," Ryan started. "The men I was with were eunuchs, basically women to us."

Cato stared at his beer can. "So, you've had a dick inside your body?"

"Hell no." Ryan laughed at how Cato said that so easily with a straight face.

"I just don't understand the appeal." Cato shook his head.

"Like I said, we thought about sexuality different then. Times have changed and people are apparently defined as gay, straight, or bisexual. Back then it was just sexual." He really hated this conversation. It was awkward.

"So what changed?" Cato asked.

"I became different. My mind somehow was molded into thinking like the mortals do now. I guess you could say I am heterosexual and I no longer find men attractive. Just different times with different mindsets."

"That's odd man." Cato crushed his beer can and tossed it into the waste bin. "I mean, when I was born it was basically the same, but my father didn't approve of man on man action at all. Just weird to think you did."

Ryan nodded. "It is unquestionably weird for me now that I think back on it."

"So," Cato started, "if that was true, than is it true you and Damian were basically together?"

He felt his cheeks flush and he wanted to crawl in a hole and die. Of all things for Cato to bring up, why this conversation, and why now? It was so long ago that he never thought about things like that. Not that he was ashamed of it, but it just was not a topic of importance anymore.

"In a way." He wanted to tread carefully around this subject. Damian really did not like this being spread around like wildfire and he knew the feeling.

Cato groaned. "So, Damian was the catcher and you were the pitcher?"

"Cato!" Ryan said a little too loudly. "Stop."

"How the hell are you guys okay being around one another?" Cato's face scrunched up, ignoring Ryan's plea.

"It was almost two thousand years ago, Cato," he grumbled. "Like I said, things changed. He's always been my best friend though."

Cato shivered. "That's weird, Ryan. Like, really weird."

"You grew up in Rome, your people did much worse, I assure you." Roman's sexual prowess was on the verge of disgusting to him. Coming from Ryan, that was saying plenty. Bestiality. Orgies. You name it—they did it.

Cato sighed. "Yeah, I've probably done worse than you honestly. Strictly with women though."

"I wouldn't doubt it," he jested.

"I also read that you were never a huge womanizer then either," Cato added.

"It wasn't really a main concern of mine. I had an empire to try and command." Ryan finished his beer and tossed it in the bin. "Then I got a taste for it and it all went down hill from there."

Ryan looked down at his watch. They were officially six hours in and he started to look around for any sign of the island. He kept his gaze on the water but still nothing. There was no doubt about it, he was ready to get this over with and get back home.

"Did you ever meet your son?" Cato broke their momentary silence.

That was a subject he avoided at all cost. He did not reply and would not. His child was taken from him too early and he never would become the man Ryan intended him to be.

121

Years he could have spent with his son were forever lost and he blamed himself for it. Had he not chosen to become Immortal, his son may have lived a full life. Actually, both of his children would still be alive.

"I didn't mean to piss you off." Cato must have sensed his anger on the subject, making Ryan drift away from his macabre thoughts.

"You didn't. But you understand why I hate my past lives don't you? Why I hate mentioning it to everyone?"

"I get it, but you can't change it. You should just accept it and help other people learn from it somehow," Cato answered. "You know something funny?" he blurted out. Cato's mind was up and down today.

"What?"

"I used to worship you when I was younger. You were my hero." Cato laughed.

Ryan smirked. "What changed?" He always had a slight inclination of Cato's hero worship. Cato's father had hated it.

Cato grunted and glanced away. "Nothing. You still are in a way, I guess. Just wish my sister was born ugly and maybe we would get along better these days."

They both laughed and Ryan felt at ease for the first time since getting on the yacht. He remembered Cato as a young child. He was short for a boy and somehow grew into the six-foot plus beast of a man he is now.

He had helped train Cato's father when he became a Warrior and they remained friends after. Ryan was sometimes invited to help train Cato to shoot a bow and have dinner. It was rare occasions given his busy schedule, but he knew Cato's parents well.

He was never close to Cato as a boy, but he must have left some sort of impression on him. As a teacher he never joked, never praised or showed any emotion. He was there to teach and nothing more.

"Your mother could not produce an ugly child even if she tried." Ryan smirked. "She was a gorgeous woman."

"Oh no, are you attracted to me now?" Cato laughed.

Ryan punched his arm. "You wish. Although, why haven't you gotten rid of your scar? They gave me that ointment to get rid of mine."

Cato rubbed the scar that sat along his face. "I don't like getting rid of them. Makes me feel superficial if I do."

"So I'm superficial?"

"You are but I don't blame you for getting rid of yours." Cato's gaze did not meet Ryan's. "Your body was pretty messed up. There was no resemblance of you at all."

"Well, shit happens and I'm over it," Ryan lied. He thought about the torture everyday and he had nightmares every night because of it. There were some things a person could move past and it was something he would never forget. The pills helped though.

"It scared me," Cato muttered. "A lot actually. I didn't like seeing you guys like that."

Ryan wanted off the subject. "What are those two doing down there by the way?"

Cato glanced at the stairs. "My guess is committing a sin against Anna's religion, but when I left, Damian was showing her how to use a sword." He looked nervous.

"Is she breaking things?" Ryan laughed at the thought of her holding a sword.

Cato nodded. "She really doesn't have a knack for it. I fled in fear."

"Girl can use a gun though, I'll give her that." Ryan approved. "Damian's lucky he got to her first. I would have been all over her."

"Holy shit, Ryan!" Cato yelled at him.

"It was a joke. I wouldn't actually go after her." Ryan could not help but grin. "Calm down."

"Not that you idiot," Cato pointed out the window. "That."

Ryan turned his attention to the window and his mouth dropped. He read about these things before and knew they were real at some point, but actually seeing one was a different story.

"Is that Scylla?" Ryan felt a shiver crawl up his spin.

"How is that possible? Isn't she supposed to be in the Strait of Messina?" Cato asked.

"Looks like she's here now," Ryan muttered.

Scylla was a sea monster with six heads on long, snaky necks and Ryan felt disgust rise in him. The six heads had three rows of shark like teeth and each looked like an odd sea monster. A woman from the waste up had an unnatural grin on her face as they swam toward the yacht. A skirt of dog heads barked and foamed at the mouth around her waste.

"Why does she have twelve feet?" Cato asked.

"No idea," Ryan muttered. "We must be getting close though."

CHAPTER X

Anna

"Take a step back when I advance," Damian told her.

She was not getting the hang of this. So far, she had slashed the curtains to death and knocked over a lamp. Swordplay was easy as a kid. Especially since they were made of wood and not life threatening. This was as dangerous as her waving a gun in his face for fun.

"I am." She took a step back and he lunged at her. "You're going too fast."

"I'm not Anna you need to move quicker."

"I'm not good at this," she groaned when he brought his sword down at her. She barely blocked it and a squeak escaped he lips.

Damian dropped his arm and took a deep breath. "You need to learn it." She could see he was forcing himself to remain calm.

She shook her head. "I sure don't." It was useless.

"Damn, damn, damn, damn," Cato, muttered as he ran down the stairs from the bridge. He was tightening his vest and jogged over to one of the duffle bags.

"What's up?" Damian huffed. "Are we there?"

Cato pulled out huge gun. "What the hell is that?" She gawked.

"An AT4," he said as he pushed past Damian. "Get ready for a fight."

"What is it?" Damian asked more forcefully.

"Scylla. Now get your shit together and come up on deck with me." Cato ran out of sight and Anna looked back at a dumbstruck Damian.

She heard dogs barking. Dogs? Were there any on the ship? "What is Scylla?"

"A Greek monster," he said simply.

Anna bit her lip. She did not know much about the Greeks but she knew their monsters looked like a jumbled mess of different animals and cracked out people. *Get it together Anna.*

"Get the hell up here!" Cato yelled down at them.

Damian snapped out of his trance and grabbed four guns out of the duffle bags. He hung grenades off of his vest and motioned for her to follow him up to the deck. Before they reached the top he turned to her. "Do not panic okay?"

"What do you mean?" Anna had a terrible feeling.

"This is a massive mythical creature and I doubt your mind will be able to comprehend it. Honestly, I thought most of the creatures would have vanished given no one believes in them anymore, but apparently they survived somehow." Damian kissed her lips and smiled. "You got this. Just breathe.

Shoot. Don't freak out."

He handed her a gun. This was scary but damn it was a once in a lifetime adventure. Not even Ryan and Damian had been up against these things and here she was, ready to fight a beast. Admittedly, she was scared as hell but the adrenaline in her body made it worth it. It was intoxicating.

They ran up on the small deck area and her heart stopped. A live, dog skirt wearing, multi-headed, tentacle freak swam their way. She froze. This was not normal. This was supernatural at its most bizarre and she had no way of processing the figure in front of them. It was everything she imagined a demon to look like and more. How did the thing even function with all the crap on itself?

Ryan was on deck yelling at Damian and Cato over the barking dog skirt. She had to make herself focus on the men instead of the she-beast coming their way. Damian nodded and Cato got down on one knee. Probably praying, or giving up, or doing god knows what, but she did not care. They were going to die.

Damian ran over to her, shaking her out of her trance. "Anna, shoot at the heads on the long tentacles. They grab people off boats with their teeth."

Lovely.

The monster was right on them and she almost fired until Damian pushed her gun down. "What?"

"Didn't you hear Ryan say to wait until we know she will attack?" he yelled over the noise.

"No." She shook her head.

"Well, well what do we have here?" A shrill, penetrating voice clung in the air. The dark haired woman with a multi-creature body must have spoke, making Anna shiver. She reminded her of Ursula with her half human body, only a much more evil demented looking version. "Two Greeks, a Roman and an American?"

"How are you Scylla?" Ryan asked casually. What the hell was he doing? This was not time to talk. This was time to shoot their hearts out and kill the creepy-crawly.

"Hungry." The woman grinned. "You smell old and stale."

Anna tried not to laugh and covered her mouth quickly. Damian nudged her as Ryan went on. "We are Immortals."

Scylla pointed at Anna. "She's fresh. I want the fresh one." Anna's heart dropped.

The dogs around her waist had begun to growl as saliva dripped from their mouths. Who the hell created this thing?

Ryan shook his head. "We need her Scylla. We are on a mission that requires the help of a female."

"Don't care," Scylla hissed. "Hungry."

"We are trying to save the world, Scylla," Ryan continued on. "If the threat we are fighting wins we will all cease to exist."

Scylla laughed cruelly. "I am nearing extinction anyways. Give me the fresh one and you can pass."

Damian groaned beside her and the three men brought their guns up toward Scylla. Anna followed suite, screaming in her head out of fear.

"Can't do that, Scylla. Please don't make us kill you," Ryan yelled as the dogs begun to bark loudly.

Cato held up his AT4. "Just let us pass," Cato added. Anna had a hard time grasping the concept of pointing guns at someone, or something, you want to cooperate with you.

"Don't talk to me Roman scum!" Scylla snapped. "You all

will die too if you are unwise."

She must have blinked slowly when Cato triggered the weapon because a huge explosion appeared in front of her. The heat that the missile gave off was intense. Not only from it's target but from the back blast.

Scylla was now missing three heads of the sharp-toothed monsters and the huge wound dripped black ooze into the ocean. She shrieked in either pain or anger, Anna did not know which, but she did know that now was the time to shoot. She pulled the trigger and fired at one of the remaining heads that started to come her way.

Sharp teeth were bared as it came closer to her and she backed up. She fired until the head was so mutilated it no longer functioned and only a black dripping substance remained on the long neck. Anna wanted to jump up and down with glee from her little conquest, but it was short lived.

Teeth sunk into her leg. She screamed, withering in agony. Another head found it's way to her and she was lifted up into the air. Somehow she managed to pull herself up to face the head that had her in its grasp and she fired right into the creature's eyes. Anna made a conscious effort not to shoot her own leg, though it was difficult to shoot around.

Scylla did not release her but instead slammed her body against the deck, bringing her back up into the air again. Black dots appeared in her vision and she blinked them away. The monster suddenly released her body and she crashed down against the upper deck of the yacht.

Anna managed to scramble up to her feet, leaning over the deck to stare at the scene below. Ryan held his sword in his hand, dripping with black goo. Cato was shooting into Scylla's chest with such a calm exterior.

Damian had apparently left the scene below as he ran up to her and pried the head off her leg. Anna didn't realize it was even there with her adrenaline at an all time high.

His arms shook as he managed to open the jaw without getting himself stabbed by the sharp teeth. It must have been a tight grip on her but thankfully her leg was fully intact. The pain of it started to drift into her consciousness as tears pricked her eyes. It had to be like getting a shark bite. She was just lucky it didn't take a chunk out of her.

"Let's get you inside." Damian picked her up easily and tossed her over his shoulder.

"You can't leave them by themselves!" she protested. Damian was having none of her objections.

Damian laughed. She thought it was out of place given the circumstances. "Scylla is headless and Ryan is going to drive the boat around the rest of her. She can't see and Cato is still firing at her. Needless to say she won't be attacking much anymore. We just need to get by her while she is subdued."

"You guys made it seem like it would be difficult." She was shocked it was that easy to destroy her.

"Well, myths make creatures like that terrifying. No doubt about that, but back then people did not have the weapons we have today." Damian adjusted her. "I didn't know Cato brought a damn rocket launcher either."

"I can't believe it only took two minutes though." Anna was in disbelief but ultimately happy everyone was okay.

Damian laughed at her again. "You hit your head pretty hard. We were at it for a good thirty minutes Anna. I was finally able to get over to you. I'm just glad your leg wasn't taken off."

"Are Cato and Ryan okay?" she asked. "Not missing any body parts?" She had a feeling even if they lost an arm or a leg those two would keep on fighting.

He nodded. "One of the dogs along her waist bit Cato, but he's okay. I don't think Scylla expected us to have guns. Or even knew what guns are now that I think about it."

She found herself being tossed down on a king sized bed in a tan room with a huge window looking out on the water. The bedspread had different colors of brown that swirled into patterns along with red pillows piled onto it. Which she just ruined by bleeding all over them.

A huge flat screen television hung from the wall in front of the bed and a large picture of a painted Italian bistro hung above the bed. Why did it all have to look so fancy? It made her feel awkward and out of place.

Damian slipped her boots off and started to unbuckle her belt. "Whoa, now?"

Damian stood up straight, giving her a disapproving look that made her feel like a child. "I'm going to fix your wound, woman. Not try to get busy with you."

She blushed. "Oh." *Damn.*

He smiled as he pulled her pants off, tossed them to the floor and crouched down to look at her leg. Part of her wanted to avoid seeing it, but curiosity got the better of her. She looked down at her right leg and nearly fainted.

It really did look like a shark bite. The sides of her leg had skin hanging off of it and looked shredded. How was the pain so minimal? She was probably still in shock of some kind.

"I'll be right back." His face looked pale as he left her in the room alone.

She stared at her leg as the blood continued to flow out of her body. Anna knew it was odd to be so calm about it, but she was. It did not even seem as if it were her leg. She grabbed a pillow and took the case off of it, tying it around her leg to stop the bleeding.

The boat seemed to be heading off their course and she wondered what Ryan was doing. They were going back the way they came, but on a different route.

After what seemed forever, Damian ran back into the room with his duffle bag and tossed it to the floor in front of the bed. He took out a bottle of rubbing alcohol and without warning, poured it over her wound. She screamed uncontrollably, the black dots appearing in her vision again. Now she felt every inch of the bite and it throbbed so terribly she felt like she was going to pass out.

"You could have warned me," she grit through her teeth.

"Just lay down and let me work, love." He sounded worried and she could tell by the wrinkles on his forehead that he was in deep thought.

Instead of protesting, she lay back and felt a pinch in her leg. The pain subsided and her leg felt numb. She closed her eyes feeling the pressure of his touch against her skin and nothing more. There was no way she wanted to look at what he was doing.

"I think this is the worst I've ever gotten hurt." She tried to laugh but it came out as a croak.

Damian did not laugh, his hands just moved against her skin and she made herself not look at him. He was in the zone or something because he didn't speak for five minutes. The yacht was back on course. They must have gotten past Scylla but if they were getting closer to the Sirens Island she wondered how she could possibly do anything.

Damian grabbed both of her hands and gently pulled her in to a sitting position. Her head felt dizzy and she was thankful her leg was wrapped up nicely. In fact, her entire shin had white gauze wrapped around it almost like a cast and she couldn't help but laugh.

"What's so funny?" Damian sighed. He looked distraught.

"Put enough crap on my leg?" She smirked, but her mood did not reach his own. He looked serious.

"I had to stitch your leg back together and the bleeding didn't want to stop." He started to dress her in a new pair of pants.

"Where did you get these?" she asked. She doubted they just had spare pants around here.

"I had Ryan turn the boat around so I transported back to the Domus real quick to get some supplies." He looked tired. "Scylla sank into the sea so she wasn't much of a threat anymore."

She let him buckle her pants and slip her boots back on her feet. "What's wrong?" She was alive yet he acted as if someone had died.

"Urbs isn't in good shape. There are riots and the symbol of the Risen are painted everywhere." He answered as he laced her boots. "The second we left all hell broke loose. It's a little too coincidental."

Anna's heart broke just looking at his face. "Why are they doing that?"

"I was able to speak to Grace for a few second before leaving and she said most of the citizens want us to either join the Risen or for us to kill the Risen now. They basically want all of us to go on a suicide mission."

Anna understood their frustration. "Why don't we?"

Damian shook his head. "If we do that who would save the mortals? This is our purpose, Anna. The Immortals come second to those in need here in the mortal world. We created the problem, we have to fix it for their sake."

"Did she say anything else?" Anna felt ashamed to even suggest it. Although, the mortal world seemed to be doing fine right now.

Damian nodded. "Yeah."

Anna waited for him to say something. He looked even more exhausted now. "Someone told her they saw Julia and Aden with a group of Warriors leaving the Domus dressed in black gear and cloaks early this morning."

Ryan

Ryan made his way to the cabin Damian and Anna were held up in, leaving Cato in charge of the vessel. They were nearing the island and they needed to make sure their ears were totally sealed from sound. Like most men that encountered the Sirens, Ryan was curious to hear their song. Curiosity would not get the better of him though. At least that is what he told himself.

He wiped his brow, drenched with sweat and water after the lovely encounter they just had. It was hot out today as well, which didn't help the sweating part. He was almost glad his hair was short now.

Scylla proved to be easier to defeat than he believed. Although he had to admit, when she grabbed Anna, he panicked inside. Perhaps he was starting to grow feelings for her as a brother would a sister. The moment she hit the deck he feared she'd bleed to death, but it looked as if she were fine once Damian reached her. Dazed perhaps, but fine.

Damian seemed a bit off when he asked for a crystal and for him to turn around for awhile, but he would feel concerned about someone he loved getting hurt as well. He just wished he could do something to comfort Damian. He hated seeing him worried like that and felt a tinge of jealousy he realized. When Damian fretted about him, Ryan felt like someone actually gave a damn about him.

He rounded the corner and caught the end of Damian and Anna's conversation. "Just don't tell Ryan," Damian said.

He leaned against the doorway, crossing his arms. "Don't tell me what?"

Damian turned around quickly to face him and then back to Anna. Ryan's eyes followed. She was pale, very pale which momentarily caught him off guard. No wonder Damian looked so worried.

"H-how weak I feel." She was almost stuttering and he could instantly tell she was lying. "I don't want you to send me back to Urbs."

Ryan eyed Damian. "I would imagine you would be all for that." He narrowed his eyes, clearly unconvinced.

Damian did not make eye contact. However, he brought his attention back to Anna, cleaning off her bloodied cheek with a washcloth. "Like you said, we need her."

Judging by the look on Anna's face, she knew that Ryan knew they both were lying. He would not push it though. He did not need to worry about whatever personal crap they have going on in their lives. If anything, Ryan figured he didn't want to know what secrets they held from him.

"Whatever," he muttered. "We are almost to the island. Cato said he could see it flicker in the distance."

"It's flickering?" Anna asked. "An island that flickers?"

Ryan nodded. "It's protected by magic so the mortals cannot see it. They have no idea it is there. Nor can they get on the island."

Damian watched Anna. "Remember the Satyrs I told you about? How they need to be believed in order to exist?" Anna nodded. "It's like that in a way."

Ryan clapped his hands together. "Let's get some wax in our ears." This fun little get together had reached it's prime.

Anna stood up from the bed with Damian's help and limped toward the door. Ryan groaned. "Maybe you should go back, Anna. I can ask Zee to fill in?" She was in no condition to do anything with her leg hurt.

"No, I can do this," Anna protested.

Damian's expression did not back up her claim, but who was he to order her around? "Fine." Ryan decided it was not his place to tell her what to do. It just meant he would have to watch her more closely now. A mission he would gladly maintain for all of his life given Damian's infatuation with her.

The three of them headed to the living room area of the yacht and Cato was behind the bar with a drink in his hand. He dumped it down his throat, wiped his mouth with the back of his hand and said, "Ready?" He grit his teeth. He had apparently abandoned his brief stint as captain.

Ryan nodded, regarding Damian and Anna as they spoke quietly amongst themselves. "Okay, Anna, you don't need anything in your ears. According to legend, which I am exceedingly familiar with, they are women that lure men. So enjoy the fact you will now be our ears, hence, the reason we needed you on this mission."

Anna's eyes widened as she nodded her head in agreement. This woman was not up for the challenge and regret of bringing her set in. They should have brought someone more experienced. He hated when he was wrong.

"So we sail to the island and then what?" Cato inquired. "Where is the second piece located anyways?"

Ryan exhaled. "You may think I know everything there is to know about everything, but I am just aware of the location, not the exact location down to the square foot, Cato."

"So we have to search the whole damn island?" Cato grumbled. "Ahmose never told you?"

"The only thing I know is that some creature has it." Ryan explained. "The island isn't exactly massive, it shouldn't take too long."

Cato took a drink straight from the bottle. "Great, so we can search around the island for days with our heads up our ass. That's just lovely." He took another large gulp. "So when we see the Sirens do we just kill them?"

Ryan nodded. "There is no reasoning with them." From everything he knew about the creatures it was that they are relentless. No man could even begin to try and bargain for his life or change their minds. To them, they were merely meat to consume.

Cato grabbed two balls of soft wax and stuffed them into his ears. After that, he placed ear protectors over his ears for good measure. Ryan and Damian did the same and he could no longer hear a sound. He hated one of his senses being gone, especially his hearing.

Anna tried saying something to them and Ryan looked at her with what he felt to be an irritated expression. She started to chuckle, which made his annoyance grow even more. She had found a piece of paper and wrote on it to explain her sudden fit of giggles.

Ryan took the paper from her and groaned.

Your ear protectors have smiley faces on them.

He took them off and they sure did the bright yellow smiley face plastered on them. After he placed them back on his ears he punched Cato in the arm. Cato merely laughed and gave him a thumbs up.

Dick.

They ran up to the helm on the upper deck and he grabbed hold of the wheel there. The island slowly came into view and he had no idea if the Sirens were singing or not. He looked to Anna, her face showed no sign of hearing anything odd so they must be out of range.

The duffel bags hung around Cato and Damian's shoulders ready to go. He was glad they had finally reached their destination. They were as prepared as they could be, armed with a significant amount of weapons. He looked to Anna. Her hair started to escape from her bun, fluttering around in the wind. It bothered him so he tucked it behind her ear.

If he wasn't mistaken, she blushed and Damian punched

him in the arm. *What?* he mouthed.

Damian rolled his eyes and Anna's blush only seemed to deepen. Well, at least they could be lighthearted while facing death.

The island was clearly in view and Anna's face scrunched up in disgust. He noticed her hand slip into Damian's. They must be in earshot and he was glad for the silence. There was nothing worse than having your free will taken from you and that's what those demons did. They lured you to them, making you crash your boat in the process and then ate you. It was dinnertime, but he was not going to be the meal.

They were now close enough for him to see the Sirens that sat on the jagged rocks ahead. He was mystified. They all looked different. As if no one could make up their mind as to how they looked.

Some of the women were large birds the size of bears with the heads of humans and others were all women except birds from the waste down with wings. He looked closer and there were others that looked like naked women with giant angel wings. There were even mermaids.

He looked at Damian and saw he looked just as stunned. They were the different versions of the Sirens all mixed together on one island. They stayed in groups around the rocks with the other Sirens of their kind. People believed in different versions of them, so it made since that every version existed, but to have them all reside on this tiny island seemed almost cruel.

They really were beautiful. None of the Warriors had any experience with mystical creatures that wanted to kill them, besides Scylla of course. People were one thing, but he had no idea what he would be up against with the Sirens. It was out of his element.

He turned the boat to go around to the other side of the island but no matter which direction he ventured, the Sirens followed them. They finally had prey that they could touch and they obviously did not want them to leave. It must be a hard existence to never be seen.

A few of them waved at the boat and he almost waved back. Their seduction was not all about their song apparently. The looks on their faces were nothing but inviting. Warm almost.

One of the Sirens looked exactly like Julia, another like Zee and another like his deceased wife. It tore at him deep down seeing her again. He never thought he would look on her face again yet there she was, sitting on a rock and waving at him. He had to get near her.

He drove the yacht straight toward the Sirens, toward his wife. He missed her even after all of these years. He shook the thought from his mind. That was not really her.

Ryan tried to change his course of certain collision, but it was too late. They crashed straight into the rocks the Sirens were perched on. The Sirens jumped onto their ship ready for their meal.

Ryan panicked. What was he thinking and why was he the only one affected by them just by sight alone? He was weak.

Cato struck him on the arm and mouthed obscenities he was thankful were drowned in silence. Ryan grabbed one of the duffle bags and draped it over his shoulder. They needed to get past these she-devils and fast. His capability to resist looking for his wife was lacking. *If I could only just look at her face once more...*

Damian had already grabbed Anna's hand, dragging her toward one of the rocks that sat away from the Sirens. It led to a pathway onto the island itself, and away from Siren territory. Ryan decided to be bait and whistled to get their attention. If anything, Anna, Damian, and Cato would get away.

The whistle seemed to have gotten their attention and they all started to flock toward him. All except the mermaid versions, who clawed at the tall rock that held Anna and Damian. Damian had his sword out and Ryan saw one of the mermaids hands fall down into the water as red blood pumped out of the stump that remained.

Ryan fell to the ground as something landed on top of him. It was one of the full bird bodied Sirens with a woman's face. It was an odd sight and felt even more odd. It was like having a giant chicken on top of him and it was hard to get a grip on the thing as he squirmed around. The woman's face was beautiful but he could not get past the immense black feathers.

He grabbed hold of the Siren's wings and managed to get back up with her still in his grasp. She managed to dig her human teeth into his arm and he roared out in pain. No one would hear him besides Anna and he had a feeling they were preoccupied with other things anyways.

With all his strength he bent the wings back on the Siren and felt them break under his grip. The face of the Siren writhed in agony and backed away from him quickly. The poor creature fell overboard into the water.

Just as he was about to descend onto the rocks, another Siren came up to him and he stopped in his tracks. His heart stopped. He felt it.

She was a fully bare human except the large white wings on her back. The terrible thing was, she looked exactly like his wife from when he was mortal. The woman he doomed just by putting her into his life. The woman who lost her life and the life of their child because of him.

His knees buckled under him and he dropped to the ground as he looked up at her. She came to him slowly with a smile on her lips that he longed to feel once more against his. How was this possible?

Her long curly black hair framed her face perfectly and her darkly tanned skin shinned like gold. Her almond shaped eyes were just as gorgeous as he remembered, dark as chocolate and full of life and want for him. Her gaze froze Ryan. Her hand reached toward him and she grasped his shoulder gently.

Ryan could not look away from her eyes. He felt a heavy weight inside him. She was exactly as he remembered. The first person he loved was in front of him and her smile was as bright as the sun.

She knelt down to his level and tenderly removed his ear protectors, then the wax in his ears. As her lips brushed against his earlobe, his eyes flickered closed and his heart sped up when he felt her breath against his neck.

"Hello my love," her voice was sickeningly sweet. *Just as I remembered.*

"You're not real." He was failing at taking control of his own mind. His body felt weak as her lips pressed against his neck, then along his jawline.

"I missed you so much my love," she chided. She hummed

a beautiful song against his skin sending shivers across his body and to the very core of his being.

He felt a sharp pain in his neck and fell backwards. She had him pinned to the deck of the boat and he could feel his blood dripping from his new wound onto the wood below. Whatever song the Sirens were singing was now replaced with the harsh cries of squawking birds and screaming women.

The woman he once loved had his blood dripping from her mouth and down her chin set with a smile so chilling it broke the trance. He scrambled up, pulled his sword from his sheath and stared at the women in front of him. Could he kill this creature that deceived him? She looked like her yet he could not do it. Even knowing it wasn't real he would never be able to plunge the weapon into her body.

So his only choice was to run from the being. He saw Cato had managed to climb atop the rock Anna and Damian were on and they waved Ryan over. He slipped in water the boat started to take on but regained his balance as he ran toward them. Why didn't they go ashore instead of waiting for him?

He managed to climb to a rock and proceeded to jump from one rock to another toward the island. It was like a stone path surrounded by water below and he really did not want to fall in. He heard the Sirens behind him, screeching in their attempt to catch him. Ryan tried to move quicker until he heard the sweetest sound erupt in his ears.

It was a gorgeous symphony of voices dancing around his senses and beckoning him back. He wanted to go back, wanted to be with those voices and bathe in the sweet harmony.

Ryan stopped in his tracks. The gorgeous women sang louder for him. Just for him. He must reach them and be with them. It was so sweet. So sweet.

He jumped back to the rock he had just left and smiled widely. He was getting closer to the sweetness. He would die without their voices. He needed them. He was desperate for them.

He jumped to the next rock.

To the next.

So close to the sweet voices.

So close.

Something grabbed him.

"No!" he screamed.

He had to get away.

Had to reach the beautiful women and their songs.

"Come on, Ryan." Cato struggled to restrain him.

He pulled his arms away, desperately clawing to get away and reach the voices. They started to get closer to him and he smiled. They were coming to him! Thank the gods they were coming to him. The perfection of their song melted into his soul making him desperate for more. There would never be enough of the sounds.

Another pair of arms grabbed him. It was Damian. "Ryan, what the hell are you doing?"

"Get off of me!" he shrieked.

"What did he say?" Damian yelled.

"What?" Cato shouted.

They could not hear the tantalizing song. It was all his and no one else's. All his. They were not worthy of the sound.

He kicked and threw his fists around trying to get them off. He needed to be near the Sirens. They would not let him go. His heart raced as the beautiful sounds grew closer. They were coming to him.

"Ryan, stop," Damian's voice strained.

Ryan felt one of them release him and he grew excited. He clawed at the ground trying to pull away and his gloves started to rip apart. He did not care about the pain. He needed the Sirens. Needed them near.

He felt a sharp blow on the back of his head and fell into darkness, away from the sweet voices he needed so much.

Chapter XI

Ryan

"WAKE UP YOU CRAZY son of a bitch!"

Someone smacked him in the face making him groan. His head throbbed and he felt like he had a hangover from hell. What in the world just happened?

Ryan's eyes fluttered open and saw a grassy meadow with flowers of every color blooming all around. Tall trees provided some much needed shade and camouflage. He was thankful the island was not one giant rocky surface, instead it was full of lush life.

Plants meant animals, animals meant water and if they were here for a long time they could hunt. Starvation was no longer a threat to his mind and he felt a little more at ease. The sooner they got out of here though the better. He had no intention on making this an extended visit.

Ryan looked up at the blue sky then groaned. This would have been a beautiful sight if he weren't aching all over. He tried to sit up but was pushed back down roughly by multiple hands.

Cato shook his head as Damian pulled out medical supplies from his pack. "Don't sit up you idiot," Cato mumbled.

Ryan scrunched his eyebrows. "What the hell is your problem?"

"You took out your damn ear plugs and went crazy." Cato rolled his eyes. "Good job there, dumbass."

He suddenly remembered everything that happened. The Siren that looked like his wife, him fighting to get away from Cato and Damian, everything. But it was like watching himself do those things. He had no control over any of it and those singing voices—they were so sweet to listen to. Just thinking about it hurt his heart.

"I didn't take them out." He shifted his legs to get more comfortable while he was forced to lie in the grass. "A Siren did."

"Why did you let a Siren take them out?" Damian asked. "You should have been completely unaffected."

Ryan did not want to talk about that. He could not. "It just happened," he said simply.

"Use your brain, Ryan. We can't keep stopping to patch you up because you can't seem to be careful." Damian scowled. "If you haven't noticed, you're the world's only chance at survival so it would be great it you quit putting yourself at risk."

"Yeah, my bad." He didn't care what they had to say. Ryan knew the reason he allowed his ear protection to be taken out. It was her. Even in death she had a hold on him.

Damian poured alcohol on his head and neck, forcing Ryan to grip the grass in his hands. He tossed the grass he ripped out to the side, but the sting remained. Nothing too terrible, he sort of welcomed the feeling as messed up as that was.

He heard movement to his right but saw nothing. It was probably just a little animal. Paranoia was setting in after their encounter with the Sirens. "I really wish you would warn me when you do that."

"Ditto," Anna grumbled to herself.

"Deal with it you big baby." Damian crinkled his nose. "Wouldn't have to do this to you if you would watch what you're doing."

"I get it. I mess up on numerous occasions." Ryan groaned. "Please continue to torture me while you patch me up as punishment instead of the consistent badgering."

Damian pulled out things to stitch him up with. "Stay still, dummy."

He lay there patiently while Damian, once again, stitched him back together. His neck throbbed and his head felt like it was going to explode. Cato had smashed him over the head with a rock apparently. Damian gave him a play by play of the events that happened while he worked.

Anna sat on her feet besides Damian as he worked and handed him things he asked for. She looked exhausted and her hair was wildly out of place. He commended her for being so well adjusted to all of this. Most would have frozen.

"Where are the Sirens anyways?" Ryan asked.

"After Cato knocked you out he threw you over his shoulder and we didn't look back. Guess they don't leave those rocks or something."

Cato studied Damian as he worked. Ryan really hoped

their earlier conversation would not make things weird between them now. Damian and he were just friends and nothing more, but judging by the look on Cato's face, he was thinking differently.

Cato caught Ryan starring at him and he frowned. "What?"

"Quit," Ryan said.

"Quit what?"

"Thinking about it."

Cato blushed and ventured away from them and out into the field of flowers. He kicked them with his boot, sending petals soaring in the air.

"What was that about?" Damian inquired while digging a needle into his head.

Given Damian's icy exterior right now, Ryan felt in the mood to make his friend uncomfortable. "Cato asked me some personal things about us when we were mortal." Ryan raised an eyebrow at him.

Damian was the one to blush now and glanced back at Anna. Her eyebrows were furrowed in confusion. Poor girl, maybe he should just tell her. At this point he felt it was becoming a nuisance just to keep the secret anyways.

"I swear," Damian began, "that is the only thing people tend to ask us about. As if that were the most interesting part of our past."

He heard rustling in the trees again, but saw nothing. Damian held out his hand and helped pull Ryan to sit up once he finished. He looked around, alarm growing inside of him. "Where's Cato?"

Damian looked behind him and there was no sign of

him anywhere. He was just in the meadow kicking flowers to death, but now he was nowhere to be seen.

Anna quickly packed up their supplies while Ryan stood up. He felt dizzy but that was the least of his worries at this point. Cato was gone without even the slightest hint of where to.

He heard rustling noises behind him once more. The spot were Anna was packing up supplies was now void of her presence. Damian instantly panicked and ran into the dense forest that was separated from the flower field.

"Anna!" he yelled with Ryan following at his heels.

Ryan heard more rustling coming from behind him. When he glanced over his shoulder as he ran there was nothing around. His attention was brought back to the front of him only to find that Damian was no longer there.

"Damian!" Ryan roared. Everyone around him was lost to the forest, leaving him vulnerable to attack. He needed to find them soon.

He unholstered his gun and stood his ground. He heard movement through the trees all around him and his nerves were on end. Whatever it was, they were surrounding him and making their presence known.

They had barely escaped death twice and now they had another problem? This island is hell on Earth.

He caught sight of a creature that ran by, it's hooves and fur were a dark brown. A twig snapped behind Ryan and he turned about. Nothing.

Another twig snapped and he turned once more. "Who's there?" he called out.

Abruptly, his feet came out from under him making him

land hard on his back. With a deep throaty groan, he managed to sit up. His feet were tied with an odd leafy green rope. "You sneaky little bastar—"

Without warning he was suddenly dragged along the ground. He still could not see who his captures were. Somehow managing to sit up, he held his gun out to shoot what he could, but saw nothing. Whoever it was, was far ahead of him. With much difficulty he holstered his gun and pulled a knife out of his flak jacket.

A rock hit his hand before he could pull out the knife. "Ahh!"

He shook his hand and reached for his knife again. Another rock slammed into his hand and he started to get angry. Leaves started to go up into his vest and his ass was already sore from being dragged.

A massive grassy mud hut came into view. It had trees sticking out of the twig roof—they must have built their home around them. He was pulled into the entrance and stopped unexpectedly. Ryan rolled over on his stomach and groaned. That was a painfully short trip.

He tilted his head up to the sight of his friends tied up against a large tree trunk. They had gags in their mouths, made of Zeus knows what, and standing guard was a creature two-thirds his size. It had the bottom half of a goat and the top half of a man. Long horns protruded from his forehead and he held a sharp spear in his hand.

"Satyrs?" He laughed. Was he really kidnapped by the little goat men that drank too much?

Two hooves came into view on the ground beside him making Ryan look up to a fat young Satyr with a slingshot in one hand and a rock in the other. "Yeah, what of it human?" the brown haired Satyr asked.

Ryan laughed and sat up. "So you're the punk that shot me?"

The Satyr nodded. "Yep."

"I thought all Satyrs did was get drunk and chase after Nymphs? Not attack humans with vines and rocks." He was being antagonistic and he did not care. Little bastard hurt his hand.

"All humans are good for are changing their minds and making everything and everyone around them suffer." The Satyr grunted. "We thought you good for nothing humans would never forget about us, but here we are, stranded on some island and it's all your fault."

A Satyr with an attitude, who knew?

Ryan unsheathed a knife from his jacket and cut the ropes from around his ankles. He stood up and looked around the hut. It was the size of a football field and each tree had small little huts built around them, obviously little homes of Satyr families.

Little ones galloped along the ground and chewed on apples while the adults glared at them in fear and disgust. There were about thirty of them altogether but it was enough to out number their group.

Barrels of fruit and other vegetation were set against the walls of the hut and the dirt floor was surprisingly cool. They were crafty little creatures, he had to give them that.

He replaced his knife back in his jacket. "What do you want from us?"

"Payback," the young Satyr growled and aimed his slingshot at Ryan.

"Enough, Ash." A gray bearded Satyr wobbled over to them with the help of a wooden cane. He was bald and missing a horn. "Excuse our inhospitality. We haven't seen humans here in a very long time. You understand our worry, do you not?"

"Doesn't mean there is a need to treat us like rabid dogs," Ryan countered. "We mean you absolutely no harm so untie my friends."

"Who are you?" the old Satyr asked ignoring his demand. Ash had lowered his slingshot but continued to glare at Ryan with loathing.

"My name is Ryan," he answered.

"The outside world has changed greatly, both language and religions alike. Yet here you stand, speaking our language and more importantly, you are able to see this island." The Satyr studied Ryan with an intense gaze, which made him uncomfortable. "How are you able to do these things? Humans pass by us without a glance yet you were capable of making it past the Sirens. A feat in itself."

Ryan looked to Damian and Cato and they shrugged in their restraints. He was unsure how Immortals would be welcome here. Given the gods were the ones to put the Satyrs on this secluded island and they were the god's weapons. He was not exactly in the position to lie though.

"Have you heard of the Immortals?" Ryan decided on the truth.

The older Satyr's stare softened around his eyes and turned toward Ash. "Cut them down and get them something to eat."

"We cannot trust them, Leif," Ash hissed. "You are putting us all in danger."

"Do what I said," Leif said calmly. He kept his eyes on Ryan and Ryan made sure not to break the contact. To look away would give the Satyr dominance over him and that was not about to happen.

He heard the vine ropes fall to the ground and Cato grumbled, "It's about damn time."

"I am sorry my friends." Leif finally looked to the now freed group that gathered around Ryan. "We have had to take precautions in this day and age. All of the creatures the Greeks believed in are put on this one island. We were once a merry and gentle race and have had to adapt to survive."

"Hold on," Cato spoke up. "All of you are on this island? The Minotaur, Cyclopes, Centaurs, even the Gorgons?"

Leif nodded. "All the above and much more. Zeus put us here when the human's belief in us had gone extinct. It is where we will all cease to exist in this world once no one is left to believe. Which is why I find it crucial to keep you all alive."

"Do you know what is happening in the world?" Damian asked. "Why we're meant to come to this island?"

Leif shook his head. "No we do not. What is happening?"

"A group has formed to disband all religions and begin a new one of their own. Anyone who defies them will be killed. The gods will die without the beliefs of mortals," Damian answered. "Which means you along with it."

The Satyrs began to whisper amongst one another. Leif spoke, "What can we do to help?"

"We are on a mission to save the Immortals from being destroyed. They have a weapon that will kill any of us that oppose them and thus kill the last chance the gods have to remain," Ryan spoke. "We need to find three pieces of a staff that can stop the weapon they intend to use. We have one piece and the second is on this island."

Leif turned to another elder Satyr and whispered something to him. For a brief moment, Ryan had hoped they knew what he was talking about. That would have been too easy.

Leif turned back to Ryan. "We cannot help you my friends. For that, I am regretful. It is something we must not get involved in to insure our survival on this island. However, we will give you whatever supplies you may need."

Ryan tried not to be offended. Could he really blame them for their need to survive?

Ryan faced Damian. "We need to locate this damn thing. We cannot travel around aimlessly with all the creatures on the island. Doing that would just get us killed. Those creatures are far too dangerous for four people to handle."

"You don't have a clue who has it?" Damian asked. He could see the worry plastered all over Damian's face.

Ryan shook his head. "It will obviously be very dangerous and a pain in the ass. Which basically describes every damn creature in our religion."

"Go team." Cato pitifully pumped a fist in the air.

Anna

Anna shifted back and forth on her feet. Somehow she sprained it when the goat dudes dragged her away and she tried to get away. Damian had given her some pills to deal with the pain that Scylla caused but it was wearing off quickly.

Anna glared at the goat dudes. They were mean little creatures.

The guys were talking to the Satyrs about the locations of certain creatures on the island and she started to wander off in thought. She had just run away from crazy birds ladies and got bit by a massive multi-headed crazed sea woman. Now she was in a big ass hut with half goat dudes that like to drag people through trees.

This was not normal. This was insane. How could people believe in this stuff still? It was so far fetched and she was surprised they still existed. They probably only exist because of Ryan and Damian. They still believed in this nonsense. Then again, she did too now that she has seen them herself. There was no denying their existence anymore.

Still, Ryan and Damian had always believed in these weird things and it gave her the creeps. She had to admit that there are odd things in Catholicism but nothing so unworldly that it bordered on an acid trip gone wrong.

Her leg started to hurt like hell and she decided to sit down in the dirt. Anna stared at her hands. These gloves were amazingly tough. Even after her climbing rocks and trying to grasp the ground as she was being pulled away by goat-men, they remained intact. Yet Ryan's were destroyed just trying to get away from Cato and Damian. He must have really been under their spell to do be so desperate.

She felt eyes watching her and looked up to face a little goat child. The little Satyr had curly brown hair and tiny horns that barely stuck out of its head. She had to admit, the little brown ball of fur was cute. Even if the bigger versions were a bunch of jerks.

"Hi." It smiled at her.

"Hi." She returned the smile. "What's your name?"

"Abies."

The little Satyr proceeded to climb into her lap and make himself comfortable. There was no fear in his eyes—he looked utterly innocent, which he probably was. "I'm Anna," she introduced herself.

Abies looked up at her with large brown eyes that twinkled. "Are you good or bad?"

Her smile didn't seem to want to go away. "Good."

"My dad says you are a bad omen." Abies looked over to Ryan. "You don't look bad though."

Anna felt more eyes on her and realized about ten Satyrs were starring and pointing at her. Why would they think that about them? Especially since they were trying to save their world, in a round about way. Maybe if she were nice to this little guy they would change their minds.

"Well I'm not bad." She patted the little guy on the back.

"I can tell." Abies smiled back at her. "You're pretty for a human."

"Thank you." She refrained from laughing at the statement. "You're cute for a Satyr."

"I know." Abies sat still in her lap, continuing to stare at Ryan and the guys. "You are looking for something aren't you?"

"Yes."

"Where is it?" He started to pat her leg softly.

"I don't know. We need to figure that out."

Abies patted his furred knees making a little drumming beat. She decided he must have been thinking of something because he remained quiet. They sat that way for a few minutes, letting both of their minds wander. Anna decided even after getting dragged for half a mile, she liked Satyrs because of Abies.

"My dad says, when people had questions they used to ask the Oracle." He looked up at her. "Did you try that?"

"Where's the Oracle?" she asked. Did this little guy really just help them? It was official. She loved Abies.

"My dad says the Oracle is high up on the mountain," he answered. "She doesn't like anyone anymore. She lives there alone and she cannot age. The Gorgons kill anyone that goes near her temple."

Anna suppressed a groan. *Of course. More monsters and a pissed off psychic.* "Maybe we will try to make her happy. Would you like that Abies?"

The little Satyr nodded. "I don't like anyone being unhappy." He leaned his head against her chest and her heart melted. This was the sweetest creature, human or not, she had ever met.

"Abies!" a black haired Satyr called.

Abies jumped up and removed a necklace from around his neck. "Dad is mad." Without any hesitation he put it on her making tears form in her eyes. It was a wooden carved leaf hanging from a thin leather string. "Goodbye, Anna."

Abies ran off and disappeared in the now crowded area. She already missed his little body sitting snugly in her lap. She would never forget that little guy.

"Anna." Damian pulled her up to standing and wiped her

cheek. "Why are you crying?"

Was she crying? She wiped her cheek and sure enough she was. "That little Satyr gave me his necklace."

Damian looked puzzled. "So that made you cry?"

Guys will never in the history of forever, understand those types of things. "Never mind. What's up?"

"Well, Leif showed us basic parts of the island. He wasn't quite sure where everything was because territories keep changing, but he knew where we should absolutely avoid." Damian sighed. "It's seemingly impossible even though Ryan looks hopeful now that he has more information."

That brought Anna back to the real world and away from the precious gift she was just given. "Abies said something about the Oracle. That she could answer our questions."

"Abies?"

"The little Satyr."

Damian frowned but turned to look behind him. "Ryan, come over here."

Ryan excused himself from talking to Leif and he seemed grumpy. "What?" he hissed as if they bothered him from a very important meeting.

"Apparently the Oracle is here as well." Damian looked at Anna and she felt oddly guilty. "Maybe we can get her to find out where the piece is."

Ryan looked at Anna with a soft expression that made her feel at ease. He never looked at her like that—usually he looked confused or annoyed. It was a nice change of pace.

"Where at?" Ryan asked.

"He said the Oracle was on top of the mountain," Anna answered. "There's just the one out there so that narrows it down significantly."

"It's the best bet we have," Ryan grumbled. "Gather up our stuff and we'll head out."

Leif stumbled over to their group with Cato. "I wouldn't go out, sir. The night is almost on us and it is most certainly not safe outside." For an old goat he sure did have good hearing.

"Why?" Ryan looked worn. Not just physically, but mentally as well. Anna wondered if he was still taking those pills for pain.

"Many evil creatures come out in the night." Leif shivered. "Arachne, Echidna, even the Harpies. It is even more dangerous at night."

"Great," Ryan mumbled, "now what?"

"Might I suggest you stay here until the day breaks?" Leif offered a spot at the very right of the hut. It had patches of grass that seemed desperate to grow even though the sun never came through the tightly weaved roof.

Cato yawned on cue and Ryan looked defeated. Why did he always look like he hated other's opinions? *Get a grip dude.*

"Thank you very much," he finally said to Leif. Anna was somewhat shocked he was being so polite when he was obviously agitated. "We appreciate it greatly."

Leif managed a smile for the first time since they arrived in the hut. As he hobbled away from their group, Anna realized the guys had made their way over to the spot Leif indicated and she followed slowly behind. Sleeping on the dirt never really bothered her; it was the claustrophobia that did not set well with her.

They were backed into a corner basically, probably so

the Satyrs could keep an eye on them, nevertheless it did not make her feel much better. She sat down on the cool earth by Damian and they leaned against the vine, dry mud wall. His hand entwined with hers and she felt an instant sigh of relief escape her lips.

It was the first time they really had to relax all day, even on the boat she felt tense and nervous, being here felt soothing. It was peaceful here watching the Satyrs wonder around eating, drinking, and making handmade tools. They were like a little hive of bees, all working and moving constantly.

"Are there any female Satyrs?" Anna asked.

Damian raised an eyebrow. "Not that I know of."

"Then how are there kids?"

"My best guess?" Damian smirked when Anna nodded. "They are known to be attracted to Nymphs. My guess is they have relations with them and boom, Satyr baby."

"So how do Nymphs have more Nymphs?" she asked.

"Quit asking questions." Damian squeezed her hand and chuckled.

He was always so amused by her. Sometimes felt he was making fun of her. Letting little things like that bother her was not worth the battle. But in all honesty, it was starting to become annoying. She has numerous questions about all of this and it was normal to ask them.

"I'm going to talk with Leif some more," Ryan blurted out. Anna could tell he was not in the mood to sleep right now. He seemed fidgety. "See if he can give us any insight on what we may encounter and the exact location." She saw him quickly pop pills in his mouth when Damian and Cato weren't looking. This looked like it was becoming a problem.

As Ryan slipped away, Anna looked at Damian. "Why does he sound regal sometimes and other times he sounds like an American skateboarder?"

Damian smirked. "Ryan has had too many changes with his speech over time. When he sounds regal, it's him slipping back to his mortal days. We used to speak with actual eloquence but speech has changed into more of a basic knowledge of your language. Most people don't understand how to speak with intellect."

"You're saying I sound dumb?"

"No, you stubborn woman. I'm just saying that it's a different time. We tend to slip up quite often." He kissed the top of her head. "I often slip from casual speech to refined. I feel like I have multi personalities. Like everything else, we have had to evolve."

"You sound like people from Shakespeare sometimes," she agreed. "It's weird."

"I am fairly certain I have never said thou, art, wherefore, or hither to you," he teased.

"You weirdo," she muttered.

"Dost thou know thy insolence?" He was mocking her. "Methinks thy will is to plague me heavy withal woe, whereto I pray thy will adieu."

"I have no idea what you just said." Anna rolled her eyes, but her grin mimicked Damian's.

He closed his eyes and she leaned her head on his shoulder. She could hear the sounds of nature outside and her eyes grew heavy. Sun no longer seeped through the doorway of the hut as night was fully on them.

Lanterns were lit inside of the hut as they finally closed

the doors off. The Satyrs moved a large piece of wood in front of the closed doors and they were officially trapped inside of the hut. Claustrophobia really started to set in and an unsettling anxious feeling filled her stomach. She grew antsy and her leg started to shake on its own. It was a terrible feeling.

"You okay?" Cato asked all of a sudden.

He almost startled her. He was always so quiet since most people could not get a word in with Ryan around. "Just hate being trapped in here," she whispered.

Damian was asleep and leaning on her. As much as she enjoyed it, he was not a light guy. She shifted out of his embrace and laid him down on the ground as gently as she could. Cato looked at her with pure amusement.

"You're good for him, you know that." It was a statement not a question.

"Why do you say that?"

"You take care of each other and work well as a team." Cato laid on the ground and put his hands behind his head. "I'm actually glad you're here."

She sat down between Cato and Damian. "Why?"

"Well for one, Ryan is a little more cautious with you around. Not much, but more than normal. Besides that, I think there are advantages to having a female on this island. Numerous Greek creatures can lure men very easily and distract us. You counter that effect."

"Thanks?" she laughed. "I feel like I haven't done anything. You guys made it seem like you really needed me for something. With wax in your ears you were perfectly fine."

"We do need you," he assured her. "You helped with the Sirens more than you know. What if all of us had lost our ear protection? We would be dead and eaten by now. Just because it didn't happen doesn't mean you were useless. Moreover, I have a feeling having a woman will be very beneficial later on."

"Why's that?" Her heart started to swell at what he was saying. She liked having conversations with Cato.

"On the off chance we run into the Amazons, or when we need to go back past the Sirens again to get off of this damn island."

"How are we going to get back?" That familiar feeling of panic rose in her belly. "Our boat is sunk."

Cato shrugged as if it were trivial. "We will find a way."

"You're awfully confident you know that?" She smirked.

"It is what it is." Cato winked. "Get some sleep. Ryan will wake us up as soon as the sun comes back."

Anna didn't need to be told twice. Exhaustion had settled inside her, making her cuddle up next to Damian on the ground and stare at him. He was so peaceful in sleep. She brushed back the hair that fell in his face and he moaned at her touch.

She smiled to herself. After everything she had been through, Damian was always there for her. He never pushed her. He was patient. Anna knew that he was a gentleman beyond measure, especially after Nathan was killed.

When she woke up on the couch after being drugged by Ryan, Damian was there to tend to her. So careful and not forceful in the least. She didn't appreciate it then but she did now. It was probably his calm nature that pulled her to him. She was used to a chaos-filled life. She still had that, but with Damian it fell into place again. He made her whole when she never thought she would be after Nathan.

Her eyelids grew heavy and she fell asleep to the sound of Damian's soft breathing.

Chapter XII

Ryan

THERE WAS LITTLE DOUBT *in his mind on how he would execute the lust he felt for the woman before him. She was a ravenous beauty. Dark hair, long lashes and a fair complexion that would make any man relish her existence.*

He grinned when she pushed him away. His advances seemed to annoy her even though he felt her desires for him. The things she did proved that. She would give him extra bread unbeknownst to the other gladiators. Those little touches drove him insane when she passed by him. He was not reading it wrong but she never did more than pull his fantasies every which way she could.

She was a tantalizing creature.

"Do not force your hand on me." Her words were meant in venom but the intended threat was missing its mark.

"Never would I do such a thing." He gave her his most dash-

ing smile. It seemed to work when her eyes softened. His hand brushed her cheek gently and her eyes fluttered. "You are exquisite."

She shook her head. "We will be punished for your actions."

"I have merely given you a compliment." *His fingers brushed back her hair from her shoulder. She shivered at his touch and his grin ignited. The blue tunic she wore did her body justice, flattering her curves. Their Dominus and his wife were fairly well off since he had begun to make them money in the arena.*

"I must go." *She turned to leave, but he grabbed her arm gently. She looked down at his grasp then back to his face. He could see the worry there.* "This is not allowed."

"No one need know." *He pressed his body to hers and he could feel her will caving to him. She was a favorite of their master, he could see why.* "Unless you wish me to cease my advances?"

She bit her lip. "I'm unsure."

"Just a taste then?" *He brushed his lips against hers, feeling the intake of her breath.*

Her eyes fluttered closed and just as he was about to lean in to her she pulled away. "As charming as you are, I know your ways with women. I will not fall victim to your vulgarity."

With that, she turned and walked away from him, her hips moving so tantalizing that he forced his thoughts on other things before his loincloth rose.

"Odilia!" *their Dominus' shrill voice yelled down the steps into the stone cellar they spoke in.*

She turned around to glare. "Not but one minute with you and I am being scorned."

"Once we leave this place, I plan to make you mine and

mine alone." His tone was more serious.

Her eyes rolled. "To be with you would mean certain anguish. We will live and die here. You sooner then I, given your body of work."

Ryan's eyes shot open as he stared around the hut. Every creature inside was in a deep slumber judging by the snores that surrounded him. Only a few torches were lit providing minimal light.

He rest his head on hands and looked up at the roof of the hut. He could not help but think of the women he just dreamed of.

He eventually made Odilia his. They would escape from the clutches of Roman oppression and her life would end before his time. Throat slit by Roman infantry as they fought for freedom and awareness of the corrupt.

She was an unexpected light in the world of death he was surrounded in as a gladiator. Her temper was that of a proud woman that took no grief from a man, which was his first attraction.

No woman could follow that spirit he loved so much, except one.

Anna

"Wake up, love." She woke up to a kiss on the forehead. Damian looked down at her with a cute smile on his face. His hair was messed up and she could only imagine what she looked like after lying on dirt all night long.

"It's morning already?" It was a stupid question due to the light shining through the open door.

"Yes. Ryan is talking with the Satyrs right now. He said to be ready when he is done."

"Demanding isn't he?" She stretched and a little squeal escaped her.

Damian kissed her gently on the lips. "You're cute in the morning." He tousled her hair.

She rolled her eyes and Damian pulled her up to stand. She felt no pain in her leg, which was surprising given it was almost bit off. She pulled up her pant leg to find the wound covered in a green-brown paste and her wound practically healed.

"What happened?" she exclaimed. Anna was so relived that her leg was better she wanted to run around just because she could. Her leg didn't hurt. The paste was gross looking, but she didn't care.

"Your little friend Abies convinced his father to use their magical healing properties on you while you were asleep. I hope it is okay that I let them. You looked peaceful and I didn't want to wake you up." Damian bit his lip. "They have a knowledge of very old natural magic lost to the world."

"Of course that's okay," she laughed. "It doesn't even hurt that much anymore."

Damian sighed in relief. "Good. I feel better now that you are in better shape while we are here."

Anna rolled her eyes but was glad he cared so much about her. Her attention was suddenly brought to what Cato was doing. He leaned against a wall as he ate an apple. Her stomach seemed to growl as if on cue.

"Apple?" Damian offered her the fruit and she happily took it. She did not realize how hungry she was. She took a bit and it tasted just like heaven.

"How is this so good?" She moaned, taking another bite.

"They are excellent aren't they?" Damian grinned and bit into his own apple.

Most of the Satyrs were now gone and she realized little Abies was no longer there. She wanted to say goodbye to him and thank him. Anna looked back down at the necklace he had given her and smiled.

Ryan shook hands with Leif and joined them in their corner. "Are we ready?" He clapped his hands together.

"Did Leif tell you everything we need to know?" Damian asked.

Ryan seemed tense, a little more than usual. His boyish charm was completely missing and replaced with a grumpy sergeant with a stick in his ass. "Yes, it's not far from here. About a thirty minute walk."

"You look constipated. What's the bad news?" Cato mused. It looks like Cato has taken over as the boyish charmer of the group.

"The Gorgons are surrounding the entrance to where the Oracle is and there are Cyclopes that live at the bottom of the mountain." Even Ryan looked nervous. Not a good sign.

"What else?" Damian eyed him. It was hard to notice how mentally entwined Ryan and Damian were.

"Well," he started, "it seems that the Sirens are not the only creatures to escape Tartarus."

"What's Tartarus?" Anna asked.

"Our version of hell," Ryan answered gruffly, obviously

agitated. "The Sirens were all sent there after they were killed way back in the day but obviously that didn't last."

"Great," Cato groaned and slung his duffel bag around his shoulder. "Let's get this over with."

"Do you have a plan?" Damian interjected.

"Sort of," Ryan answered. "Let me think along the way and we will discuss it once we get there."

Great.

They left the hut. The sun was so bright that it took her eyes awhile to adjust. The safe confines of the hut were now behind them and the danger was very real once again. What sort of God would put these creatures on this island to suffer in fear? It was terrible. Especially for creatures as sweet as Abies.

Ryan took the lead as they made their way north with Cato at the rear. Damian walked by her side and she felt her nerves start to increase. Her mind wondered off trying to remember any creatures she learned about in school. When she'd paid attention at least.

Her and Nathan had history class together and they never paid much attention in it. When it came to ancient civilizations, she was interested, but Nathan had always kept her otherwise occupied by sending her notes and acting out in class.

The one creature she really remembered was Medusa. A crazy eyed snake-haired lady with a depraved attitude. How can she be real? How can any of this be real?

Ryan held a sword in his hand while Damian and Cato held guns. What was Ryan thinking? Guns were a lot quicker. She was starting to question Ryan's leadership skills at this point. Zee must have been wrong about him. A great military leader? *Yeah, right.*

They did not seem to want to hide themselves either. Twigs kept breaking under their feet and the crunching of leaves was a dead giveaway. It only took five minutes to get out of the forested area and back to the meadow they started in.

It really was gorgeous here. They were somewhat occupied the last time they were here, stitching up Ryan and whatnot.

Purple, pink, and yellow were all mixed in with one another creating a blanket of color along the ground. The meadow was only the size of a basketball court and she did not want to disturb the flowers. Not even the patch Cato was kicking around the day before looked disturbed. She would have expected at least a trail of flattened flowers left in his wake, but there was nothing to indicate they'd been here.

Without a care to the scenery in front of them, Ryan and Damian trudged through the flowers. Her heart dropped a little seeing their feet step on the little beauties and Cato nudged her forward. She purposely followed behind Ryan and Damian so she would not ruin any more of the flowers than they had to.

Men. They never care about things like this.

"You okay?" Cato whispered. He was obviously trying to avoid the others hearing him. He probably thought she was in pain or shock or something.

She nodded—there was no point in saying anything about it. At some point they would grow back and it would be perfect once again. Hopefully.

"Damian come here," Ryan beckoned. Damian jogged up to him and Ryan put his arm around his shoulders as they walked. They had such a bromance it wasn't even funny.

Cato scoffed.

"What?" she asked.

"Nothing," he muttered.

She rolled her eyes. Cato was a complicated creature, but she wasn't going to push it with him. "Okay."

Ryan and Damian continued to talk between themselves and left Anna and Cato to walk in awkward silence behind them. They made it past the flowers and she looked toward the mountain. It was not horribly massive, but she could tell it would take awhile to climb. Trees covered most of it and had spots with rocky cliffs that she could see. At least there was plant life on it and not just a gigantic mound of rock. It reminded her of pictures of Colorado.

She squint her eyes and she could tell there was a temple on the top of the mountain. The white marble seemed to shine in the sunlight and she was amazed it looked fully intact. Well, as far as she could tell anyways. It was the size of a quarter from where they stood.

"You think they will ever confide in me about plans?" Cato asked her out of nowhere. He seemed passive.

"They don't already?" That was odd. After how long they had been together it was weird to single him out.

Cato shook his head. "It's always been just the two of them. Sure, we are like family, but I feel like the youngest brother and they are twins. They just mesh whereas I am on my own. It's no fault of their own. I know they are happy with me on the team, always have been."

"I don't think they even realize what they are doing. Those two are oblivious to almost anything other than battle."

Such as Ryan's pill popping habit and Damian's constant need to baby grown men.

"Maybe not." Cato stared at his gun as he marched and she felt bad for him. He did look like the little brother the others siblings didn't want to play with.

"Get up there and get involved then," she suggested. "Make them include you."

"Thank you Anna, but I do believe it is a losing battle. They will include me when they are ready." Cato smiled warmly. "Besides, I don't want to sound like a little girl. No offense."

Anna punched his arm. "I take offense." But she smiled when Cato grinned at her. He was so much taller than her. Probably six foot four or something from what she judged, just a bit taller than Nathan.

"Take offense all you want, sweetheart, but you are a woman not a little girl." Cato winked as he gave her a little nudge on the shoulder.

After the meadow, they found themselves in rolling hills of grass. It reached to the very end of the mountain were she saw a large cave, which stuck out like a sore thumb. There was nothing but grass. No trees or rocks to hide behind, they would be more than noticeable to whatever wanted to chop off their head at this point.

"I don't like this," Cato murmured.

"Me either," Ryan agreed. "The Cyclops are going to see us coming."

Ryan looked around and she could see his wheels turning. He surveyed the area like a hawk and she could almost see what Zee had revealed about him. Still, it was hard to think of this man in front of her as a great and powerful leader. Mainly because all she had gathered about him was that he's a hot-head with a sarcastic mouth and an addiction to sex.

"We should have come at night," Cato groaned.

Damian ran his hand through his hair. "Agreed."

"At least the grass is tall, we can crawl through it slowly," Ryan pointed out, but Anna thought it was hardly anything to be positive about. "Flank the mountain on each side so we don't draw attention to one large area."

Damian grimaced. "I don't see any other option."

"Anna with Damian and Cato with me," Ryan decided. Anna was perfectly fine with that arrangement.

"What are we doing? Just reaching the mountain and climb up until we meet?" Cato asked.

"Sounds good to me." Ryan nodded. "If shit hits the fan, cover one another."

Anna groaned. This was an insane plan. She did not see any other option though. They could go around the other end of the mountain but who's to say what is over there. Ryan seemed to think this was the lesser of two evils and she had to trust him. She was thankful, however, that she was paired with Damian.

"Come together a safe distance above the mouth of the cave. The Gorgons will be near and I want to regroup for the plan after that." Ryan checked his weapons.

"Why not go over the plan now?" Anna asked.

He looked at her with an intense and stern glare. "One step at a time. Concentrate on what we are doing and don't be seen."

Ryan and Cato took the right side and ventured off without a word. Anna turned with Damian as they headed toward the left side. "Stubborn, isn't he?"

Damian chuckled. "I think that last part is mainly for you to be honest."

"Why? I can remember what we are going to do next," she protested.

Damian squeezed her hand but instead of assurance she felt disdain. She hated that Ryan did not trust her or believe in her ability. He was such a chauvinistic pig.

"Even *he* is nervous about facing these creatures, Anna. They are something we have no experience in fighting and if he is nervous, I bet he assumes you are as well." Damian stopped walking. "He doesn't want to overload your brain with things we have to do and have you make a mistake. Do you know who the Gorgons are?"

"No."

"That's precisely why he is avoiding telling you, love. One suicidal mission at a time."

She racked her brain trying to remember who the Gorgons were. What was so terrible about them? Oh well, she would find out and she needed to put all her concentration on getting past the Cyclopes.

Damian dropped to his knees and she followed suite. They both held their rifles in their hands and got on their stomachs. This was scary. Would she even get to see the monsters? Damian crawled foreword in the tall grass. She had no idea if Ryan and Cato had already far ahead or not.

"I wish Ryan would stop trying to protect me all the time," she grumbled as they moved through the tall grass. She looked behind her and was glad the grass was slowly popping back up toward the sky.

Damian stopped briefly to move the hair out of his face. "It's not personal, Anna. It takes years for him to trust a person."

"So he doesn't trust me?"

"He trusts you," he grunted as they crawled ahead. "Just not when it comes to the job."

"That's messed up," she mumbled. How dare he judge her?

Damian paused to look at her. She didn't even bother to mask the anger she felt. She was pissed and he would just have to deal with it.

"Would you trust someone with your life you barely know?" Damian asked. "Let alone, trust a person you barely know to help save the entire world? Would you trust someone with all of that if you were unsure of how capable they are in battle?"

He just had to put it that way. "No."

"Exactly, my love. It's not personal at all, he just being cautious." Damian kissed her cheek and they moved forward. The field was the size of two football fields at least and she grew tired of crawling for so long. She was thankful that their gear included kneepads but her backpack grew heavier the longer they crawled.

The wind picked up and long blades of grass swept over her head. It offered additional cover and she hoped the wind stayed this steady until they reached the mountain.

When would they reach the end? Part of her felt they were not even going in the right direction. She could not see anything down here with the grass flowing over her head. It blocked out most sights and the uneasy feeling of being lost built up in her gut ready to burst into a full on panic mode.

"Are we close?" she managed to croak out.

Damian shushed her and she pushed herself up to try and see over the grass. She fell back into the ground as Damian pulled her back and she gave him a dirty look. He shook his head as they crawled forward, but at a slower pace.

That answered her question. If he would not talk they must be nearing the caves and her nerves made her legs shake. Monsters were up ahead. Real, honest to god, killing machines that scared the living crap out of her and she had no idea what to do. Where did she need to aim if they saw them?

As they got closer she heard grunts and was able to make out the cave to their right. Her heart beat so hard she literally feared it failing. She was scared. Beyond scared and she froze up. Damian seemed to have noticed because he turned back to her and grabbed her hand.

He looked into her eyes with such a guilty expression it broke her heart. "You will be fine my love. I'm so sorry you are here," he whispered. "Please stay calm and don't look at them. Just look at me and follow."

Anna did as she was told but curiosity got the better of her. She looked into the cave and saw the backs of giant hairy men the size of three-story buildings. They were massive and dirty, not to mention they only wore loincloths. Some were bald and others had long hair that was a mess of tangles.

One turned around and she gasped. The one eye in the middle of its forehead looked around the grassy landscape. The sight bothered her more than she thought. She kept telling herself they would look silly like that. Even thought she would laugh at the sight of the monsters but there was nothing funny about it. They were large and terrifying. Her breath caught in her chest, unable to escape. Never in her life had she been more frightened then now.

"Damian," her voice was barely more than a whisper.

Damian pressed his forehead against hers. "Breathe, Anna, baby." He had somehow managed to turn around to face her.

She nodded against his head and inhaled deeply. Her mind was not made for this type of thing. These cannot be real and yet here they are, large and extremely dangerous looking. They could squash her like a bug with ease.

Ryan and Cato were probably already making their way up the mountain. She needed to pull herself together and quickly. Damian remained with her. His calm seeping into her being like it always did.

He gave her another look of pity and she forced herself to move forward but the closer they got the clearer the conversations of the Cyclopes became. "We should find them and eat them." She stopped in her tracks.

"No," another Cyclops responded. "People don't come here. It's bad luck to eat them."

Damian put his arm around her and squeezed her gently. He had to be frustrated with her, but she knew these monsters were talking about them. No doubt about it.

"Maybe they are a gift? A delicious and meaty gift." She could barely see a bald Cyclops licking his lips as he spoke and revulsion set in. His teeth were jagged and rotten looking.

"Keep moving," Damian whispered.

They crawled onward as she tried desperately to block out their conversation. However, certain words managed to slip through, such as stew and skewer. She was glad Damian stayed behind her now, it felt reassuring and he was basically forcing her forward.

"Do not go looking for them," one Cyclops insisted.

"I smell them. I do not see them, but I smell them." The bald one's chuckle boomed through her ears.

She heard a loud smack against flesh. "Do not. Stay here and enjoy the Centaur meat."

As they reached the edge of the mountain, Damian took the lead and climbed up past her. She followed his steps and the managed to sneak around the mouth of the cave unseen. The Cyclopes were still arguing about how to eat them and she was glad there was a small dirt pathway through the grass to follow up along the cave. It was worn out and she decided this must have been a usual route for other creatures on the island around these guys.

They finally reached a point where they could stand up and they ran up the path toward a group of trees far above the cave's entrance. She was safe for now and she felt tears almost sting her eyes out of joy.

"You did great." Damian kissed her forehead and she couldn't help laughing.

"Yeah, except I almost peed my pants." She rolled her eyes. She just wanted to just go home. This was not for her at all. Combat, she could handle, but mythical creatures, not so much. "That was sort of easy I guess."

"They are somewhat dimwitted creatures. I'm glad for that," Damian muttered as he looked around for the other two men. "Well, at least the mountain has trees and such growing all over it. Better than a rocky landscape."

"Lots of room for things to hide though." She cringed.

"Hey guys," Ryan called over to them as they jogged toward Anna and Damian.

Anna did not feel like moving, neither did Damian it seemed, so they waited until the other two came over.

"How'd you manage?" Cato huffed. His lip was bleeding. She was about to ask him what happened but Damian interrupted.

"Good. Had a nice little dirt path up along the way here." Damian grinned. She was thankful he left out how she nearly peed her pants.

"Lucky," Ryan groaned. "Ours was steep and the grass was slick. Nearly fell twice."

"You did fall." Cato wiped blood off his lip. "Your boot landed on my face."

"Get over it," Ryan groaned.

"Okay then," Damian interjected. "What now?"

Ryan took his pack off of his back and unzipped it. He took out several small shards of a mirror, no bigger than a sticky note. "Here." He handed everyone a piece.

"What's this for?" Anna asked.

"The Gorgons," he said it like it was obvious and not out of the ordinary.

"Where did you get this?" she asked.

"The Satyrs have been collecting things for many years. I guess when people have come to the island and the Sirens had their fill, they collect what is left. They found these mirrors intriguing and kept them. They let me have them."

"Okay, so what do we do with them?" she asked.

Ryan rolled his eyes at her. Ever since they got on the yacht he had been acting like the worlds biggest prick. His attitude was terrible and she'd much rather have his smart-ass comments than making her feel like an idiot. "Well, I have no idea where they are and I really don't want any of us turning into a statue so we are going to have to navigate around using these."

"Cool, things that can turn us into statues. How exactly do they do that?" she asked.

"By looking you in the eyes," Damian muttered in her ear because Ryan's annoyance was plastered all over his face. This was not going to work but she honestly could not think of another way. If these things turned you into stone just by looking at you then she would follow whatever Ryan thought best.

"I wouldn't use it the entire time. I plan on just looking at the ground and using my peripheral vision until I spot or hear something," Ryan instructed. "Unless that's what you want to do."

Anna rolled her eyes and was glad when Damian put his arm around her. He felt so safe and reassuring. She loved him. She really did.

CHAPTER XIII

Ryan

NOTHING LIKE LOOKING AT the ground for thirty minutes while hiking up a steep trail to make a person feel utterly lost.

Ryan was having a difficult time trying to navigate, given he could not really see where he was going. Once they got past the Gorgons he would be happy. Vision was the one sense he could never do without.

They continued up the small worn path through the tall grass and were about halfway up the mountain. It was taking a long time, mainly because of his lack of vision but additionally because it was steep and somewhat slick.

"So these Gorgons," Anna said interrupting his thoughts. "Who are they exactly?"

Ryan took a deep breath. He had to continuously tell himself it was not her fault, that she knew nothing about

Greek culture and beliefs. Really though, America failed in its education.

"Their names are Stheno, Euryale, and Medusa. I think you have heard of her at least." Ryan looked at Damian, who rolled his eyes at Ryan being impatient.

Anna scrunched her eyebrows. "Medusa. I've heard that name before in school. Snake-haired lady right?"

"Good," Ryan mumbled. "At least your culture hasn't failed as much as I thought in educating the masses."

"Okay Mr. Big Shot, if I told you I needed to find a WiFi hotspot for my smartphone to sync, what would that mean?" Anna smiled as she teased him.

Ryan looked to Damian and Cato, both shrugged in as much confusion as he was. "I think you are making words up."

"And you think *I* am stupid." She trudged along with her prying. "So they can turn people into statues?" Anna asked.

When are the twenty questions going to end? "Yes."

"What do they look like?"

Ryan gave Damian his best, 'I'm thoroughly exasperated with your woman' look and he thankfully took hold of the reins. "They have the body of women but their skin is scaled like a snakes. On their back they have golden wings that allow them to fly and snakes for hair," Damian explained.

"That doesn't seem too bad," she said. "Kind of creepy, but not bad."

"Don't forget the fanglike teeth and bronze clawed hands," Cato added.

"What the hell is wrong with your people?" she groaned. "Did you guys ever think up nice monsters? Things that didn't give every child a nightmare? Maybe a fluffy bunny that cuddles with children when they are sick or something."

"Centaurs and Nymphs aren't too terrible," Damian suggested. "And of course Satyrs."

"Nut jobs. All of you," she laughed.

Ryan could not help but laugh. "Yeah, like your religion is all peaches and cream."

"Who even says peaches and cream?" She punched him in the arm.

Ryan rubbed his arm and lightly pushed Anna away from him. She was growing on him. Like an annoying little sister he couldn't get away from. Anna was almost like one of the guys. Except for the breasts of course.

He stepped on a slick spot and lost his balance. He fell down hard on the ground and felt a sharp pain shoot through his ankle. Why did he always manage to get hurt? His agitation level was already through the roof. All of his problems had begun to pile up on his mind and eat away at him.

He needed solace. Calm even. He needed things to get fixed in his life and dammit he needed his pills now.

"You okay?" Damian over rushed to him.

Ryan nodded. "Just twisted my ankle." He was glad nothing broke. That was the last thing they needed.

Damian and Cato pulled him up to standing and he put his weight on his ankle. He winced, but they did not have time to rest.

"You sure you're okay?" Damian worried as always.

"Yeah," he answered, "let's keep moving."

With Damian's worried glances, they trekked into a forest of trees and Ryan spotted what looked like a statue. He forgot to keep his eyes down on the ground and the statue was a slap in the face to wake up and pay attention.

As they got closer, curiosity won out and he looked at the perfectly made marble figure. It was a man, possibly around his age and sporting what looked like a hippie leather outfit, flowers and peace signs included. He had long hair and beard to match, and a look of terror on his face.

"How the hell did this guy get here?" he muttered.

"Maybe he was one of those weird guys that decided to believe in old religions," Anna suggested. The all looked at her like she was crazy. "What? Modern day people are weird."

"Sounds like it," Cato snickered

They continued on. Ryan was hoping that perhaps the Gorgons had no desire to kill people after all these years. That maybe, perhaps, they decided to be with one another in peace and away from the other creatures on the island. He was obviously wrong. That man was not even one hundred years old.

No, they were obviously still vindictive as ever and he kept his eyes low. As many times as artists have created his likeness, he was not thrilled to have an exact replica with him stuck inside. Especially when no one would be able to see it.

"There's a Satyr over here," Damian whispered from behind, "nestled behind a tree."

"Alive?" Cato called.

"Statue."

They progressed along the path, however, the Gorgon's works of art seemed to multiply. Women and children in togas with their faces frozen in fright. There were men with armor that dated back to before Ryan's time. All of them had different expressions permanently petrified forever on their cold marble faces.

Fear, shock, even the lack of emotion was upon their faces as they ventured through the cemetery of statues. It was a sad but beautiful sight. There was so much history right in front of them that he almost felt a slight desire for the past.

The women dressed in Greek clothes, their hair in wonderful curls that framed their faces and jewels that must have been set in gold. The men in armor made him miss the glory of battle. Just the feeling of strapping it to your body and preparing for war was exhilarating and the prospect of feeling your enemies warm blood over your body, made him feel more alive then he had ever felt.

He missed those days. Longed for hand-to-hand combat. In a sadistic way he longed for the bloodiness of it all.

"What are you doing?" Damian whispered.

Ryan turned around to face Damian. "Nothing."

Cato and Anna were looking at a large statue of a man, who was peeking over his shield. His mistake in curiosity would forever be frozen in his shameful inability to resist the urge. Something he could relate to after his visit with the Sirens.

Ryan turned back to the statue he was standing right in front of while thinking about war. The frozen man in front of him was a clean-shaven, had long hair and was dressed in full Greek battle gear. His sword was up and ready to strike, his shield was held in his left hand.

What looked like a gash on his brow must have been new when he was transformed into a statue. A trickle of blood had started to come down to his eye before the Gorgons released their evil on him.

"Looks like you," Damian acknowledged, "when you

were mortal."

Ryan had to agree. "It's almost as if it's a bad omen."

"Could be." Damian put his hand on Ryan's shoulder. "Or it could for once in our lives be a coincidence. You are always so negative."

"Hard not to be." Ryan stared at the statue. "Excuse me." Ryan made his way behind a nearby tree, out of the other's sight and pulled out his pill bottle. It was getting low which sent his nerves on edge, but he needed to take them.

He knew it was becoming an addiction of his but he could not stop. Nor did he really want to. Ryan was fully aware the pills made him constantly on edge and not himself, but he had to do what he had to do.

He popped two pills in his mouth and swallowed them dry. It may have been a placebo effect but he already felt better having taken them. He leaned his head against the tree, closed his eyes and listened to his surroundings as the other's rested.

A shiver trailed down his spin. Something inside him was sensing danger and he turned around to face his group. They were all wandering around looking at statues and he felt guilty for not keeping them on track. They should not be looking around—it was putting them in danger especially in the Gorgon's hunting ground. "Get together. Get your mirrors out."

They did as he was told without hesitation and the four of them stood in a circle with their backs facing outwards. Ryan looked through his mirror and saw nothing but statues. He knew danger was near. He let his guard down just for a minute and he could feel it as his instincts kicked back in.

"What did you see?" Cato asked.

"Nothing," Ryan whispered. "We were careless just looking around. Be ready."

He saw movement in his mirror through the trees. His heart leapt. These creatures were what he feared most. They were quick and ferocious. Vision was so important in battle and they took it from him. He needed his other senses to kick into gear and fast.

Ryan strained to listen to the world around him. The rustling of leaves and the breathing of his friends all raced in fear of what was to come. His eyes were glued to the mirror.

A snap of a twig behind him made his mirror jolt in that direction. That's when he saw her in his mirror but just briefly as an evil smile spread on her lips. "They are here." His voice was small and uneven.

He heard the intake of everyone's breath, even his own, but the release was prolonged. Another twig snapped and a flash of red followed by black and then green scurried by in his mirror. The sounds of snakes hissing surrounded them, as it progressively grew louder. Every so often Ryan could he the maniacal laughter of a woman break through the hissing.

They were playing with them. Feeding off their fear. Ryan knew they wanted their group to break up and run in fright. It would be easier to corner them that way but he stood his ground, thankful the others did the same.

Deep breathes in and out. Now was the time to concentrate. The plan. They needed him to come up with a plan.

Evil winged women are surrounding us. They can fly and turn people into stone. What is their weakness? Two of them are immortal. Medusa can die but that would anger them.

What options do we have?

Crush them? With what?

Set them on fire? The two are immortal.

Tie them up? It was the only option he could think of.

"Okay," he looked into his friend's worried eyes. Anna looked on the verge of fainting. "We need to tie them up and cover their heads."

"Why not kill them?" Ryan could see tears straining down Anna's face as she spoke.

"Two of them can't die and if we kill Medusa they will follow us the entire time we are here looking for revenge. We need to subdue them and get away," Ryan answered and turned to Cato. "Do you have rope?"

"Duh." He rolled his eyes. Ryan resisted the urge to smack him upside the head.

Ryan waited for Cato to move. "Then get it out, dummy."

Cato removed his duffle bag from his shoulder and dropped it to the ground while Ryan kept his eye on his mirror. The Gorgons were slowing around them, enough for him to see their faces. They were gorgeous women in the face, minus the sharp fangs of course.

It was a sad fate they were dealt and he understood their hatred for the Gods. Life was rough and they needed to accept it already and move on.

The one with black snakes for hair stopped and looked directly in the mirror at Ryan. Her face was beautiful. Ryan found himself mesmerized until her snakes came to life and hissed at him. The woman's black eyes were lifeless and her malicious smile stayed put.

"Okay, now what?" Cato's voice squeaked. In normal circumstance Ryan would have made fun of him. He held a massive amount of rope in his hands.

"Did you really just pack a duffle bag with rope?" Ryan laughed.

"Hey, you never know when you might need three hundred feet of utility rope," Cato said.

"Anna, how do you feel about being bait again?"

"Hell no," she said simply.

"Okay." Ryan looked to Damian. "You're up."

"No." Damian looked at Anna. Okay, so he wanted to stay by her side. Ryan understood that.

"Okay fine then." He'd much rather be on the trapping end of the plan so he could make sure nothing went wrong, but he would have to work around that. "I am going to taunt them away from here. Meanwhile, Cato is going to set up a trap." Ryan kept his voice low enough that the Gorgons wouldn't hear him.

Cato was an expert at trapping and honestly, Damian was terrible at it. With a grin on his face, Cato nodded and started to work with the rope as they stood in the circle. He wasted no time as he made different knots that looked utterly complicated.

"Are you sure you should be doing this? You won't be able to see very well and they are fast," Damian protested.

"I'm going to run where the trees are thicker so they cannot fly. They will have to chase me on foot and those big wings will slow them down." Ryan grasped Damian's shoulder. "I got this. Besides, Cato is doing the trapping and you and Anna were pretty clear about not being bait."

"Maybe I should go. You twisted your ankle," Damian said worriedly. "Yeah, I should go. I changed my mind."

"No, this is my job." Ryan grinned and broke the circle

before Damian could say another word. "So I hear you ladies hate Poseidon and Athena. I must say, those are my two favorite Gods. So kind and generous to everyone."

The hissing died and Ryan looked in his mirror. All three Gorgons stood side by side behind him and he inhaled sharply. They each had a different color of snakes for their hair, red, green, and then black. A small white toga barely covered their shapely bodies, with golden shoes laced up their shins.

"Close your eyes," he whispered to his friends before he turned and started to walk toward the trees. "How lovely to meet you ladies! Might I add how disgusting you look today? I mean I cannot even imagine how you looked before. I think Athena might have done you all a favor."

"Easy," Damian whispered before he was out of earshot.

"I mean it as a compliment, of course." Ryan proceeded, ignoring Damian's advice. "I think she made a vast improvement."

"How dare you," a voice hissed. The words came from a musical voice yet they dripped venom.

Ryan made it to the thickest area with trees. To his pleasure, they slowly followed him and they looked particularly unhappy. Things were going as planned. It made his mind clear up when things went as planned—even if these were creatures he had nightmares about as a child.

"Poseidon had every right to take your purity from you Medusa. He is a god and you were just a plaything for him. You should have given yourself willingly when asked. After all, you are just a woman. Put on this planet to amuse men." Any women he knew, ancient or in modern times, would not appreciate what he'd just said. It's not as if he really believed it, but he knew how to piss a woman off better than anyone.

The one with black snakes moved quicker than her sisters. She had to have been Medusa. Her face was the most beautiful, it was also the angriest.

"He raped me," Medusa hissed, as she got closer to Ryan from behind. He picked up his pace. "Athena should have stopped him. I prayed, begged even and she did nothing. She blamed *me* for it!"

"Why wouldn't she blame you?" Ryan laughed as he continued through the trees. "You were nothing to her. Let me rephrase that, you are *still* nothing to her."

All three Gorgon's hair hissed at him and their faces went from beautiful to terrifying in an instant making him jump in shock. They were far enough into the trees that he could not see his friends anymore. How long would it take Cato to set up a feasible trap?

"Come here you scum," one of them hissed. At this point Ryan did not bother to look in the mirror. His main concern was to get away because he could hear them getting closer. He trudged through the trees, making sure he didn't trip over anything on the ground that would cause the end of his life.

"What did I do? I'm just telling the truth," he yelled over his shoulder. "Maybe if you didn't flaunt yourself around, Poseidon wouldn't have gotten the wrong impression."

In truth, he felt bad for Medusa. The poor woman was raped by a god and cursed by another. Athena could have protected her, but she didn't because Medusa was raped inside of her temple and Athena saw it as sacrilege. Poor Medusa had no chance to fight for herself. It was a terribly miserable story.

If she did not go around turning people into statues, he

may feel bad for her, but she took revenge to a whole different level and killed innocent people. He could only imagine the pain she must have gone through, both mentally and physically. But it was no excuse to kill, especially innocent people just as she used to be.

Ryan broke into a run when heard the women scramble behind him to catch up. They shrieked in anger. He was being terrible to Medusa.

The trees were less dense here so he decided to turn around and head back to his group. Hopefully Cato had plenty of time to finish the trap. Hope was the key word that popped in his mind but given the fact he had been off on his own for about five minutes it would take five minutes to get back. It had to be enough time.

His ankle throbbed in protest when he made a large turn around the Gorgons so he wouldn't run into them. To his surprise they made no attempt to cut him off but just followed directly behind him. They were either idiotic or just hell bent on killing him.

Ryan jumped over a large tree branch, as he landed his knee buckled from under him. He fell to the ground crushing leaves below him. To his horror, he felt a body jump on his back and flip him over.

Ryan squeezed his eyes shut as hard as he could, to the point of it almost being painful. He would not die this way. There was no way in hell he would be turned into a statue for the Gorgon's amusement.

Hissing surrounded his face and he could feel her body firmly pressed against his. "Well, isn't this a treat sisters? An Immortal with a little something extra inside."

He had no idea what she meant by that. "Get off me."

Her body pressed into his even harder and his breathing became labored. "You will pay for your disrespect, Immortal. What better way to reap revenge than to take it out on one of their most prized possessions?"

"I am no one of worth to them," he tried to lie.

"You Immortals are their pride and joy." The hissing of snakes grew louder in his ears and he could tell her face was getting closer to his own. "Open those pretty eyes of yours."

"Not going to happen," he said.

He felt a sharp pain radiate in his arm as if a lion had dragged its claws across it. Ryan bit back the urge to scream. The gorgon's laughter filled the air making him uneasy. They were enjoying this much more than he remembered being in their character.

From what he knew, they hunted to turn you to stone, not torture you, but he could be wrong. That, or they have changed to something far more sinister than even the fates could have imagined.

"Open," she commanded again.

"Medusa?"

"Clever." She licked his earlobe sending a shiver down his back. "Yes?"

His guess was spot on. She was obviously in control of her sisters and after the things he said she probably wanted to hurt him the most. "Can I ask you one question before I open my eyes?"

Medusa's breath tickled his neck. "I must say, it is a pity to loose such a specimen of the male form. You will be fun to look at for eternity."

Ryan tried not to throw up in his mouth at the thought. "May I ask?" he repeated.

Medusa gripped his bleeding arm tight with her hand. "If you must, I see no reason why not."

"If you must, I see no reason why not," Ryan said.

"What?" Medusa asked.

"What?"

"What are you doing?"

"What are you doing?" Ryan mimicked.

"Stop it!" Medusa's anger was apparent in her voice.

"Stop it!"

"If you do not stop I will cut out your tongue."

"If you do not stop I will cut out your tongue." Ryan forced himself to smile to annoy her further.

She shrieked in outrage and stood up from his body. A swift kick to his ribs had him wrapping his arms around his torso. "Try and repeat my words now," she hissed along with her snakes.

Ryan grunted. "Try… and repeat my words now."

He listened to the leaves beneath her feet shift as she brought it up for another blow. Ryan forced himself to sit up and managed to grab hold of her leg judging by the sounds she made. She let out a squeal of protests but he brought his fist into her kneecap as hard as he could.

"Sister!" The other two Gorgons had made their appearance finally known. Ryan was already setting off opposite of their noisy location with his eyes wide open when he knew he no longer faced them head on. His arm throbbed in pain.

"Get back here you swine!"

Ryan laughed. "Who says that anymore?" *Probably beings*

who had no concept of evolving language, he thought to himself.

"When I catch you I will make sure you do not turn to stone," one of the Gorgons shrieked. "I will kill you slowly!"

"I hope not," he muttered to himself.

The pills in his system must have taken full effect as his ankle became more than tolerable. He kept at a steady pace, occasionally bringing up his mirror to make sure he was far enough ahead. They weren't as quick when they were enraged and their wings would occasionally get caught up on low branches.

A few times he laughed out loud when they fought with one another to be ahead of the rest.

Being chased by enraged women, just another day in the office.

As soon as Ryan was out of sight with the Gorgons, Cato dug in Damian's duffle bag and pulled out an axe.

"So glad you fucking packed this," Cato grumbled.

"Me too," Damian answered

Cato started to swing at the tree with all of his might. "Get the rope," he grunted as he worked. "Tie it around the trunk of this tree high up. Not that end." Damian almost grabbed the overly large circle Cato tied together and grabbed the loose end.

Damian climbed up and tied the rope around the tree

trunk while Cato hacked away. "Now what?" When he was finished he waited for further instructions.

"Do you see that thick branch up there?" Cato nodded his head up to the center of the statue meadow. Damian saw a large tree branch sticking out of a massive tree.

"I see it," Damian answered.

"Hoop the rope over it like we are going to hang them because we sort of are."

Damian worked as quickly as he could, putting the rope exactly where Cato instructed. All the while Cato was hacking at the tree like his life depended. Anna stayed clear of them both while they worked. There wasn't much for her to do without getting in the way.

In about ten minutes Damian was done and he quickly covered the large rope circle on the ground with leafs and turned to Cato. "Are you sure this is going to work?"

Cato nodded apprehensively. "Pretty sure."

"We don't need pretty sure with this one," Damian groaned. "Will it or not?"

"I am doing what I can in the few minutes I have, Damian. We made the circle wide enough to catch them if they are near one another. Just make sure you can push the tree over." Cato wiped the sweat from his brow. "If I had more time to make it properly I would say it would definitely work."

He had just swung his axe one last time at the very tall somewhat skinny tree. It was so close to falling over that Damian stood clear away from the direction it would fall. Cato was rather experienced in this sort of thing in his past. He knew exactly how to fell a tree.

Damian heard Ryan yelling in the distance and he ran

over to the nearly sawed down tree with Anna. Cato stood across from them ready with more rope waiting for Ryan to come into the small clearing. "Are you ready?" Damian called to Cato, who was hiding behind a tree ready to pounce.

"Yeah, I'm not going to lie. It might not work," Cato yelled back. "Just so you know."

"Dammit, Cato," Damian grumbled, but he didn't offer a better idea. It was amateur work at its best but it was all they could do within their time frame. Cato had hacked the hell out of the tree in record time, which was commendable.

"Are you ready?" he asked Anna.

She nodded and he gave her a quick kiss on the lips. He hated her being here. This was no place for anyone, not even them.

Ryan ran into the clearing, sweaty and exhausted. He was clearly ahead of the Gorgons and he stopped in the middle of the circle rope trap. Damian heard the Gorgons coming closer and Ryan seemed to look around for Damian and Cato.

"Get out of there you idiot!" Cato whispered harshly.

Ryan studied the ground and took a step just outside of the circle. What was he doing? He needed to run.

The three snake women came into view. Thankfully they faced Ryan, who had his back to them and they paused. From what he could see of their faces they were furious and ambivalent. Good lord they were terrifying.

"Do you give up?" the one with black snakes for hair asked.

"I've been thinking," Ryan said. "Maybe Athena just brought out the evil in you that was already there. What sort of person enjoys turning innocent people into statues?"

They slinked closer to the middle of the rope circle. "I suffered and so shall everyone else."

"You have children in your collection," Ryan growled. "Children are above all innocent in life. You deserved your fate. You deserve misery."

The Gorgons stepped closer to Ryan as a group. Once they reached the middle, Damian nodded to Anna. They pushed as hard as they could against the tree. Cato had it cut perfectly to where it was no trouble to push over quickly. He turned back to see the rope circle close so fast around the Gorgon's ankles that he barely saw it happen.

They shrieked as they were lifted into the air upside down and their heads knocked against one another. He had no idea how that worked so well but it did. Cato ran out of the shadows with a large branch in his hand, and hit the Gorgons in the head repeatedly while keeping his head low.

Ryan picked up a branch and helped hit until they stopped moving. They both dropped the bloodied branches on the ground, heaving heavy breaths.

Ryan fell to his knees and then laid on the ground. He looked exhausted as his chest rose up and down. "I like them better when they are severely unconscious," he breathed heavily.

"I didn't know you could knock out an immortal being, but I'm glad it worked," Cato added. "I just wanted to hit them."

The Gorgon's snake hair hung down limply brushing against the ground. Damian was glad their eyes were closed and very swollen. Even if they were able to get free and search for them it would be difficult. He wasn't a fan of beating women, but they hardly counted as such anymore.

"Cut the rope," Cato ordered.

Damian cut the rope off the fallen tree and heard the bodies drop limply to the ground making the sounds of crushed leafs waft in the air. He grabbed Anna's hand and inched toward the bodies' of the Gorgons. Their wings lay limply on the ground and Cato and Ryan were tying their clawed hands together.

"See it worked. It wasn't so bad." Cato stood up after he was done tying their hands together.

"Easy for you to say." Ryan punched his shoulder. "They pretty much hate me with a passion."

Damian rolled his eyes. "Along with many other women in this world, Ryan. Why not the Gorgons as well?"

They all stood back and looked at their handy work. These poor women never had a chance in life to be whoever they wanted to be. Their destiny was this. What would happen if he ever displeased the gods? Would he suffer a similar fate?

"Let's tie them to a tree and move on." Ryan dragged one of them by the feet while Cato dragged another.

Damian had no desire to help. It felt wrong to treat a creature like this. Sure, he had killed his fair share of people, however he never treated them like a piece of garbage. Tied to a tree might be the way they spend the rest of their lives. It felt wrong.

Cato placed his empty duffle bag over their heads and tied it tightly around their necks. It was an incredibly snug fit and probably choked them. Then they started to wind the rope around the Gorgon's bodies and the tree.

"Are you okay?" Anna looked up at him with her gorgeous brown eyes. She was so beautiful. He never could have imagined himself so lucky to find a woman like her.

"Of course." He tried to smile the best he could and kissed her forehead. "I'm glad you weren't bait."

"That makes two of us." She grabbed his ass and he jumped in surprise.

"What was that for?" he laughed.

Anna winked at him. "I don't know. Feeling kind of frisky I guess."

"I do believe lust is your deadly sin, my love." He grinned. "I think battle might turn you on, ma'am."

She grabbed his ass again and he grabbed hers back. Anna squealed playfully until he pulled her into his arms. How was he so lucky?

"Hey lovebirds," Ryan yelled over to them as they finished tying up the Gorgons. "Let's get moving."

CHAPTER XIV

Ryan

AFTER TAKING ON THE Gorgon sisters and walking for however long, he felt the need to rest. That was a stupid idea on this big mountain, given the alarming amount of creatures on it, but he needed it. He pushed his body to go on until he felt weak in the knees. Everyone looked equally exhausted and had yet to complain. It was only a matter of time until someone collapsed, so they had better take a break.

The trees didn't seem to let up much the entire time they walked. He was constantly pushing his way through branches, bushes, and tripping on fallen debris. Ryan sighed in relief once he saw a small area with a little pond. It was odd to see it on the mountain, but Ryan didn't think anything of it. If he tried to make sense of the island he would lose his mind. Nothing here was normal. Well, not normal for the mortal world he had adapted to.

"Can we stop for a bit?" Damian suggested. He didn't seem particularly tired but he looked at Anna as if she were the one that actually wanted the break.

Ryan shrugged, trying his best to look relieved. "Yeah, for a few minutes."

Anna and Damian sat down as Damian leaned against a tree trunk. They were some distance away from the little pond, and Anna made herself comfortable between his legs, leaning against him. They entwined their fingers together and Damian brought her hand up to his lips. Anna smiled as she tilted her head back and Damian brushed his lips against hers.

Ryan rolled his eyes. His jealousy of their relationship was growing so much so that he felt pain in his chest every time they did something intimate. For the longest time he avoided a relationship like theirs and now that's all he wanted.

Ryan decided to leave them alone to avoid his growing frustration and made his way to the pond. Cato followed behind him. "Didn't want to watch the love birds together?" Cato seemed to sense his mood. "Those two are insatiable."

"Disgustingly so," Ryan grumbled.

"At least Damian is happy." Cato jumped over a fallen branch. "For awhile he just seemed to be going through the motions of life. Not really enjoying himself."

Ryan was oblivious to that until Anna came into the picture because he never realized how true it was. Once she arrived, Ryan knew Damian had changed. He was excited and more passionate. He talked back to Ryan more often then not these days. He never really realized how submissive his friend used to be until now.

They made their way through the bushes and now had

a full view of the pond. Flowers of every color decorated the surrounding area, the smell of honey drifted through the air. The first thing that looked off about the place was the fact there were pine, ash, oak, and fruit trees in the surrounding area. They mixed in with one another in an oddly beautiful way. It was unusual to see so many different trees flourishing together.

The pond was barely the size of a boxing ring with a rock fountain trickling in the middle. Lily pads floated along the surface, with yellow flowers sticking out of them.

"Well, this is cool." Cato crouched down to look into the pond. "There's a bunch of little fish in here. Wanna catch some and make a snack?"

Ryan rolled his eyes. "It's always food with you isn't it, you big bastard."

"Hey, I may be tall but I am anything but fat, shorty," Cato countered as he looked down into the water.

Ryan leaned up against the pale trunk of an ash tree and crossed his arms. Perhaps he could get some sort of a nap in while they rested for a few minutes. The light sound of water trickling in the pound was soothing enough to make his body feel heavy.

Arms wrapped around his body from behind him. Ryan was in a sort of daze from exhaustion that he didn't process in his mind as to who it was. He looked down at the arms and his eyes widened. They belonged to a woman whose skin was a pale green color.

Ryan jumped away from the tree and whoever had a hold of him. He was shocked to see arms protruding from the trunk of the ash tree. He almost backed up into the pound until Cato caught him by the shoulders.

"What the hell?" Cato whispered to him.

Ryan watched with fascination as the arms dropped back into the trunk and disappeared just like a ghost would. Only seconds later a figure came striding out of the tree in the image of a gorgeous woman with pale green skin. She didn't look sickly, but startlingly artistic. Leaves that matched the ash tree were woven throughout her pale blonde hair in such a way he swore it grew that way naturally. It probably did.

Her figure was hard to look away from. Her curves were intoxicating. More leaves covered her private areas as if they were winding up around her body, but not enough of her was covered. He still felt himself blush at the sight.

"Whoa," Cato breathed.

Ryan nodded. "Whoa."

She tilted her head to the side and looked at them. Her eyes were a bright red color which was a stark contrast compared to the rest of her.

Ryan cleared his throat. "Hello."

Her eyes were on Ryan as she was silently studied them.

Cato bumped into him almost violently. Ryan turned to see another gorgeous figure stepping out of the small pond.

This new woman had deathly pale skin and hair that was a deep blue-black and floated around the air as if she were still submerged in the water. Her body was barely covered by a very thin piece of cloth and it left nothing to the imagination.

He realized his jaw hung low and he tried to snap out of the trance as more women seemed to emerge from around the area. There were ten of them, each resembling a different flower or plant that decorated the area. One was the color of honey and another had flowers placed delicately in her hair. They were all equally intoxicating to look at.

They eyed Cato and himself as if they were some alien-like creatures.

"Nymphs?" Cato's eyes were glued on the women.

"Yep," Ryan answered, but his voice was so low he didn't know if Cato could hear him.

He felt very cautious around anything on this island, including Nymphs who were mischievous but not know to be evil. Judging by how long all of them were crammed on this island, it wouldn't surprise him if they had changed.

The Meliai Nymph that grabbed him came upon him almost suggestively. She placed her hands on his chest and he inhaled sharply. Ryan had no idea why they were affecting him so much. Being surrounded by beautiful women that were no threat to him tended to do that that to a man.

"Greetings," her voice dripped in honey.

"To you as well," Ryan managed to say with confidence.

"We have two fine specimens before us." She looked around to the other Nymphs. Ryan felt like he was either the luckiest man on the planet or the most unfortunate. Both Zee and Julia were still firmly planted in his mind even though the sight before him was beyond tempting.

He glanced at Cato, who was getting quite a bit of attention from the Naiad Nymph that climbed her way out of the small pond. Her hands were venturing in areas the made Cato's cheeks turn red even though he didn't back away from her touch.

Ryan was surprised that his memory on the different types of Nymphs had flooded back into his mind. It had been so long since he really thought about his beliefs other than just the gods.

"Is there something we can do for you?" Ryan tried to sound unaffected and failed miserably.

"You are of our faith, are you not?" the Meliai Nymph asked. Ryan nodded. "Free us from this prison then."

"How?" Ryan felt himself stuck in some sort of trance. The need to help them no matter the cost flourish inside him.

More Nymphs came around him to touch his body and although it was uncomfortable, he had a hard time pushing them off. They seemed transfixed on him and Cato. He would be stupid to push them away, but he felt like it was more of a curiosity of theirs rather than something sexual.

"The gods will listen to you. Free us," her singsong voice chimed against his ear. "We need to be in the world and make it full of life once again. It is dying without us. We can feel it wasting away."

She grazed his earlobe with her teeth. It was odd to be somewhat turned on by a mythological creature. This was definitely something he was going to keep to himself. Her once curious demeanor was definitely turning sexual.

"I'll do what I can," Ryan managed to choke out the words and cleared his throat. He had no idea why he was agreeing without another thought. "Definitely."

"Me too," Cato groaned when the Naiad Nymph cupped his groin while he was trying to back away from her advances on him. "Whoa."

"Thank you," all the Nymphs' voices chimed at the same time in a musical way. They begun to retreat from Cato and Ryan with satisfied looks on their faces.

Ryan didn't want them to leave. It was strange but their presence made him feel more alive. Perhaps that was the point of them. Bringing life into the world was their existence in a nutshell.

"Wait," Ryan blurted out.

The Nymphs slowly stopped in their tracks, turning around to face them once more. The Meliai Nymph grinned at him with bright white teeth.

"Yes?" she cooed.

"That's all you wanted?"

The Meliai grinned wider. "What do you wish of us?"

Ryan's brain drew a blank. It was odd just for them to have that simple request and then leave. He expected more from them. She studied him and he looked right back, until he suddenly had a thought.

"If I do this, will you fight on our side?" Ryan asked.

Cato raised his eyebrow at him. "Huh?"

"Will you?" Ryan went on.

The Nymphs looked amongst one another until the Meliai Nymph spoke up, "We are not warriors by nature, sir."

"Not by nature, but you can fight with nature," Ryan insisted. "If in the final battle we need you and the other creatures, we want your assistance."

"How will we know when you need us?" she asked politely. He took it as a good sign they were considering it. After their brief meeting it seemed like a very good trade off.

"We will send someone. Trust me, you will know when it is time." Ryan had a game plan in his head. It was crazy but it could work.

"As you wish," she walked up to him as the Naiad Nymph

went up to Cato.

Ryan and Cato both received a kiss on the lips, sealing their promise as well as causing some frustration as the Nymph's nearly naked bodies rubbed against theirs.

Ryan's nymph pulled away to look at him. "You remind me of your father."

Ryan blinked. "What?"

"You will find out one day." She grinned. "He was fond of our kind as well."

Ryan wanted to ask what she meant by that, but they retreated as they sunk back into their respective homes. The tree Nymphs melted into the trunks, along with the Naiad into her pond. Nymphs of the earth seemed to just disappear like ghosts all together, leaving Ryan and Cato standing awkward and alone.

"Did they make you—" Cato started.

"Yep," Ryan interrupted.

"Is that weird?"

"Yep."

"Can we never talk about this?"

"Yep." Ryan closed his eyes, getting himself back in control. "That was an odd turn of events."

Cato seemed to have some sort of trouble with his trousers. "A fast, amazing, weird turn of events."

"Let's get back to Damian and Anna." Ryan shook his head out of the oddly satisfying situation they were just in.

"Hold up, I need to adjust myself," Cato grunted.

Anna

Anna groaned as they climbed further up the mountain. It was becoming increasingly steeper and she was exhausted. They had spent most of the day on this damn mountain and she was sick of it. It was hot, she was sweating, and she was cranky.

"What's wrong with you?" Ryan called back. He was a lot further than her and Damian, but he must have heard her groan from where he was. Thank god Damian stayed behind with her.

"I'm tired," she yelled up to him. "So suck it."

"Just a little further." Damian pulled her after him and she was thankful for the help. "Are you okay?"

He was probably worried about her attitude, as always. "Yep."

The further they got up the mountain the rockier it became. The temple was so close that she felt like just sitting right here and waiting for them to talk to the Oracle. They did not really need her there anyways, right?

Her foot slipped on a rock making her slide back down a few feet. "Great." Anna sat down on the ground, she felt like a child but she didn't care. The event didn't help her current cranky mood.

Damian came after her and knelt down. "Get on." He turned his back to her, looking over his shoulder for her to jump on.

"No," she laughed.

Damian rolled his eyes. He was so cute. "You're a big

tough girl, okay? I get it, just get on my back."

Agitated and grateful, she lay her body horizontally across the back of his shoulders in a fireman's hold. This could not be easy for him. He was probably tired too and she felt like she was holding him back. As he begun to climb faster up the mountain, she realized she had held him back. Damian didn't seem even remotely tired or maybe he was just putting up a front for her sake.

She could no longer see Ryan and Cato through the thick trees ahead. Damian and her must have fallen so far behind and it was all her fault. Panic rose inside until they made it past the thickest part of the trees and into a large clearing. In an instant her breath was caught in her throat at the sight before her.

"Holy shit," she mumbled.

In front of her stood a massive white temple with marble stone pillars. It looked straight out of some ancient Greek movie or something. Ryan and Cato were waiting on the stairs for them as Damian jogged over. She could not take her eyes off of the building.

How the hell did they make this thing?

"About time," Ryan teased.

"Shut up," Anna grunted.

"Pretty nice for someone banished to the island," Cato added. "I expected something smaller. Especially for just one person."

"It looks like the Parthenon doesn't it?" Damian's eyes traveled up the tall pillars.

"Let's just get this over with." Ryan was obviously as moody as she was.

They walked up the steps and were soon in front of a pair of large wooden doors. Some guy riding a chariot was carved on the doors and the sun beamed behind him. She was about to ask who it was until Ryan pushed the doors open and they piled inside.

It immediately made her feel like she was in a museum. Her surroundings were cold and lifeless and their footsteps echoed around the room. Statues of what she assumed were the Greek gods, lined the walls, towering over them.

At the very end of the temple sat a wooden tripod chair and on the ground beside it was a pile of blankets and pillows. They looked dirty yet comfortable at the same time. It was a wretched little home for the Oracle, who was nowhere to be seen.

As if reading her mind Cato spoke. "Where is she?"

Ryan gazed around the room like a hawk. He was tense, much more than usual as of lately. Ryan seemed to be progressing into a constant state of pissed off and angry at the world. Maybe he was just taking things more seriously like everyone kept badgering him about. He was more cautious and less carefree. She preferred the latter if she had to be honest.

Anna heard a loud crash to her left and turned to see a shattered clay pot on the ground. It appeared to have fallen off a little table that sat next to a statue and Ryan bolted to investigate. Anna finally slid off Damian's shoulders, and placed her hand on her gun's grip.

Ryan started to walk behind the statues base but stopped in his tracks. He glanced worriedly back to Damian. "Come here." His voice was strained.

Damian released her hand and trudged over to Ryan.

She didn't even realize he had hold of her, "Oh gods," Damian muttered loud enough that Anna could hear. He crouched down. "Ma'am?"

"It's okay," Ryan cooed to whatever was back there. "We won't harm you."

A small and weak laugh came from behind the statue. "You can't kill me you know," a hoarse voice said.

"I wasn't going to try, ma'am." Ryan crouched down with Damian. "What happened to you?"

Anna was damn curious now. Cato seemed intrigued as well as he made his way slowly toward the small voice. Anna stood her ground but as soon as Cato got closer, a crazed woman pounced out from behind the statue with a loud shriek and slashed an old knife at Damian and Ryan. She had made contact with Damian's shoulder and Anna instantly lunged into protective mode.

She pulled out her gun and aimed at the wild woman. "Don't move."

The woman glared at her, confusion on her face as she looked at the gun. "Leave me be."

"Can't do that, you weird chick. We need your help," said Anna.

She gave Anna another odd expression. "Why are you referring to me as a baby chicken?" She glared at Ryan when he chuckled.

"It's an expression, Oracle," Ryan said calmly, though the amusement didn't leave his eyes. It was good to see some humor in him after his mood lately.

Her eyes glared fiercely at him, which wiped the smile off his face. Anna decided instantly she liked this woman. She didn't know if she was starting to become protective of these guys or what, but she didn't like it when people gave them death glares.

Her long brown hair was wild, as if she hadn't taken care of it in years. She probably didn't care much about her appearance given she was the only mostly human being on the island. It was obviously she didn't leave her sanctuary much either. Her skin was extremely pale, her big doe eyes were clear and she looked healthy for the most part.

"Get out of here," she ground out through her teeth. "I cannot help you."

"Why not?" Cato probed.

The Oracle eyed him suspiciously, the dagger in her hand wavered. Anna didn't drop her gun, the Oracle had attacked Damian, which was unacceptable.

"People use me and leave me," she summarized. Her thin body began to shake. "I will not help."

"Oracle, we need your help. It's life or death," Ryan disputed her decision.

"It always is," she retorted with a small laugh. "You make me lose myself and let the gods take me over. I won't do it anymore. It's exhausting." Her fiery eyes seemed to have only disgust in them as she looked at Ryan.

Anna tried to be patient with her—she must have been alone for centuries. She was probably bat shit crazy at this point. However, time was precious and they needed answers. The damn world depended on her help at this point and Anna intended to get it.

"Here's a thought, help or I will shoot you," Anna offered the choice. "Sound fair?"

The Oracle, cocked her head to the side. "Shoot me?"

"Yeah." Anna nodded.

"Anna, she doesn't know what a gun is," Damian said softly as he clutched his bleeding arm.

Well now she felt stupid.

"Would you like me to demonstrate?" She smiled wickedly. It made her angry seeing Damian bleed.

The Oracle gave Anna a look of complete disgust. "You can threaten me all you want, but I cannot die. Apollo made sure of that."

"Oracle, please." Damian leaned closer to her like she was a frightened animal. "What can we do to change your mind? We will be totally lost without your guidance." Buttering her up seemed to work a bit.

The woman studied Damian up and down. Anna felt the green-eyed monster rise up. She needed to stop batting those long dirty eyelashes at him right now. If she couldn't die then shooting her would be perfectly fine. Right?

"Bring me away from here," she blubbered as she jumped into Damian's arms and had begun to cry. Anna could feel her face turn red and her finger was tempted to squeeze tightly. Ryan was next to Damian and she saw him bit his lip with worry. Great, now she was the loose cannon out of the group.

The knife in woman's hand fell to the ground and Ryan kicked it away from her. Damian cradled the woman in his arms and tried desperately to soothe her as he whispered into her ear.

"What the fuck Damian?" she called out.

Damian ignored her and continued to rub his hand up and down the woman's back, while his other hand tried to smooth down her wild hair. Full-fledged anger built up inside her body as she stormed to the entrance and sat down on the top of the stairs. How could he do that in front of her? Touching another woman like that was not okay.

After a few moments Ryan followed her outside and took a seat next to her. Anna tried to control her breathing. "I'm not in the mood for your shit right now. Whatever smart ass, dickhead thing you have to say, keep it to yourself."

"I was actually just checking on you." He seemed sympathetic, which made her question who was actually sitting next to her.

"I'm being dramatic, I know." She grit her teeth—it was hard to admit. Still, part of her felt justified for getting mad. Damian ignored her while he wrapped his arms around some strange woman.

Ryan put his arm around her shoulder, pulling her against his side like a buddy would. "I would be pissed too. Don't worry, we can be dramatic together." He ran his hand along his head. "Hell, I tried to kill myself after I saw Julia with Aden. I do believe I exceed your degree of crazy."

In an odd turn of events, Ryan of all people was making her feel better. "You tried to kill yourself because you hit her, you dummy."

"Even so." He waved his hand in front of them. "Being dramatic is a part of being human."

It started to nag at her consciousness. "What are they doing in there anyways?" The wind blew around them, grasping her loose hair in waves.

"Cato and Damian are trying to convince her to let them get her cleaned up." His voice was thick with conviction.

"What!" she shrieked. "They are going to see her naked." A lump formed in her throat that ached with every breath she took.

Ryan tightened his grip on Anna when she tried to stand up. "It's just a body. It's not like his male appendage is going anywhere near her." Their eyes met, but his was a fixed expression.

Breathe.

Nope, breathing was not going to work and she tried to remove Ryan's arm. She wanted to get Damian away from the naked girl that pushed her body against his. She elbowed him in the ribs, which only made him use both of his arms to clamp tightly around her. It was like being in a bear hug and there was no escape.

Anna wriggled around until Ryan ended up on his back, his arms still tightly around her body. She lay on top of him with her back to his front. It was incredibly awkward. "I don't like this position." Her voice cracked.

"Really?" he asked in a husky voice. "I do."

"You are nasty."

"You are correct." Ryan chuckled, amused with himself.

"What the hell is digging into my back?" she squealed, trying to move away from him.

Ryan burst out laughing. "It is just the hilt of my knife, chill out."

"Ryan, let go of me." Her breath came in ragged gasps. His hold on her was tight making it difficult to breathe properly.

"If you calm down, I will. Damian is not doing anything but showing kindness to that girl." She felt him sigh underneath her.

"Then why don't you go and show your kindness instead of him?" she retorted with a little more venom than she intended.

"She doesn't seem to like me much." Anna rolled her eyes. The girl did seem slightly agitated by Ryan's presence. She relaxed and just laid on top of him, giving up her struggling. Ryan patted her head like a dog. "Good girl."

"You are so annoying," she muttered.

Ryan sat up and finally slid her off of him. "Yeah, I get that often."

"I'm being dumb, huh?" she asked.

"Like I said, I would probably be pissed off if I were in your place." He scratched his cheek. "But come on, it's Damian. Mr. Nice Guy. He would never do anything to really hurt you, Anna. You have to know that."

"I guess."

"I think after the whole gun episode you probably frightened her," Ryan added without a hint of annoyance in his voice. "Damian has a calming soul. She probably was just drawn to it after being so scared when strangers showed up out of nowhere."

That was true, but Anna let her feelings get the better of her. "Well, she was being uncooperative." She really was.

Something like a sigh escaped his lips. "She has been alone, surrounded by monsters for over two thousand years, Anna. She has the right to be somewhat uncooperative."

Whatever.

Ryan spoke again, "Can I ask a favor from you?" Ryan's voice turned low and uncertain as he stared at his feet.

Apprehensively she said, "Sure, what?"

"If something were to happen to me, and I am not saying it will, but just in case, please look after Damian. Even if someday you two decided not to be together just make sure he is happy. He is the best of us both and he may need to step up in the Immortal world one day."

"Why are you talking like this?" She frowned.

"Like I said, this will be a difficult battle and if I don't make it I want to make sure those I leave behind are properly attended to. Sort of like my unwritten will, I suppose." His smile didn't reach his eyes. "I'm not going to kill myself, Anna. I just want that peace of mind. Just in case shit hits the fan."

Feeling choked up she nodded. "Okay, but let's hope the shit stays clear of the fan."

"Agreed."

CHAPTER XV

Ryan

AFTER SITTING IN SILENCE for what seemed like forever, Damian came outside to retrieve Anna and Ryan. He was relieved Anna had calmed down. She was a hot head and he blamed her heritage. Call him what you will, but Hispanic women were crazy when it came to their men.

Ryan's eyes made their way toward the Oracle when they walked in. She sat on the ground, looking like a completely different person. Her dark hair was brushed and clean, lying over one shoulder as it fell down to her waist. Her thin body was scrubbed clean and her white chiton hung from her body in the most flattering way. He could tell why she was chosen to be the Oracle now. They only picked the most beautiful women.

The sadness still remained in her eyes from years of loneliness. No matter how naturally beautiful she was, all he could see was her anguish. Attitude was a very attractive trait and when your looks are washed over by depression, it is all anyone ever sees. He pitied her.

When the Oracle saw Ryan and Anna come in she worriedly looked to Cato with wide eyes. Cato gently put a reassuring hand on her shoulder, talking in her ear as his eyes narrowed in on Ryan. He could not tell what Cato said, but it seemed to calm her down.

"How did you clean her up?" A throbbing headache begun to develop beneath his temples. He needed pills.

"There's a natural spring behind the temple and we found some clothes she just hasn't bothered to wear," Damian answered. He leaned in to whisper, "Doesn't seem like she cared about her hygiene for a very long time. It was not pleasant."

Ryan could have guessed that from the first steps he had taken toward her earlier. She looked much better now. Except for that fact she was basically clinging to Cato in fear of him and Anna. Her round eyes were huge and darted back and forth from him to Anna. Ryan had no idea what he had done to make her so frightened of him.

"Is she going to help us now?" Anna's voice was hallow. She looked less irate after seeing how the Oracle clung to Cato instead of Damian.

Damian crossed his arms over his chest. "Cato has been talking with her the entire time. I sort of just fetched things when he asked for them. She seems to like him the most."

A smile dangled on the corner of his lips when he noticed Anna relax more. "Cato finally found a mate and it happens to be the damn Oracle. Great."

"Cato has never had problems with mates, Ryan, he just

doesn't boast about it." Damian's brows knitted but Ryan could tell he held back a grin.

"Quit saying mate," Anna interjected, "it sounds weird."

"What should we say? Sex buddy? Maybe cuddle buddy?" Ryan asked.

Anna's eyes flashed with annoyance, as did Damian's. All right, he was being ganged up on, time to change the subject. "Has she said anything?"

"Just little things here and there. Not much that makes sense," Damian answered.

"Guys, come here," Cato called them over. He had his arm around the Oracle and she crushed herself against him. Ryan could not figure out what she was so wary of.

They neared her with hesitation and the Oracle let out a stifled squeal. "No, not him." She pointed at Ryan.

He held up his hands in surrender. "Okay, what did I do?"

"You are a killer. A murderer," she begun. "So many have perished by your hands. You have no soul. You are an empty shell."

"Shit." His body stiffened at the remark.

"You betrayed all that you loved for your ambition. You cannot be trusted. All those around you will cease to exist due to your insolence. I will not chance the same fate."

Ryan's jaw clenched. Everything he knew to be true about himself was being confirmed by her. Others had always told him that he put unnecessary blame on himself, but the Oracle only confirmed his fears. She knew the truth of the world and she saw right through him. He needed to leave. He had to get away from her.

As he looked around the room, he realized he had begun to back away from everyone without knowing. None of his friends said a word on the matter. They must believe her words and never had the heart to tell him. They all thought he was a monster.

He needed his pills, now!

Damian's face hardened as their eyes met. Ryan continued to withdraw from the temple but Damian roughly grabbed him by the arm and forced him back where he stood.

"No." He tried to pull away from Damian. "I don't want to be in here."

"You will remain here and face the issue like a man." His eyes bore into his with a determined stare. "You do not back down. Not from anyone. You are not a coward so quit acting like one."

Ryan stole a glance at the Oracle. Her eyes were narrowed to slits, as she looked right through him. She knew his true self better than most people living and it frightened him. You could not hide a thing from a person that could see all and knew all. It made him uncomfortable. She could ruin him with his past if she pleased.

"Damian, please," he begged.

"No." His voice was thick with anger.

He looked back at the Oracle, and to his surprise, her expression was now perplexed. Her head was tilted to the side and although her voice was low, Ryan heard her say, "Interesting."

"What?" Cato asked gently as he stroked her arm. Ryan tried not to take his actions to heart—he knew Cato was being overly friendly to win the woman over.

A wicked smile spread across her lips. "He has been

tamed."

Ryan heard Anna muffle her amusement. He found nothing funny about that statement. In fact, he felt extremely insulted. "Excuse me?" He grit his teeth.

The Oracle's smile remained. "You are no longer interested in your preservation. There is a difference in you. It is faint to see, but you are damning yourself on purpose. Do you wish to die? Are you now allowing other's to take command of you?"

"Stop." His voice cracked.

Damian's gripped tightened on his arm. "Keep going."

"No." His voice was low and grave. He never told anyone he was thinking of becoming mortal again. Never gave much thought about it, but he felt it. There had to come a time when he would cease to exist as everyone else born was meant to. The only person he even thought about telling was Julia in the training arena, but they were interrupted before he could say anything.

Everyone said he was being less cautious when it came to battle, which was true. He was at the point in his life when dying seemed like the natural thing for him. He'd existed for so long, lived through so much, that part of him felt it was his time to go. Yet, he was still standing.

The Oracle no longer smiled. No one said a word. Ryan needed to escape before she told them more.

"I will do this for you," the Oracle said. "But after your mission, you must come back for me. I will not be stuck in this purgatory any longer."

There was no way in hell Ryan wanted to come back to this damn island. It did not seem he had a choice in the matter though. Cato's charm could only go so far with a woman on a mission.

"Agreed." He turned to leave. He needed out.

"You will stay," the Oracle hissed. "The others will leave."

"I don't think that is a good idea," said Cato.

The Oracle smiled kindly at him and pressed her palm against his cheek. They looked in one another's eyes for an uncomfortably long time. Ryan rolled his eyes at the thought of Cato falling for the Oracle. Cato was supposed to keep it together for all of the lovesick morons in their group. He could see his affection for her though.

After a moment of awkward starring Cato finally turned toward Damian and Anna. "Let's go."

"We will be discussing this later." Damian scowled at Ryan, but followed Cato and Anna out of the temple, closing the doors behind them.

Ryan was left in the eerie temple with a deranged Oracle. There was an awkward silence between them and he started to feel as if the statues were closing in on him with their weapons raised high. Death by the very thing he was trying to save. How ironic would that be?

"May I ask you something?" the Oracle finally spoke.

"Might as well," he grumbled.

She made her way toward him slowly with a glint of interest in her eye as she studied him. All fear she had not minutes ago, had seemed to melt away. He felt her eyes wash over his body and he tried to concentrate on the sound of her bare feet softly padding against the floor.

"Why have you changed your name?" she asked. "Ryan may be a good name, but it isn't you. It doesn't fit."

"I don't like it anymore," he answered honestly. "I don't want people to recognize me."

"It is a strong name though," she said, as she got closer to him. "I am certain there are others with your name. Why would they realize the truth behind it?"

"It's better to avoid it altogether, Oracle."

She smiled. "Is it?"

Ryan simply nodded. She was becoming brave with him now. There must be something she sensed about him that was different than the man she knew him to be in his past. Was he weaker? He didn't like that thought.

"You've grown soft," she answered the question in his mind. "The thirst for blood and battle has wavered. I wonder what it has been replaced with."

"Are you going to keep asking questions or are you going to help us with our mission?" he asked harshly. She was playing a sick, twisted game. He had no intention of playing along with it.

The Oracle stood directly in front of him. Her proximity was bordering uncomfortable. "Attitude is still intact though."

"Well, not everything can change," he admitted. "Let's get this over with, please."

She turned on her heel and slipped away through a small doorway behind curtains that hung from the walls. As she returned, he noticed a small bowl and leafs in her hands. "Can you make fire?"

Ryan tossed her a lighter from his pocket. She looked at it with extreme interest. Dear god, she has no idea what it was. "Okay, I'll do it."

Ryan took back his lighter and flicked it on. A small

flame burst into the air and the Oracle gasped in awe. She had dropped her tools to the ground and stared at the flame. "Oh my."

"Yeah, I make fire," he said in his best caveman voice.

"Apologies. I have seen the mortal world as it is now, and the technology they now possess in my visions, but things such as this have always been fascinating." She looked bashful for the first time.

"I can imagine how odd things look now. Believe me." Ryan found it odd he was giving her comfort when just minutes ago she was spilling his secrets out to everyone that mattered to him.

"That weapon the woman had," she started, "I have seen it on many occasions. I just could never imagine seeing something like that in life. It felt false."

Ryan understood completely what she was saying. It still amazed him how far humans had come since his time with their technology. It was baffling and frightening. "What am I lighting?" He changed the subject.

She sat down, never taking her eyes off of the lighter and pointed at the leafs. "These."

"Jimsonweed?" He laughed. He had not dealt with that stuff in ages.

The Oracle nodded. "Yes, now sit down and breathe it in with me."

"Why?"

"I will not make this journey alone. I am usually only allowed to give advice but now you seek an exact answer. I want company," she stated simply. "It takes more concentration."

"I don't get why I have to do it too," he groaned. Getting

hallucinations did not sound appealing right now.

"Because I said so. Now sit."

Anna

"Why did we have to leave?" Anna protested.

"Who knows and who cares as long as she helps us." Cato crossed his arms. "But like always, she was obviously enamored with Ryan."

Damian laughed and smacked Cato on the back. "She is intrigued by you. Trust me, those puppy dog eyes of hers were glued to you most of the time. Ryan was just not what she expected."

"What would she expect from him." Her curiosity set in again.

"Well, when Ryan was mortal, everyone loved and feared him. He was not a merciful person. I guess you could say but he did what he had to do. Regardless of who got in his way, even friends," Damian answered. "He most certainly loved battle and how it made him feel."

"A little too much," Cato agreed. "He would charge straight into battle without a second thought and come out of it drenched in blood."

"How would you know?" Damian laughed, but not unkindly.

"I read." His eyes rolled skyward. "Am I wrong?"

Damian did not answer and Anna had a feeling Cato was right. Did Ryan really enjoy killing that much? It took a special type of person to be able to murder so many people and he obviously did not feel the guilt of it all. Who in the hell wanted to be covered in blood unless they enjoyed it? She suddenly felt herself a little afraid of Ryan now.

"So what do we do? Just wait?" she asked. Anna wasn't exactly in the mood to hear about how much Ryan like to kill people when she annoyed him so much.

Damian sat down on the steps and dropped his bag to the ground. She barely noticed the weight of her pack anymore and she left hers on. If something happened she was not in the mood to lose what little they had left.

He handed her an MRE. Her nose wrinkled as she took it from him. "I thought I was done eating this stuff."

"Meal ready to eat. A lovely invention, I must say." Cato grinned. "It's not that bad."

"Garlic herb chicken?" Anna grinned.

Cato was already tearing his package apart. "Duh, this shit is great."

"Whatever you say." She couldn't help but laugh at how excited he looked to eat. Cato was great.

They sat quietly and ate their meal together. Anna couldn't hear anything in the temple going on, it made her uneasy. It seemed like they had been in there for hours.

Damian finally interrupted the silence. "Come with me." He grabbed her hands after they were done eating. She followed him away from Cato. It was getting dark outside and going off into the trees seemed like a depraved idea. Oh well, you live and you learn.

"Where are we going? Shouldn't we stay with Cato?"

Damian squeezed her hand. "He will be fine I promise."

They were deep enough into the forested area that Cato disappeared, but the temple could still be seen in the small clearing of the branches. She looked at the sky above and smiled. It was filled with pinks and oranges, mixed together with white clouds, the sun barely able to peek through. For a brief moment she forgot where they were and enjoyed the view.

"What are we doing?" Her voice was low and uncertain.

"I just want to be alone for awhile, Anna." Damian stopped their ascent and grabbed her face gently. "I cannot wait for this to be over with so we can vacation somewhere. I want you all to myself for a few weeks. Is there anywhere you want to journey to? Somewhere you have always wanted to see?"

She kissed him softly. "I just want to be where you are. But if you must know, I would love to see Egypt. Don't ask me why, but it sounds cool."

Damian arched a brow. "Odd choice. I never really cared for it much. Ryan loved it though."

"Of course you've been there." She sighed. "Is there anywhere you haven't been?"

He nodded. "Antarctica."

"Well, I hate the cold so that is definitely not happening."

Damian pulled her against his body. "Wherever you want to go, I will bring you there. It doesn't matter if I have been there before. We will make new memories together and I can guarantee they will trample any account I had there."

"I'm going to hold you to that." Their lips met once more and she could not help but intensify it. She craved his touch, it kept her sane throughout this mission and she needed it fiercely. She needed the reassurance that she was fighting for something worth saving in such a cruel, unforgiving world.

He broke away from her to catch his breath, his forehead pressed to hers. "Calm down, love," he growled against her lips. His eyes were closed and he bit his lip, it was his habit to control his urges she'd learned.

She wasn't going to let him push her off so easily. Anna placed her hands on his chest, pushing him roughly into the tree trunk behind him and heard a groan escape his lips. "You calm down." She locked her eyes on his as she pressed her body against his.

"I'm working on it, but you are not making it easy." He bit his lip again.

She took his earlobe between her teeth. "How's that going for you?"

"Not very well." A small moan escaped him.

"This wasn't your intention when you brought me out here?" She trailed kissed down his neck. The stubble on his chin felt rough against her lips, but she didn't mind.

"Surprisingly, no," he admitted. "But I won't complain about the turn of events."

His strong arms wrapped around her waist, pressing her firmly against his body. She desperately wanted to take her gear off. It was in the way. He must have had the same idea because he started to take off her vest and dropped it gently to the ground.

"You sure this is a good idea?" She smirked as he undid his vest. "It might not be safe out here."

"I don't really give a damn right now." His flak jacket fell on top of his vest after she removed it.

"What if Cato comes looking for us?" He was taking too long to undress her so she stood back from him and did it herself, down to her bra and panties. The ground around them was soon littered with their gear and weapons.

"Who cares?" Damian groaned and pulled her into him once more once against his bare chest.

Instant relief washed over her when his hands caressed her bare skin. She grabbed the longer hair on top of his head and yanked it down. His chin veered up giving her perfect access to bite his neck.

His fingers dug into her back making her groan. "Take your pants off."

"You, ma'am," he kissed her roughly and continued, "are getting rough and demanding."

"And?" She unbuckled his pants.

"I'm enjoying it." He grinned and kicked off his pants.

He turned her around and pushed her against the tree. The force of it stole her breath—she loved it. Normally he was so gentle with her, as if she would break from his touch. She loved that, but this she liked more. Damian letting loose and being forceful was a turn on.

The sun was gone now and they were left naked in the trees with one another. She was happy the island did not have any people on it. Otherwise she would probably feel really nervous about being so exposed. She could hear the rustling of leaves and nothing else.

Damian brought her arms up, pinning her wrists against the tree trunk leaving her neck exposed for his gentle kisses. She could tell the need in him was growing after every kiss he planted on her body. His hands never stopped caressing her.

When he paused for even a second she groaned in protest.

"I don't know how you affect me so much," he started, "but I can't seem to get enough of you, Anna."

He let go of her wrists and started to kiss down her stomach. "Not that I don't love what you're doing, but hurry up and let's do this." They did not have time to explore each other's bodies right now.

"As you wish." Damian took her by surprise lifting her by her ass as she wrapped her legs around his waist. He pushed her back against the tree and thrust himself deep inside of her.

She yelped in surprise as her body quickly grew accustomed to him. "I love you, Damian." She knew it was too soon to feel this way, but she did.

Not stopping his movements, he gazed lovingly into her eyes. "I love you, too."

Chapter XVI

Ryan

NOTHING WAS HAPPENING AND his patience was being tested. There, in front of him, sat the Oracle with her eyes closed while he sat there awkwardly breathing in the burning plant. He drummed his fingers against his knees, waiting, yet nothing was happening.

The rest of them had walked out of the doors maybe twenty minutes ago and he heard no sounds of distress. Ryan didn't like them being out in the dark like that. Especially after Leif told him how dangerous nighttime was. He figured one of them would be smart enough to interrupt this drug session if there was danger.

He felt anxious in his stomach from sitting so long and his legs begged him to stand up.

"Sit," the Oracle commanded.

"Nothing is happening," he dropped his body back down

to the floor before he could fully make himself upright.

"Are you sure?" Her voice was something like a sigh.

"Pretty damn sure." Anger crept into his voice.

"Then why are you slapping your hand all over your body?"

"I'm not." He rolled his eyes. When he looked down at his arms he felt panicked. He was indeed slapping at his body without realizing it. Hundreds of black spiders were crawling out of the cracks in the ground and up his body. His heart galloped.

Ryan rolled over onto his hands, pushing himself to stand and begun to stomp his feet at the little creatures. He desperately tried to get them off of his body, but they just kept coming, faster and in larger numbers. He did not like this one bit. This was a bad sort of high.

The Oracle remained seated without a worry in the world. Completely ignoring his outbursts of frustration and disgust. He was about to say something to her then the spiders disappeared.

Ryan looked around the room and saw the statues of the gods begin to move. Zeus walked toward him carrying a large lightning bolt and Poseidon looked ready to throw his trident. They were heavy in their movements and he felt them glaring down at him with fury in their eyes.

Ryan backed away and bumped his back into something hard. He looked up to see Athena glaring down at him. She outstretched her hand trying to grasp him and he scrambled away before she could touch him. A scream caught in his throat as he made his way back over to the Oracle. He was going insane.

"Make this stop." His breath came out in ragged gasps. "Please."

"I cannot." She smiled wickedly with her eyes closed. "I believe you need to face your demons. Perhaps you will find your way out of the darkness of your past, *Ryan*," she said his name harshly.

"I have no idea what you are talking about." He did but he wouldn't admit it. He was thankful the statues were no longer moving.

"No?" Her hair rose around her as if she were in the wind. "Find your way to forgive who you were and become a man worth being."

"This is stupid, I need to find the second piece of Brahma's staff, not go on a journey of my soul," he hissed.

"I cannot control what happens to you or what you see. I will not show you what I see until you face your fears." Ryan was on the verge of slapping her. "Only then will you be worthy of the information."

He literally growled. "This doesn't make any sense. What do you care if I face this?"

"You're right, the Oracle does not care but her patron does." She smiled widely.

"Apollo?" Ryan's voice was low and grave. He couldn't possibly be talking to Apollo through her. Could he?

"Ryan." Her eyes remained closed and her smile disappeared into a grimace. "Remain strong."

He almost asked what that meant until a petite hand appeared on his shoulder. He didn't want to look whom it belonged to but his curiosity won out in seconds. There, in front of him, stood his first wife. The woman who started his heart so long ago and who also ended it just as quickly, when her last breath fled her lips. She stood there grasping a young boy's hand—he was no older then twelve.

He backed away as they both stared at him blankly, their pale, dead hands outstretched to him. He needed to get away from them. He'd avoided this his entire life. He could not face the harsh reality that they were dead because of his choice to become Immortal. He left them to die.

Their eyes were wide and frozen with death. Every movement they made sounded as if their bones were cracking. Their skin was barely rotten, and he could see the maggots wriggling in the most decayed flesh. He was frozen in fear as their corpses came closer.

Just behind them he could see his other son, almost eighteen years old with bruises along his neck. His dark hair was shoulder length and he had the beard of a man, even at his young age.

"No," his voice barely a whisper. He hadn't realized he was holding his breath as he continued to back away from them.

They did not relent. They continued their slow decent upon him, their ragged clothes drug along the floor leaving blood in their wake. It made no sense.

He turned to run and ran directly into the next figure of his nightmares. It was his wife from when he was Spartacus.

Her dark hair was draped behind her back giving him the perfect view of her throat. It was slit open so wide, her head was nearly cut clean off. Not a word came out as she tried to speak to him except for a blood-curdling gag. Her clothes were drenched with her blood and left puddles of blood at her feet with every step she took.

Ryan dropped to his knees. She placed her bloodied hands on either side of his face gently, and he could feel the warmth of the fresh blood against his skin. She bent down to get closer to his face, her blood continued to spill out of the wound in her neck and threatened to fall on his face.

He yanked himself from her grasp, crawling backwards to get away from the women he had wronged so deeply. Slipping in the blood that covered the floor, he fell on his stomach, landing at the feet of another woman. He didn't want to look but his eyes betrayed him as they looked up at the strawberry blonde smiling down at him.

She was another woman in his life for a small amount of time when he replaced the real Thomas Culpepper until his execution day. The priests in Urbs managed to make him look like the real Thomas Culpepper with their magic and held him hostage for Ryan's entire mission.

He had purposely caused her to be beheaded so that the king of England would move on from such an immature, childish woman playing queen. She was so young when she died and it was his fault alone that she died. Kings did not take kindly to other men sleeping with their wives.

She inched closer to him and the blood gushed from her mouth as she spoke, "Hello, Thomas."

He tried to crawl away from her but it was no use. She seemed to glide toward him with an eerie smile plastered on her face. "Leave me alone, Catherine." He was panting.

Her head cocked to the side and slid partially off her neck. "I don't want to ever leave you. I love you, Thomas. I died for our love." Nausea worked up his throat.

Ryan managed to stand up, drenched in blood and accidentally ran straight into his first wife and son. They grabbed his arms and pushed him down to his knees. All he could do was comply. The fight in him was leaving as he looked up at the people he'd wronged. Part of him wanted to succumb to whatever hell they had planned for him. It was the least he deserved.

More women appeared from his past. Their dresses were in tatters and their decomposing bodies were wounded with whatever killed them. He couldn't breathe. They were going to kill him.

They made no effort to hurt him as they gathered around his slumped form. Instead, he saw only joy in their eyes. His heart ached for them. He could have made their lives better yet he'd brought nothing but sadness to them. If he didn't exist they would have lived long and happy lives.

He glanced around the bodies for the Oracle. She was sitting in the same spot with her eyes closed, completely calm. "Help me." His voice wavered in fear.

"Not yet." Her tone was so casual it infuriated him.

Being surrounded by all of them broke him inside. Ryan instinctively curled up into himself and closed his eyes. He rested his head on his knees and felt his body automatically begin to rock. He was going insane. They were talking to him, bleeding on him, grabbing at him in gentle ways he didn't deserve.

And then the touching ceased. The blood that he been drenched in disappeared and all was quiet. After a moment he dared look up and all the women from his past were gone. Relief came over him until he saw two soldiers standing in the corner facing him.

One had his throat slit wide open and the other had a spear driven through his center. After so many years he still remembered their faces exactly. They were dressed in the same linen armor from when he was mortal.

"Hello, your highness," one of them spoke, although the slit in his throat made it come out sounding raspy.

"Leave me, Parmenio," Ryan's command came out weaker than he intended.

"I think not." Parmenio's ran his hand over his thick dark beard.

Ryan stood up and tried to calm himself. This cannot be real. They were long dead and it was just the drugs in his system. Yet, the women were able to touch him. Could that just have been a trick of his mind as well? *Pull yourself together you coward!*

"You must pay for your actions," the speared man spoke. His long dark hair fell into his face, but Ryan could see the angst on his face.

"Cleitus," Ryan said low and timid. "Why are you here?"

"You must pay for your actions," he hissed.

Ryan shook himself of the memory. "Have I not shown how sorry I am for killing you?" He could not help but stare at the spear stuck in the man's body.

Cleitus laughed. "Just because you did not maintain yourself for days, does not mean you are forgiven. You must suffer as we have."

"I will not." Ryan pulled his gun from his holster and pointed it at the men. "Go away, now." He tried to ignore how much his hand was shaking.

"Look what has become of you," Parmenio laughed coldly. "A disheartened slave to others. Your mother would be ashamed."

"He has grown weak," Cleitus agreed. "A mere shimmer from who he once was. He is nothing now. Not even worth the effort of caring."

"Leave." Ryan's voice hardened.

The two men crossed their arms over their chests. "A pathetic baby, solely dependent upon others. You are nothing. A fraud. Pitiful." Parmenio's lip curled in icy contempt.

"Either way, he will die." Cleitus laughed. "When he does, we will do whatever we please with him."

Ryan tried not to show fear. He could not look weak in front of these men. He commanded them long ago and they could not see him back down. "I am ordering you to leave now. If not, when my life ceases I will make your afterlife worse than your life was." His voice was firm with a hint of anger. "Do not test me or think me weak. You both have made the mistake before."

Both men disappeared before his eyes. Relief flushed over him, as all his demons were gone. He was left alone only with the Oracle, whose face was contorted in confusion. He didn't feel any better about facing all those people from his past. If anything, it brought their memories up further in his mind, making him even more reluctant of himself and the people around him. He had caused so much pain.

"Come here Ryan," the Oracle said dreamily.

Reluctantly he made his way back to her and she held out her hands to him. He took his seat in front of her and placed his hands grudgingly into hers. There was not even an ounce of his being that wanted to touch her after what he had just witnessed, but he hoped now he would get the answered he sought.

"Now what?"

"Close your eyes." Her face was now void of expression.

Ryan did as he was told and saw nothing but endless black behind his eyelids. This whole experience was tiring. He could sense night was here. Sleep wanted to take over. It almost did.

He dreamed of Julia.

She was hazy, but he knew it was her. Her lovely blonde hair was pulled back tightly. It was so unnatural for her.

She was with Aden. They were holding hands and both wore long black cloaks that trailed along the ground. He had no idea where they were. It was all so fuzzy.

They were moving toward a stone pillar. Attached was a man. It was Ahmose. He was bloodied and bruised. Almost identical to how he and Damian were when they were held prisoner.

Julia kissed Aden on the lips as they stood in front of Ahmose. She smiled. Why would she smile?

"Has he really turned?" Julia asked.

"He has," Aden returned the endearment. "Jesse is on the way to help clean him up. He has seen the truth."

The scene changed.

Zee stood with Grace and Colette. All of the women looked distraught and dirty. Where have they been?

"We cannot keep risking ourselves for the mortals right

now," Colette groaned. "Urbs is in chaos. We have to concentrate on finding the Risen and killing them."

"Our problems are much deeper than that." Grace's voice was hollow. "The Risen has obviously infiltrated the mortal world. Their numbers are rising and I would bet anything mortals are now converted to their cause."

"What are we supposed to do then? Sit around and wait for the world to end while those four are running around Europe?" Colette's voice was thick with displeasure.

"They are doing what they must." Grace was calm and collected. "We will continue to fight here and in the mortal world, Colette. There is no other way."

Colette stood up and laughed, but there was no humor behind it. "You do what you will Grace, but unless we find the Risen and kill them, no one will be safe. I will hunt those bastards down myself."

"You will do as I say," Grace spoke harshly. Colette left the room and Grace seemed to age twenty years from exhaustion. "Continue to keep the Immortals at bay, Zee. Send six teams out tonight to patrol and keep the peace. As always, if anyone starts a conflict, arrest them and bring them here for detainment."

"Are you sure? We have already lost five Warriors to the civilians." Zee looked apprehensive.

"This is why we were chosen." Grace smiled warmly. "We do what we must. Colette and I will be leaving to the mortal world. Please stay safe."

Ryan wanted to speak to them. To say anything to the women he left in charge. He could feel his mouth moving yet no words would form.

The haze all around them thickened and the scene

changed once more.

It was a horned creature with a man's body. He could not see its face. Who was this man? The haze covered what Ryan wished to see most even though he felt himself drawn to the creature. He followed him.

From what he could tell, they were in a long corridor and they sped through it at an impossible speed. There were so many different rooms connected to an enormous amount of directions to go. It seemed never ending until they came to the end of a corridor that led into the light.

The man walked out into the daylight and Ryan could barely see the green grove in front of him. Far across the grove was the very mountain he was on right now and there was a spring directly in front of the horned man. It seemed peaceful.

As the creature turned his back to Ryan, he felt himself gasp. Something stuck outside of the man's back, barely covered by a thin layer of skin. It was protruding out from the middle of his spine and in the shape of the first piece of Brahma's staff.

The scene faded away and Ryan desperately clung onto the Oracle's hands to see more. Nothing came. Had he just witnessed Julia's betrayal or was it just something he feared once again? One thing was for certain, he knew where the second piece of Brahma's staff was and it was not for the faint of heart to acquire.

Chapter XVII

Ryan

"**O**PEN YOUR EYES RYAN."

He winced, brow furrowed tight with pain as his heart felt like it was twisted like a screw. Managing to open his eyes, he saw the Oracle sitting in front of him with a look of concern in her eyes. Her brow was creased and her lips were in a tight line. He had no idea what she was worried about, but he imagined he didn't look to well after what his mind went through.

"Sorry for falling asleep," he mumbled as he rubbed his eyes clear. She would not look away from him.

"You did not sleep." The Oracle screwed up her face. "I shared my vision with you after you faced your own journey."

A throbbing headache developed beneath his temples. He tried to massage it away with his fingertips but it wasn't helping. She handed him a cup of water. He didn't question where she got it.

"Does it always feel like that?" he groaned. He downed the water quickly. It was surprisingly cool and it made him feel better.

"Always." She nodded. "You seemed very distraught when you were on your own."

"That would be an understatement." He couldn't help but laugh. "I think I was put in hell for the entire time it lasted."

"Have you figured out the next step in your plan?" She already knew that answer yet she asked it nonetheless.

"What? No riddles, messages, or undecipherable poems?" Ryan laughed. The Oracle never gave a straight answer. It was always for the priests to decipher out the message.

"I've always known the answer. The priests deciphered them as they saw fit." There was bitterness in her words. "There are no priests here though, are there?" She smirked.

"No."

"Then I am sure you know who you must face, without the riddles or messages."

"The Minotaur," they said together.

He rubbed a hand over the stubble on his chin. "Can things ever be simple again?"

She looked sad for once. Ryan had to admit it worried him. Gloomy looks from someone who could tell the future was not exactly a good thing.

Getting to her feet she strolled over to the statue of Zeus. Ryan felt a slight sense of panic come over him as she touched his foot. Thankfully, the statue remained still. He didn't know if he would be able to look at the statues the same ever again.

"It may," she said with weary resignation. Darkness had

fallen and her face reflected the light of the torches on the walls. "Decisions have yet to be made and our fate has not been decided. It is a unique matter you face, Ryan. While you were on your own, I tried my hardest to find the outcome of this battle."

"And?" he pressed on.

"I see nothing. It is as if there is a block on the world." She turned away from him.

"That doesn't sound good." He stood. "So what now? Do I give you some cash and go on my way or what?"

She laughed. It was honestly a sweet sound. "Cash. You have adopted barbaric speech. You used to be so intelligent and philosophic."

"Two thousand years away from people with outstanding intellect will have its effects on a person," Ryan said. "So what do we do now?"

"You will keep your word and bring me away from this place when the battle is won." She faced him. "If it is won."

"If." He walked toward her. "I don't like that word. Not one bit."

Her mouth turned up a fraction of an inch. "Then be triumphant. You are used to victory."

Ryan took her hand in his. She flinched at the contact, but let him hold it. With no hesitation he brought her hand to his lips and kissed it gently. She was a wonderful woman, and did not deserve the hell she has been through. He would take her away from this place. She deserved that much.

"What are you doing?" she whispered.

"Showing you the respect you initially deserved when we first came here. I am truly sorry for everything, Oracle. I wish you didn't see me as the monster I am."

She placed her hand on his cheek. It was a motherly affection he was not accustomed to. His mother was not exactly the most loving woman. However, regardless of her actions he always knew she cared deeply for him. "My name is Amara."

"Well, Amara." He covered her hand with both of his. "Would it be fine if we stayed the night in here? I was told it is rather dangerous at night."

"Yes, that would be perfectly alright," she spoke in a quiet tone. "You have truly altered from the man I have seen. I imagined a barbarian, a mad man. It was terrifying when I first laid eyes on you."

"You've seen me before?" He couldn't help but grin at her mischievously.

"It gets rather dull here alone. I have seen every one of you before in my visions of the outside world." She blushed. "Except for the woman."

"Oh?"

"Cato is rather splendid." She bit her lip and nervously giggled. She was leaps and bounds better than when he first saw her. She was no longer as crazed as before, still odd, but less insane. "He seems strong and very underestimated."

Ryan burst out laughing and immediately felt guilty by the embarrassment washing over her face. "Sorry, it's just odd."

"Why is it odd?"

"Cato is as capable as us all." Ryan truly meant it.

"That's not why you laughed." She crossed her arms. "Is it because he is not as kind as Damian or as utterly handsome as you?"

"I'm not saying that."

"You are thinking that."

Ryan could admit that Cato was never the one in the spotlight. It was always he and Damian. He never complained though and why would he? It was not their fault

Did he think Cato was ugly? Of course not. Was he kind? Well, that much was up for debate. If anything Cato's personality mirrored his own.

"Sorry," he said quietly.

"Don't be." Her eyes seemed to look right through him. "But please do not underestimate him. I have seen him protect you at all costs. That much is known about your future. Now gather your friends and get a good nights rest. You are going to need it."

Everyone except Ryan sat around the small fire pit they created inside the temple. There was a small opening in the ceiling for ventilation. Ryan was far away in a corner, either sleeping or avoiding them. Damian had asked him what happened inside the temple and the only response he was given was a shake of the head.

Damian would not push it. He knew better than that. With time he would tell him.

They had come to figure out the Oracle's name is Amara and he was glad. It was a hell of a lot easier than calling her the Oracle all of the time.

They had just finished a hefty meal of figs, cheese, and

bread. According to Amara, Apollo provided her with things she needs to survive and live somewhat comfortably. He was not particularly hungry given they just ate an MRE but it was rude to refuse.

Anna seemed hesitant with the figs, which she stated she'd never had before. It surprised him. Either way, he managed to get her to try one and she ended up becoming very fond of it.

Cato and Amara seem to have an attachment and sat rather close to one another. Occasionally, Damian saw him brush her thigh with his fingertips or Amara slap him on the knee playfully. It seemed they all were incapable of falling for women on missions.

"That is Aphrodite." Damian pointed out a statue of a woman

"She's gorgeous." Anna was staring at the statue and Damian decided to educate her on his beliefs.

"She's a very beautiful woman." Damian nodded. "Her and Ryan had a small affair a long time ago. He bragged about it for decades."

"Whoa, what?" Anna laughed.

Damian put his arm around her. "Our Gods were very involved with us. They even had children with some mortals."

"That's like, really weird." She knit her eyebrows together in either disgust or deep thought—he didn't know which.

Damian liked to watch her expressions. She was such an interesting woman. Independent and had the mouth of a sailor. Sure, he loved a woman with a classy grace about her, but Anna was refreshing. She was a lady, even if she would never admit it yet also not someone stiff to be around. She was fun.

"Is there anyone he hasn't slept with?" Anna grumbled as

she tossed her nearly eaten fig in the flames. "That guy has to have a disease or two."

"I haven't," Amara spoke up.

"It was rhetorical," Anna said.

Cato rubbed Amara's back. "He is pretty bad, but he isn't that terrible. Well, okay, maybe he is pretty bad. Besides that, we cannot get diseases remember."

"You guys are getting too technical." Anna shook her head. "I was being somewhat sarcastic."

"Sarcasm is a dangerous weapon." Damian grinned and kissed her lightly on the lips. "You are probably the master of it from what I have gathered."

She rolled her eyes once more. "So, what's the plan for tomorrow?" He didn't know why, but her annoyance seemed to be growing.

Damian glanced back over his shoulder at Ryan. "I'm not entirely sure. Ryan wouldn't say."

"He had a busy day." Amara tucked her hair behind her ear. "Getting visits from your past will mess with anyone's mind."

"What exactly happened?" Damian knew they were all curious. Hell, he was probably the most curious. It was rare that Ryan would seclude himself from others like this. It must have been something terrible.

Amara took a bite of bread. "It is his journey. It is his choice to share or not."

Anna's lip curled up. She did not think much of Amara noticeably. "Well, it must have been very traumatic," Damian said.

Amara nodded. "Indeed, it was. Although, I will never

understand how you and Alexander haven't suffered a mental breakdown from your lifestyle." She popped a piece of cheese in her mouth. "I mean really, surrounding yourselves with death for thousands of years should have affected you psychologically somehow. It doesn't seem to be the case though."

Damian's eyes snapped toward Anna. It was apparent by the look on her face she caught the name Amara had just said.

"Alexander?" Anna asked.

Amara waved her hand. "Yes. I sorry, I mean Ryan. I keep trying to call him that but it just isn't him."

Damian and Cato exchanged nervous glances. This was the last thing they need. A mad Ryan was not a good Ryan.

"What was his full name again?" Anna dug on for information. Damian had no chance to stop it. The damage had been done. "I forgot."

"Alexander the III of Macedon." Amara looked up at the ceiling in thought as she crossed her legs. "I suppose most people in the modern world refer to him as Alexander the Great."

Damian felt his hand being squeezed very hard by Anna who looked like a child getting candy.

Ryan should not mind her finding out. It was not that big of a deal. Was it? He made it seem like such a secret, but was it really that bad? No matter how hard Damian tried to convince himself of those words he couldn't. Ryan would be furious.

"So who the hell are you?" Anna's eyes bore into him. His mouth felt dry. "What's your real name, Damian?"

Perhaps this is why Ryan did not like people knowing his past. Damian did not want to go into who he was as a mortal.

He was not taken very seriously and was a constant shadow to everyone else back then. Not only that, but there were certain things about his lifestyle he wished to remain secret, especially with Anna.

"We were friends growing up and set out to war together. No one important." Damian tried to remain calm and casual.

"Don't talk down about yourself." Amara was now sitting on Cato's lap, who looked both pleased and worried about that subject at hand. "You did great things, Hephaestion."

Damian laid his head in his hands at this point. He hated his original name. "Why must you say these things, Amara?"

"Pardon?" She looked around the group dumbfounded. "Why can't I call you your given names?"

"Ryan and Damian have issues with their pasts and apparently don't want people acknowledging them by said names." Cato tucked a hair behind her ear. "No one really gives a damn, but those two do."

"Right, because people don't constantly ask us about our history and what it was like living then and so on and so forth," Damian growled. "Constant questions about our lives instead of who we are now. It's tiring. Not to mention Ryan is constantly held on a pedestal he doesn't desire to be on anymore."

"He still is Damian. Everyone knows who you both are. It's about time you get over it." Cato was right, but Damian could not give up the fight for Ryan's wellbeing so easily. He had to stand up for him.

"Ryan's expertise was in warfare. Hand to hand combat and military brilliance is what he is known for," Damian started. "Now, everyone believes he should be the best Warrior we have when in reality, he was never trained to be an assassin.

Which is what Warriors are now."

"Calm down, Damian," Cato groaned. "We get it."

"I don't believe you do." Damian was getting unusually nasty with Cato. Be it the stress or the fact that their secret was out, he didn't know.

"Don't get your panties in a twist." Cato gazed at Amara— she looked back at him just as loving. Damian was baffled to see actual affection there. "I am perfectly aware of what you guys specialized in. It's not like it was any different for me."

"I would like to speak with you," Anna interrupted. Damian grudgingly followed her out of the temple doors and to the edge of the thick tree line. "Alexander the freaking Great is Ryan?"

He really was sick of the hype. "Yes."

"And you're Hephasty?"

"Hephaestion."

"Who was that?" She tilted her head to the side. "Or you I mean. Whatever."

He wasn't surprised about her lack of knowledge. "I grew up with Ryan and was a commander of part of the military on occasion. I really only deserved my ranks because Ryan favored me. There were other men much more qualified."

Anna laughed, quickly covering her mouth. "I can't believe this."

She seemed so excited that it worried Damian. One part of him felt so insecure that she would go running to Ryan now because of his fame and the other part of him called himself an idiot. This woman wants him. Not Ryan. End of story.

"Well, now you know," Damian said.

"I have read so much about you guys." She grinned. "I

cannot believe I haven't put it all together. I mean, it makes sense, but at the same time it's crazy."

"How do you know so much about us?" Damian tried not to panic. *Please don't know about all of it.*

"In school it just sounded really cool. Don't get me wrong, history can be pretty damn boring, but I thought Alexander the Great was cool. Not to mention I loved the movie with what's his face in it." She paced back and forth.

"Movie?" Damian groaned.

"You know, the one with Jared Leto and that Colin dude." Anna stopped in her tracks. "Hold on. They were together in that movie. Like, together, together."

Damian held his breath. He and Ryan both had avoided the cinema especially when it was about Ryan. They didn't like how phony it all was and quite frankly movies confused them.

"Were they?" He tried to play dumb. This truly was a part of his past he wanted kept secret.

"Yeah." She eyed him suspiciously. "They were."

"Interesting," was all he managed to say.

"You and Ryan… were you guys together?"

Filled with frustration, Damian ran his hands through his hair in exasperation. Such an awkward end to what seemed a magical evening.

"In a way I suppose, but it wasn't like that then," he assured her.

She blinked repeatedly. "What?" Tears begun to fill her eyes. "You just failed to mention we have been hanging around your ex boyfriend all this time?"

"It wasn't like that," he insisted. How could he make her understand it was not seen that way then?

"Then how exactly was it?" She laughed, but there was no humor behind it.

"It was a different time and things were seen differently then." By the look on her face this was not making matters any clearer or easier. "We were close friends that admired one another. There was no attachment as far as a relationship was concerned."

"So you guys were freaking friends with benefits or what?" She tried to contain her yell.

"I suppose." It felt weird to say. He was on the verge of giving up with this conversation. He felt like he was digging a hole and there was no way out of it. "We were never together, not like that."

"You slept with him Damian." She laughed. "My boyfriend has probably been with more guys than me. That doesn't feel good to hear. You should have told me."

"Anna, stop. It was not like that at all. Please understand," he begged. "It was so long ago that we never even think about it anymore."

"How can you look at him and not feel anything?" She started to walk down the path they first came up here on and Damian followed her like a pathetic puppy.

"Because we are friends. Nothing more." He tried to find a way in front of her to cut her off, but she managed to get ahead of him. "Please stop, Anna."

"Ugh!" She made a fake vomiting sound. "It's so... ugh!"

"Homophobia is an awful trait." Damian tried to lighten the mood with a smile. She was having none of it.

"I'm not homophobic, Damian. It's just weird that I am with a guy that has... you know."

Damian managed to get around her and grabbed her shoulders. He looked deep into her eyes and tried to look as miserable and pathetic as possible. He needed to make her understand.

"I am not gay and neither is Ryan. We never have been gay. Sex was viewed different back then and we always knew that women were the only relationships in our lives. We were both married when we were mortal."

"Ryan was asked to join the Immortals and confided in me about the whole ordeal. We were close as friends and I told him I would miss him dearly and wished him the best. I made sure he knew how important he was to the world and he refused to join the Immortals without me joining as well."

"Cute." She rolled her eyes.

"We faked my death and he then had to act like he was losing his mind as if he was slowly deteriorating from his common sense and priorities." He continued on, "In a way he was. I waited in Urbs until the Gods decided it was his time to leave the mortal world. They faked his death because it was becoming very difficult to convince others he was aging when he wasn't."

"Why are you telling me this?" Anna's tears finally spilled over. It pained Damian.

"I want you to know everything, Anna." He wiped away her tears with his thumb. "I love you with everything I have and I don't want you to think I have feelings for someone when I don't. Nor have I ever in that sort of way."

"You two had sex," she whispered. "It's weird."

"I get that." He tried not to laugh. "Trust me, I find it very odd as well after all these years have passed by."

"Did you like..." she started. "You know?"

Damian's eyebrow rose. "What?"

"Like," she paused, "who did what when you did it?"

Damian rolled his eyes and let his hands drop from her face. Why would that be her concern right now? There truly has never been a more complicated and uncomfortable conversation in his life.

"I really don't think that matters, Anna," he answered.

"Sort of."

"No." He shook his head. "It doesn't."

He could see her forcing a smile. "I mean if you like certain things, I don't think I am willing to provide that service."

Damian grabbed her vest and pulled her into him. He kissed her passionately and felt her body tense. This was not a good sign.

He placed both hands on either side of her face, tracing her bottom lip with his thumb. She had to see that she was upset for no reason. She had to see what happened between him and Ryan wasn't romantic. "Anna..." His voice was barely a whisper, but he had no other words to say.

She gently pulled her body away from him. He let her but it was difficult. If she were done with him he would have to accept it. In all honesty though, could he handle her leaving him?

"I need to think about this," she murmured. He saw another tear fall down her cheek. "This is hard to process right now."

"Anna, please," he groaned.

She took a step back from him and he saw a forced smile once more. "Let's get some sleep, okay?"

Damian did not move as he watched the love of his life turn and walk away from him. He had to make her see, even if it was the last thing he ever did. She was now his world.

Chapter XVIII

Ryan

RYAN TIGHTENED HIS VEST and made sure he had everything in its place. He was glad the others left him alone all night. He still didn't feel in the mood for company, but solitude was not obtainable for now.

He couldn't get what he saw out of his mind. His wives, lovers, children. They haunted him even in his sleep. He doubted he could ever get away from the guilt he felt. If anything it made it stronger. Whatever they tried to accomplish, they made it worse not better.

The others were getting themselves ready inside of the temple and he made his way to Damian. Putting his hand on his shoulder Ryan said, "Ready?"

Damian jerked away from Ryan's hand and said, "Yeah."

"What?" Ryan was taken by surprise. "Did I do something?"

Damian looked over at Anna, who was by herself at the entrance, and then back to Ryan. "No." It was all he said.

Ryan frowned, his eyes wondered over to Anna, who was eyeing him suspiciously. *What was their problem? Did they get in a fight or something?*

She turned on her heal and stalked out of the temple. He had no idea what to think, but decided it was not worth his time trying to figure out. Instead, he made his way over to Cato, who was kissing Amara's hand. Honestly, women were such a distraction.

"We will come back." Cato held onto her hand. "I promise you."

"I think I believe you." She smiled sadly. As she turned her attention to Ryan she placed her hands gently on his chest. "You have become a great man. I see that now. When the time comes you will do the right thing."

"What are you talking about?" he asked quietly.

"When the time comes, you will know." She had a dejected look in her eyes. "Do not second guess yourself, Ryan. You must do what you have to."

"I have no idea what you are talking about," he groaned. "Riddles?"

"Riddles." She nodded. "Apollo has ordered this information to be a secret. I am sorry."

"Well, thanks for the creepy, unhelpful warning." He winked, trying his best to seem upbeat instead of depressed. "See you in awhile, I guess."

"I do hope so." She shook his hand and then gave Cato a hug. "Goodbye."

They left her in the temple and found Anna just below the

steps. Damian looked as if he'd aged twenty years. Ryan was tempted to press for information. He left it alone though.

"Ready?" Ryan asked Anna. She nodded, refusing to look at him. It felt like he was the source of her animosity. "Did I do something?" He seemed to be asking that a lot today.

Her eyes burned with anger as she said, "No, let's get going."

Trying his best to ignore it, he led them behind the temple. From there, he could see the springs not too far away and a small cave opening. It was exactly as he saw it in Amara's vision. He was glad it would not take long to get there. With the way their group was feeling, he wanted to get this over with and get back home.

They walked by the small natural spring Amara must have bathed in. Her old dirty clothes laid on a rock, abandoned to nature, as it should be. The thing was grotesque.

Down a narrow path with a sparse amount of trees, they walked in silence. At least Cato was at his side. Anna and Damian walked apart from one another—it was not a good sign. This must be something serious.

Ryan led the group, and he felt eyes were on him. Either from Anna or Damian was his guess and it made him self-conscious as they continued on. He almost tripped over a root that stuck out of the ground before Cato caught him.

"What the hell is up with them?" he whispered to Ryan as he stood him up straight.

Ryan shrugged. "I have no idea, but it seems to be focused on me."

"You think?" Cato asked.

"Either that or I am feeling very on edge."

"Well, let's hope they work it out," Cato grumbled. "They won't be worth a damn if they are both pissed off."

"Agreed." Ryan continued to walk with Cato behind him and he begun to think about what he saw in the temple.

His child, from when he was mortal, was killed because others feared his claim to the throne Ryan had created. So young and innocent to life, murdered because of who his father was. His older son didn't stand a chance either. The people Ryan surrounded himself with were as power hungry as he once was.

Then there were his friends who he murdered because of hearsay. He could never live that down. Their blood was directly on his hands and no one else's. So much death surrounded him that it became normal, as natural as breathing. Even as a child, he was bred to become a killer, a ruler. There must be a curse on his life, never allowing him to find happiness and destined for only blood.

"You okay?" Cato's voice was low, his tone uncertain.

"Just thinking." A headache flared at his temples.

"You've been quiet for about forty-five minutes," Cato went on. "It's just weird for you."

It had already been that long? Apparently, because they were at the bottom of the mountain and he did not even realize it. A lush green field lay before them and he started across it. He decided the creatures probably stayed away from this place. If the Minotaur lived here, it would be suicidal to come near it.

"It's a lot quicker going down than up, isn't it?" Ryan wasn't in the mood to speak, but for the sake of morale he forced himself to.

"That's what she said," Cato mumbled.

"That made no sense," Ryan retorted.

"Does it ever?"

With ease, they made it through the field and came upon the spring, which sat off to the side of the cave. Ryan was apprehensive of going in, but they had no other option. He peered below and saw steps leading down into darkness. They really should have brought their helmets for the night vision. He regretted that.

"Go on," Cato said. "Lead the way to our deaths."

"Not funny," Damian mumbled.

"Not laughing," said Cato. "How are we going to see down there?"

"Just going to have to use our flashlights I guess," Ryan said. "Unless there are torches down there."

"Let's get moving," Damian grumbled. "I want to get this over with."

Ryan rolled his eyes and made his way down the steps with his flashlight in hand. The stone walls and floor were carved perfectly. All of it was smooth and evenly built. It was remarkable.

"Do you know where we are going?" Anna asked suddenly.

"Nope," Ryan answered.

"What the hell?" she said. "We are going to just walk around underground again? Good plan, Ryan."

"We are looking for the Minotaur, a moving creature not an unmovable object," he growled. He was getting sick of her always questioning him. "There really isn't a way to look for him besides exploring down here."

"You went from, man with a plan, to playing it by ear," Anna sarcastically laughed, "Impressive."

Ryan stopped in his tracks causing Cato to run into his back. "What did you say?"

Anna cleared her throat. Ryan could barely see her in the dim light of the flashlight. "Nothing."

"No." He veered toward her, ignoring Damian's obvious tension. "What the hell did you mean by that?"

"Nothing." She looked down at the ground. He shone the flashlight in her face and he could see she was turning red.

Suspicion sunk in, he looked at Damian who avoided eye contact at all costs. They were hiding something and he had a good guess as to what.

"How about this Anna," Ryan started. "You either tell me what you meant or I make you tell me."

"Damian—" She looked worriedly to his friend but Ryan wasn't having it. His hand flew up to her face, gripping her jaw in his hand tightly, forcing her to look at him.

"Now." He was livid.

"Release her now." Damian tried to step in between them but Ryan blocked him out.

Ryan did not let go of her. A burning feeling of anger built up through his entire body. His brain had been through too much lately to process any kind of restraint at this point. He wanted to hurt her. He wanted to hurt all of them.

"Now," Ryan repeated himself.

Anna looked frightened. A thought in the back of his mind told him to release her. That whatever she knew about him was not enough to get this upset about, but the anger in him overruled it. She knew something. It was obvious and he squeezed harder.

She squealed in pain. "Let me go!"

A familiar click came from behind him and he turned toward Damian. His gun was pointed at Ryan's head, ready to fire. "Let her go, Ryan," he said calmly.

Ryan felt a growl escape his lips as he let go of Anna. She rubbed her chin and he could see her skin flaming red from where he touched her. He knew he was losing it. His mind was no longer coping with things well and he needed help. As mad as he was, there was no excuse to put his hands on Anna like that, but his anger had yet to subside.

The only thing he could do was turn and walk away. He continued down through the halls, not even bothering to see if they followed. He turned corner after corner, hoping and praying that they would find the Minotaur soon so he can get away from them. He needed to be alone and he was willing to fulfill this mission by himself.

"Wait up," Cato called to him.

He did not stop, he kept moving, almost wishing to lose them. Anna knew about him. Deep down he felt it after what she had said. It was not untrue though. He always had a plan of action and now he never did. For so long he had counted on his ability to think on his feet. Plans seemed obsolete.

"Dammit, Ryan." Cato grabbed his shoulder and turned him around. "Will you stop?"

Ryan punched the stone wall and felt that familiar sharp pain stab into his hand. "Shit." He shook his hand as if it would actually help.

"Feel better, cupcake?" Cato asked. "What is your deal?"

"She knows, doesn't she?" He groaned.

"Yeah, Amara said it without thinking," Cato answered. "It's not that big of a deal, Ryan."

"It is," he insisted. "I want that person gone and the more people know, the longer my past sticks around."

"It is always going to be there whether you like it or not. You need to realize it and move on," Cato said gently.

"I can't." Ryan punched the wall once more. "It's a plague. A goddamn disease following me around that I can't shake."

"Just calm down and let's get this mission over with. We have to work together otherwise we are all dead. Okay?"

Ryan took a deep breath. He needed to calm down, but his mind was screaming to hurt something. He really was starting to lose his mental stability.

"Fine." He wanted nothing more then to kill something right now. "Where are they?"

"Just around the corner."

They made their way back and found Damian and Anna as far away as possible from one another. They both looked down at the ground not moving one bit when Ryan and Cato came up to them. *Good, they should be ashamed.*

"Let's get this done and leave." Ryan made a point to slow down so he wouldn't lose his team, even though, he really wanted to get away from them. It was difficult keeping his mind off what just happened seeing as he could smell Anna's perfume and heard Damian clicking his tongue. They were taunting him. He could feel it.

Ryan had come to the conclusion they were in the Labyrinth. An endless maze of tunnels and rooms that held gods know what in it. He had a feeling it was the Labyrinth in the vision and had hoped he was mistaken. This place was full of danger and probably ran as big as the island, maybe even further under the ocean bed. There was no guarantee for them even being able to leave this place without getting lost for ages.

He saw something up ahead and shone his light on it. It was the bones of a Satyr, probably from long ago. Its ribs were broken inward—obviously it didn't die of natural causes.

He moved on, hearing Anna gasp behind him. Would she ever stop being so weak minded? Everything shocked and bothered her. She needed to grow up. If she wanted to get any-where in this new life of hers she needed to deal with death. It's just another part of life.

Ryan took a deep breath. He knew he was being some-what dramatic about the entire ordeal. He was still pissed.

"What's that?" Damian asked.

Ryan looked ahead and saw an opening to a room. He was hesitant to walk in, but at this point, didn't give a damn. The least he could do was be the first one in to make sure it was safe. They leaned up against the wall. Ryan had his pistol close to his body, peering into the room to check it out. Satis-fied it was safe, he waved them in behind him.

It was a large room built like a massive prison. There were jail cells covering every wall, some were enormous enough to hold a Cyclops. Torches lined the area and Ryan turned his flashlight off. He did not want to make them more noticeable with the foreign light in the room and he'd rather use a torch anyways.

He looked into one of the jail cells and it was empty. So was the next one and the one after that. He came upon one that was in the middle of one of the wall and he heard some-thing weeping inside.

"Hello," he whispered.

The weeping stopped and silence filled the cell. A small man with long tangled hair crawled from the darkness and into the light. The only clothing covering his body was in rags and he was nothing more than skin and bones. He clung to a half eaten apple as if it were his life.

"It will not work," the man said. "It will not work."

Ryan looked back at Damian who shrugged. "What are you talking about?" Ryan asked.

"The apple!" the man yelled showing his yellowed teeth.

"Oh." Ryan looked back to Damian again. He looked just as lost as he was. "Will anything else work?"

"No," the man muttered to himself. "It never works. Nothing works. Ever."

The man started talking to himself, or possibly someone that was not there and Ryan felt like he knew whom this was. He could not put his finger on it. All these stories of his beliefs seemed to have hid in the back of his mind throughout the years. There was no doubt he was loyal to the gods. No one could deny that, however his knowledge on the legends had wavered.

"What is your name?" Ryan asked.

The man laughed. "Name? He wants to know my name." He was talking to his imaginary friend. "What is in a name really? It's just a word. Letters that are mixed together to form meaning to our ears. Words, words, words."

"Let's just go," Damian whispered. "He is crazed."

"I am King Erysichthon. Bow before me." The broke out into fits of laughter. His ribs were protruding out and it was a ghastly sight to see. "Bow down swine! Bow, bow, bow." He erupted in more giggles.

After hearing his name, Ryan moved on without a second glance. "Let's keep moving."

"Wait," Anna protested. "Shouldn't we help him?"

"No," he said simply and made his way toward the only other exit from the room besides the one they just came in.

"Hold on." He heard her rattling the jail cell. "I'll get you out." Ryan didn't worry about it too much. There was no way she could get him out.

"Anna, no," he heard Damian say calmly. "He must stay here."

"Are you guys serious? He is starving to death," she said.

Ryan groaned loudly for effect, making his way back to the cell. He pushed Anna away from it. "Leave him. Let's go."

"No." She tried to push past him, but he blocked her way.

"Damian, get a hold on your woman right now or I swear to Zeus I will force her," he hissed. Damian tried to gently pull her away, but she yanked herself from his grasp. "The Gods put him here for a reason, Anna. There is nothing we can do. He is paying for his crimes."

"Your gods are heartless." She shoved Ryan's chest, but he didn't budge. "There is no reason for this sort of punishment. This is cruel, disgusting, and inhuman."

He couldn't help it—he laughed. Not out of humor, but he felt himself growing cold inside. His breaking point was on its peak and Anna was pushing him too far.

"Little girl," he started, "you don't dare speak about my Gods like that, or anyone's gods for that matter. You are Immortal now and you better show some respect or you will find yourself just like this scum right here. Do you really think for a second that I give a damn about what you think? You are lucky to even be here given your lack of experience you pathetic, disrespectful, little child."

"You fit right in with your Gods," her suddenly brave attitude didn't seem to waver. "Heartless and cruel to the people that love you. Ever since we came here I've experienced nothing but hell from the creatures your gods created. They enjoy your pain just as much as you do."

"Anna stop." Damian tried to pull her away from him. Erysichthon was mumbling and laughing to himself all the while.

"Don't stand up for him!" She pushed Damian off of her. "This is wrong Damian. You cannot treat people like this."

"It's not for us to decide," he interjected. "Ryan is right."

"Just stand up for Ryan like you always do." Ryan saw a tear run down her cheek. "Just stand up for your boyfriend instead of your girlfriend since he means so much to you."

"Ahh." Ryan laughed. "Now your little attitude makes sense." So that was what she was upset about.

"Shut up." Damian glared at him. "Anna, I am not taking his side. It was the Gods decision to imprison him and he must remain. Regardless of what Ryan believes, it is what I believe."

Anna surprisingly slapped Damian. That was a little uncalled for. "The only reason you believe it is because he does. Still love sick, Damian?"

"Did you not just see me put my gun to his head for you!"

"Will you all just shut up," Cato yelled. "We have a damn mission to fulfill and you are arguing about your damn love lives. Excuse me, but there are millions of people that need our help and your petty problems need to stop. This is ri-god-damn-diculous."

"Petty, petty, petty," Erysichthon repeated over and over. "Petty, petty, petty."

"Cato is right," Damian urged. "Let's get moving."

"I don't want to leave this guy here," Anna insisted.

"You will leave him here," Ryan said. "End of discussion."

"I hate you," Anna said.

"Grow up, Anna." Ryan eyed her. "You're making yourself look pathetic. However, the more you speak the more the feeling is becoming mutual."

"I'm sorry." She laughed. "I just found out my boyfriend has slept with his best friend, who happens to be a guy, and I am finding it a little hard to get through my head."

"Well, get it through your head because you are over analyzing nonsense and hurting yourself for no reason." Ryan stormed away from the group.

He was sick of Anna being with them. She seemed like someone he could really get along with at first and apparently putting her and Damian together just made her bitter. It bothered him that she was becoming very frustrating to be around.

CHAPTER XIX

Anna

"PLEASE JUST LEAVE ME alone right now, Damian," Anna hissed. "I don't want to think about it anymore."

"I just don't understand why you are making such a big deal about something that happened so long ago, Anna." He groaned.

They were still in the jailed area and Ryan and Cato were off arguing about something across the room. She had every right to be mad. They were freaking together! Two guys. Her boyfriend. It was a hard thing to get past.

"If you were in my shoes would you be able to get over it?" she asked. He gave her a shy smile and she rolled her eyes. "You are gross." *Typical man.*

"Anna, please," he begged.

She was trying her hardest to get over it but it was difficult. All the little things they did kept popping up in her head. Like when they constantly shoved each other and joke around. Or when Damian freaks out when Ryan gets hurt. They loved each other, she knew that much—she just didn't know in what way.

"I just need time, Damian. I've never had a boyfriend that likes guys too. Especially when he is constantly around his ex."

"I don't have an interest in men, Anna." He rubbed his temples. "I have no idea how to get you to understand this."

"You slept with a guy. You must like guys," she said. "It's pretty cut and dry to me."

Damian rubbed a hand over his face. "It was viewed differently then. There wasn't a defined sexual preference. We did not have a certain sexual orientation like people do these days, Anna. It was nothing but a physical act."

"You keep saying that but it doesn't make sense to me." She groaned. "Just please, leave me alone for awhile. I need to think."

Damian looked upset. She could tell he was trying to contain himself. "Fine, but I want you to know that me and Ryan have been nothing but friends for more than two thousand years now and we don't have the slightest interest of reliving those days. As far as the modern world is concerned, we are one hundred percent heterosexual if it makes you feel better to put a label on it."

Damian walked away from her toward Cato and Ryan. She felt a twinge of jealousy and tried her hardest to push it away. She was with a wonderful man who'd never lied to her about anything. A man that treated her like a queen and she somehow could not manage to believe what he was telling her. What is wrong with her?

She wandered around the room looking in the jail cells. All of them were empty until she came upon one straight across the room from the king guy. She would not even bother trying to say his name.

"Hello?" she whispered.

All she could see was a woman with long red hair with her back to Anna. She did not seem to be wearing anything and looked cold. How could they put these poor people down here?

"Miss?" She tried to get her attention. "Can I help you?"

"Please, let me out," the woman cried. "I'm so weak."

Anna looked for a lock on the gate and found it. Pointing her gun at it she said, "Watch out."

The woman hastily stood up, her knees shook and Anna was surprised at how pretty she looked. Why was everyone so beautiful in Greek stuff? *What a bunch of perverts.*

Before she could squeeze the trigger, Anna's gun was maneuvered out of her hand and she turned to face Ryan. He shook his head. "Don't."

"She needs help," she said. She looked across the room and saw Damian and Cato in a conversation, leaving her to face Ryan's wrath alone. "There's no reason for a poor, frightened woman to be locked in here."

"Yes," Ryan declared, "there is."

"You are so cold-hearted."

"Would you like to know why these creatures are down here?" Ryan laughed. "I'd be happy to provide you with some insight."

"Fine." She crossed her arms. "Let's hear it."

He pointed across the room. "His majesty over there cut

down the sacred grove of the Goddess Demeter. Everyone knew what the place was, but he was full of greed and wanted to build a feast hall for himself. So she punished him for his insolence."

"Seems pretty harsh," she said.

"He isn't a good man. Let's just leave it at that."

"And her?" She pointed to the redhead.

Ryan leaned against the cell's door. "Hey." He gripped the bars and gave the woman a knee-buckling smile.

The woman eyed him, a grin immediately replacing her look of sorrow. "Hello, sir."

Ryan beckoned her forward. "You are very beautiful."

"Thank you," she cooed. Was she trying to seduce him? Her rolling hips told Anna yes.

"Come here," Ryan urged. His tone was seductive and low. It made her uncomfortable to hear.

The woman did as she was told and came closer to Ryan. She placed her hand gently on his cheek through the bars and grinned. "Will you release me, my love?"

Ryan reached out to her, caressing her neck gently as he spoke, "Oh, my dear." Without warning his grip tightened on her neck. Fangs popped out from her teeth, making Anna's eyes widen in horror.

The woman's hair turned into fire and her legs were suddenly oddly shaped. One looked like it was made out of brass and the other resembled a donkey or horse's leg. What the hell is this thing?

Anna stepped back in shock and Ryan released his grip the creature. The thing banged on the bars in fury and receded back to her cell. "What the hell is that?"

Ryan rubbed his hands together. "That lovely creature is an Empousai."

"How did you know?"

"She is beautiful and luring. She was not a Siren because she wasn't singing. I didn't know for sure until she turned though. One thing is for certain, these things belong here and that means she was someone bad."

"So this place cages monsters?" She wanted to believe these creatures didn't belong here, even if it still seemed cruel to her.

"I guess." He shrugged.

Anna turned from Ryan. She was about to make her way back to Damian, but she stopped. They were running toward her with their guns drawn, both looked determined to reach them. She turned to find Ryan gone; his knife was lying on the ground. She bent down to pick it up when twelve sets of hooves appeared in her vision. Then her world slunk into darkness.

Damian

"Dammit!" Damian yelled out loud and punched the wall. "Where did they take them?"

They had been chasing after the Centaurs for what seemed like hours inside of the Labyrinth. Cato had rolled his ankle, forcing Damian to stop his pursuit. He would not leave Cato alone in this hellhole even if it were eating at him to follow Anna's captors.

"I don't know," Cato groaned as he finished wrapping up his ankle and slipped his boot back on. "All I hope is when they escape, they don't kill each other."

"That's not funny," Damian grumbled.

"Once again I'm not joking." Cato laid his head against the wall.

Damian had to agree. It was by far the worst pair of their group to put with one another. Why didn't he stay by her side, despite her wishes? It was a stupid decision.

"Can you walk?" he asked.

Cato took a deep breath. "Sure why not. Who needs their ankle anyways?"

Damian felt terrible, but they had to keep moving. He had to try and find Anna and Ryan even though he knew it was a lost cause in this place. It was vast and full of unknown terror. If there were a hell on Earth, it was probably the Labyrinth.

Damian held out his flashlight and led the way for him and Cato. He tried to ignore the soft grunts Cato was making as he pushed himself to keep going. There was no choice. He must find Anna. Even if it cost him his life, he had to make sure that she was okay.

"Do you think they're fine?" Damian asked.

"Well," Cato grunted, "I imagine so. Ryan isn't exactly easy to kill and he knows how much you care for Anna. So I doubt he would leave her behind in spite of what she was saying."

"I don't blame her for being angry. I don't know how to fix this."

To his surprise, Cato laughed. "Damian, she had no right to be angry. What happened back then was between Alexander and Hephaestion, not Ryan and Damian. You two are one hundred percent different now."

"I bet you are sick of all our drama aren't you?" Damian said.

"Pretty much." Cato chuckled. "But life is full of drama. If it weren't I would be worried."

Cato had a way of making Damian feel better. Damian had always thought he was the buffer between Cato and Ryan, but as of lately it was quite the opposite. Cato was putting up with him and Ryan for so many years, it was a wonder that he even stuck around.

They turned a corner and found a bullet lying on the ground. He couldn't help but called out, "Anna! Ryan!"

There was no answer. Just Cato's steady breathing filled the hallway. He felt defeated and sat on the ground. He was famished and extraordinarily thirsty. There was no doubt in his mind that they were long gone from being found. He would just have to hope.

Cato sat down opposite of him and they proceeded to drink from their canteens and eat some of the bread Amara had given them. It was a taste he never thought he would experience again and he took his time enjoying it. It reminded him of when he used to sneak bits of food from the kitchens before his family was served when he was a child.

"I wonder what time it is," Cato spoke up. "Feels late."

Damian looked at his watch but it had stopped working once they had got on the island. "No idea. My guess is mid afternoon."

"What took them?" Cato asked. "Looked like horses."

"I think it was a Centaur." Damian almost laughed at the

notion. "Looked like one anyways."

"Aren't they supposed to be outside? Not underground?" Cato asked.

"Who knows what is going on with all these creatures here?" Damian grumbled. "All I know is, we need to find Ryan, Anna, and the piece of Brahma's staff and get the hell out of here."

Damian stood up after a few minutes and brushed himself off. Cato followed suite and they continued through the tunnels. He had no idea where they were or how they were going to find Anna and Ryan—let alone how to get out of this place.

This was just like the Catacombs. A huge mess when they split up but at least Ryan was able to find him and Anna. Damian was not so resourceful or lucky. With his luck they were already dead. *Quit thinking like that.*

"How do you think everyone back home is doing?" Cato finally asked.

Damian forgot to tell him what Grace had said. "Not good at all."

"Why's that?" he asked.

"Do you really want to know or would you like me to lie?" Damian asked.

"What?" Cato grabbed his arm. "What's going on?"

Damian told Cato how he went back to get Anna some new pants and what happened when he ran in to Grace. Although he felt like he should avoid telling him about Julia, he had to.

"Julia was leaving with Aden wearing long black cloaks?" Cato looked like he smelled something foul. "Maybe there was a reason for it? She was cold or something?"

Damian's lips set in a grim line. "Possibly." He really doubted that was the case.

Cato was quiet for a minute. "She's different," he finally said. "She isn't herself. I think she is the enemy."

Damian did not want to agree, but he did. Julia was gone. "She looks different and acts different." It was all he could say on the subject without possibly angering Cato.

"She was so sweet and pure and now she is tainted. I can see it. Everyone can see it."

"I hate to say it but I think Julia is gone, Cato," Damian said. "I do believe she has joined the Risen and I also think Aden has a great deal to do with it."

"I'm going to kill him. I don't care what my punishment is. When we get back I will murder that little bastard," Cato said matter-of-factly.

"I don't think many people would be opposed to the idea," Damian said.

They were coming up on another room and Damian felt very hesitant. After all the creatures they had run in to on this island, in such a small amount of time, he knew something bad was bound to happen.

With their guns ready, they shuffled into the room. It was empty. A little fountain trickled in the corner with the statue of a life size nymph above it. Damian sighed in relief.

"That's odd to have a water nymph shrine down here." Damian noticed Cato's cheeks flushed.

"I have a feeling this entire place doesn't make sense," Damian replied. "It's Greek Wonderland."

"You Greeks believed in some sadistic stuff," Cato said.

Damian laughed. "And you Romans copied us. So I believe you're a sadist as well."

"Too true." Cato ventured over to the fountain and looked down in it.

Damian looked around the empty room. It was small, barely the size of a child's bedroom. "Let's get going."

"Come look at this," Cato called him over. "I think the nymph is in there."

Damian inched over to the shrine and looked down into the fountain. Down in the bottom was a miniature looking woman, swimming around along the bottom and he laughed. She looked like a little mermaid but with no fishtail and blue hair.

"That's odd," Damian mumbled.

They made their way out of the room and continued down a hallway. A room with an arched doorway came up and although Damian wasn't in the mood to try their luck again, they ventured in to it. Damian felt like a child in a candy store immediately.

Unlike the former room, this one was massive, filled with weapons of mass quantity. Swords, daggers, spears lined the walls. There were shields of different shapes and armor from the time of the Greeks. No guns. Ryan would love this room.

Damian looked over at Cato, whose mouth was open in awe. "Whoa."

"Whoa indeed." Damian looked around.

He recognized weapons from when he was mortal and brushed his fingers along the top of a helmet. It all looked brand new, as if someone was keeping them pristine.

Damian looked at Cato, who pulled a gold dagger off of

the wall. "You my pretty, are now mine." Cato sheathed it in his belt.

"Let's get a move on," Damian said.

They started toward the door when iron rods shot down out of the archway, and caged them in. They were in their own personal jail surrounded by deadly weapons.

Cato grabbed hold of the bars and tried to shake them. "Shit."

"Don't panic," Damian said. He looked around the room for any possible escape. There was nothing. The walls were solid stone and the only exit was now barred.

"Live, or die tryin'," a voice boomed throughout the room.

"Great," Damian mumbled.

"Is now a good time to panic?" Cato asked.

Julia

Julia rubbed her temples. She kept getting headaches and thankfully Aden was on his way to give her a tonic that helped. There were brief moments that she fully regretted joining the Risen and it bothered her.

She had to be doing the right thing and there should be no doubt in her mind. Yet, sometimes there was. This whole thing was tiring and she could not wait for it to be over with. She didn't like was that so many mortals were dying. Thankfully, children were totally spared because their minds could still be molded. She didn't know if she could handle their deaths as well.

She sat on her bed in the Domus and groaned from the throbbing pain on her temples. Visions of her and Ryan's bodies wrapped together popped in her mind and she smiled. She started to crave the feeling of his hands on her body.

As always, that feeling did not last and she suddenly realized she despised him. He was stuck in the old ways of life and could not see the error of their beliefs. The Gods were evil for making them do their work dirty work. What was their reward?

They received nothing for risking their lives and were not even known by the mortals for the good they did. She was sick of it. Done with it all.

"Ugh!" She groaned as the pain intensified.

"Julia?" Aden proceeded into her room casually. She was glad to see he held the familiar tonic in his hand. "Are you okay?"

"Yes." She held out her hand to the tonic. It was like her addiction at this point and she drowned the little cup quickly. "Thank you."

"Your welcome." He sat next to her, placing his hand on her leg and rubbing it soothingly. "You look tired."

"Well, after a night of torturing government officials, I imagine I do." She smirked. "Has Australia joined yet?"

Aden nodded. "They are going to address the citizens today and declare what the new laws are."

"Good." She laid down on her bed and stared up at the ceiling. "Has Ahmose woken up yet?"

"Yes, he has. He is still getting used to the idea right now but he seems convinced fully. It is hard for him to realize he's lived a lie for so long."

"At least he realizes now. That's all that matters and we can finally get rid of all those deity loving idiots in Urbs."

Aden leaned down, kissing her on the lips. She grabbed the back of his neck and pulled him closer into her. "Why Miss Julia, are you getting impatient?" He groaned against her lips.

"Impatient?" she asked.

"We promised no physical activity until after all this is done." He grinned.

Julia smacked her lips. "Who would ever find out?"

Aden smiled and kissed her roughly, briefly pulling away from her to say, "No wonder I love you."

CHAPTER XX

Anna

ANNA WOKE UP WITH a pounding headache. She tried to reach up to rub where she had been hit, only to realize she was tied to a post with her hands behind her back. The familiar feeling of panic rose in her as she tugged hard on the ropes. All it did was painfully tighten the ropes on her wrists.

She took in her surroundings. She was in an odd sort of room. The floor was filled with straw. Opposite of her were stables on one side of the room, and someone else. She realized it was Ryan.

He was hanging from a beam by his wrists with a metal chain, his boots were gone and his feet barely reached the floor. Oh God was he dead? He was not awake and he had a gash above his eyebrow. *Please don't be dead.*

There was no one else in the room with them and she stupidly pulled on the ropes again. They would not give at all.

"Dammit," she muttered.

She looked around for anything to cut the rope and realized that all her weapons, and what she assumed were Ryan's, were on a table behind his hanging body. He was stripped of all his gear and only wore his pants and undershirt. What was going to happen to him? She was fully dressed just missing her weapons.

"Ryan," she half whispered, half yelled. "Wake up." He did not move an inch and hung there lifeless. That had to be painful on his wrists. "Ryan, wake the fuck up!"

A door slammed shut behind her making her jump. Her chest moved up and down rapidly and she barely refrained from screaming. She did not want to die down in this stupid maze place where no one would ever find her body. Especially when the last thing her and Damian did was fight.

No more sounds came from the room, which only served to build up her anxiety more. She decided to focus her attention on Ryan since he was the only familiar thing in the room. She now fully understood why women liked him. He was handsome, very muscular and had a very active spirit. She would never be able to think of him in any sort of sexual way though.

Anna realized that his face was starting to get scruffy. She had never seen him with facial hair and it sort of looked good on him. It grew in thickly instead of in patches like Nathan's used to. Maybe he needed to break away from his clean-cut look.

She heard multiple knocking sounds hitting the ground after so much silence and dared to look around the back of her pole. Three horses were coming her way. Wait, not horses, they were half man half-horse guys. Where the horse's head should have been, was the upper body of hippie looking men with long hair and beards, but breaking from the hippie effect was the spears in their hands.

She was sick of this Greek bull crap.

"The girl is awake," one of them said.

"Don't touch her," the black horse looking one said. Anna was instantly relieved. "Wake the man."

One of the brown horse guys held a large bowl in his hand and tossed water on Ryan's head. He gasped awake and shook the water out of his face the best he could. His face went from dazed to calm pretty quick. Was that a good sign?

"Who are you?" the black horse guy asked. "Why are you here?"

Ryan obviously ignored the question, looking around the room until his gaze fell on her. She could not see any concern in his eyes, but that never meant anything with Ryan. He was the most complicated person she had ever met.

"Speak!" a brown horse guy yelled.

"My name is Ryan," he said simply.

The third horse guy punched Ryan in the jaw. He spit blood onto the straw and wiggled his jaw around. "Answer all questions, human."

"My business for being here is just that. My business," Ryan stated calmly.

Another hit to his jaw made her wince in pain for Ryan, but he showed no expression on his face. That man was dumb. What was he thinking?

"Why are you here, human?" the black horse guy asked again.

"Why do you care?"

"We have claim over these walls and you are trespassing," the brown one said.

"I thought this was the Minotaur's territory."

The third one scoffed. "We are at battle with the beast."

"Then we have something in common," Ryan stated. "Let us go and we will help you hunt him down."

"The human must want the territory as well. Kill him," the third spoke to the black horse.

The black horse seemed to be deep in thought until he finally shrugged. "Fine."

"Wait," Ryan's voice was low and demanding. "You cannot do this."

"Why not?" the third one asked.

"We are Immortals."

The three horse guys looked at one another and begun to argue about something in an awkward huddle away from them. Ryan gazed down at her, giving her a reassuring look. He mouthed, "*Don't worry.*"

The black horse guy came up to Ryan. "We know no Immortal by the name of Ryan. This name is unfamiliar. You are lying and claiming honors you do not deserve."

"I swear to you we are both Immortals," Ryan protested.

The third horse guy slapped Ryan on his cheek. His poor face was already looking bruised. He was not even being rude and obnoxious like he usually was either. Maybe people, or in this case creatures, just feel like hitting him for no reason. She could understand that feeling.

The brown one was somehow able to grab Ryan's short hair, yanked his head back and held a knife to his neck. "You lie."

"I do not," Ryan spat. His teeth looked bloody and he stared directly in the creature's eyes. *Damn he is brave.*

She instantly hated herself for thinking that way about him. She needed to hate him, but she could not. Jealousy was a terrible trait and maybe she needed to believe that Ryan and Damian's friendship is just that, a friendship and nothing more.

With a hit to his gut, Ryan desperately tried to catch his breath after the horse guy let go of his hair. She could not take watching this man go through any more punishment. He really was a good guy deep, deep down. Jesus, he is a freaking legend!

"Stop it!" Anna yelled.

The horse guys turned toward her with bewildered faces. Ryan lifted his head. His eyes pleaded with her to be quiet, but she could not. He did not deserve to be hurt all the time even if he was a gluten for punishment.

"Pardon you?" The black one looked surprised.

"We are Immortals, dammit," she hissed. "That is Alexander the Great right in front of you."

Ryan hung his head, probably moping about his poor little past life. The horse guys seemed to be studying him up and down. It made Anna feel as if she did something wrong. Would her revelation make it worse for Ryan? *Crap, did he have beef with the horse dudes?*

"You stated your name was Ryan," the brown one said. "Did you lie?"

"No." Ryan shook his head. "It is the name I go by now."

"We have no proof this is King Alexander," the third one

stated. Anna really did not like him or the brown one. "Kill them and be done with it."

"We must take into account what they have said," the black horse said. "If this is truly King Alexander, we cannot murder him."

"He must prove it," the brown one agreed.

"How the hell do I do that?" Ryan laughed.

"Answer some questions for us," the black one spoke. "Who were some of the women in your life?"

Ryan looked pale, but he answered, "Roxane, Barshine, and Statira."

Anna had no idea who these women were, but he did not seem to want to talk about this. He looked aged almost instantly. She was glad to hear about him. He was such a mystery and she was finally learning about someone very important in history.

"Your children?" the black one asked.

"The ones that did not die at birth?" Ryan growled when the horse guy nodded. "Herakles and Alexander IV."

Anna was ashamed at how curious she was. Ryan looked devastated at the mention of his children. It obviously broke his heart and she guessed it was why he did not want anyone to know about his past. Something must have happened with them. She couldn't picture him as a father.

"Mother and Father?"

"Philip II and Olympias," Ryan spat. "What else?"

"Your horse?"

"Bucephalus."

"Let me see your hand," the black one said.

Ryan laughed. "You're going to have to look yourself. I'm

sort of tied up at the moment."

The horseman looked at Ryan's hand then nodded. "He has the wound of the Immortals. Check the woman."

Anna had never been so thankful for a scar in her life. She still remembered the horrible sting she felt at her ceremony when she became a true Immortal.

The brown horse guy came over to her and gently grabbed her hand even though it was tied behind her back. He had to kneel down. "She does as well."

As if he weighed nothing, the black horse lifted Ryan off the ground, taking the weight off of his wrists and unchained his hands. "I apologize, your highness. It is difficult times we live in on this island."

The Centaurs honestly looked a little ashamed and scared. What sort of power does Ryan have exactly? Apparently a bunch, because she was cut free of her bindings as quickly as possible and they were both given a wooden box to sit on.

Ryan rubbed his jaw, resting his elbows on his knees. For some reason she wanted to make sure he was okay and she gently grabbed his face making him freeze at her touch. "What?" She felt like Damian's concern for Ryan's well being was rubbing off on her.

"Nothing," he mumbled and let her examine him.

His jaw was intact and so were his teeth, just a little bruised and a definite headache later on. "You're a tough little shit, you know?"

Ryan smirked. "Yeah well, I think some parts of me have begun to turn numb after all these years."

"I wouldn't doubt it. You're like a magnet for getting hurt," Anna said.

"Comes with the territory."

"Most Immortals I see don't get hurt like you do," Anna stated. "I think you like it or something."

Ryan laughed. "Yeah, it's fun. Let me tell you." He shook his head.

Anna believed he either liked the pain or liked the attention he received from it. Either way, it was sort of pathetic, but then again he always took the brunt of everything. Damian and Cato rarely received as much torment as him.

"Sarcasm suites you," she added. "So why do you always get hurt and taunt the people wielding the power?"

"I think I'd rather myself get hurt than anyone else honestly," Ryan said. "Cato is a good man and he has done nothing in his life worth deserving pain. Damian of course is my best friend and I am protective of you because of Damian's affection."

Anna felt guilty once more for thinking it was the attention. Ryan got enough of it as it was without getting beat on. "You do so much for Damian." She sounded bitter. "No wonder he cares more about you than anyone else."

"Anna stop," Ryan said forcefully. "Damian is literally like my brother now. We have lived for thousands of years. Trust me, countless things change over time. There is nothing between us in that sense anymore. Not even a little. It's like you are looking for a reason to dislike him."

Anna blinked. She wasn't entirely sure how to respond to that. It happened a long time ago and she was acting as if it happened last year. The pain in her heart from hearing the news subsided.

"It's just difficult," she said.

"I don't see why." Ryan stared at her. "Those people are gone. The person I was then, and the person I am now would not get along. Guaranteed."

"What makes you say that?" She laughed.

"For one, I thought much differently about sex." Ryan looked like he was accessing a memory as his eyes glazed over. "My mother had to bring a woman to my bed to have sex with me because my parents were worried about my lack of a sexual appetite."

"What!" Anna burst out. She couldn't help it. Ryan was a slut.

Ryan grinned. "It's true. My focus was warfare and my studies."

"Well shit sure changed."

"It sure did."

She would have never guessed. They never studied Alexander's personal life in school. Just his military exploits.

"Your highness," the black horse came up behind them and held out an offering of apples on a small clay plate. "Please accept our apologizes."

Ryan held up his hand. "Honest mistake."

"It is unforgivable to touch a man of your stature that way," the brown one added. "We were not kind."

"I've had worse," Ryan said. "Please don't call me highness anymore. I am no longer a king."

The three horse guys looked among one another. "Sorry to disagree with you, your highness. However, you will always be royalty. It is a matter of your blood."

"Not much good it does," Ryan said. "It's an empire long destroyed."

"It is good," the black one countered. "You are a royal descendant of the Gods."

"My mother fed me that nonsense when I was a child. I no longer believe it." Ryan smirked and took an apple. "I highly doubt my father is actually Zeus."

"How do you not realize that he is?" the black one asked.

Ryan took another bite of his apple and seemed to want to ignore the horse guy. "Can you take us back to our group?"

"I am afraid we do not know where they are, sir," the third one timidly spoke. Anna was glad. He was a little jerk from the start.

"Alright, well we better get going then. Please inform the rest of your kin that we are not the enemy," Ryan said. "Let's go, Anna."

"Wait," the black one called. "Let us help you."

"I think it wiser if we progress alone. But if you do find the beast and kill him, I would be very grateful if you came and found us," Ryan said. "He has something we desperately need."

"As you wish, my lord. Let me give you something to help on your journey."

He handed Ryan an odd looking dagger. It looked like it was made from an animal horn and had a makeshift leather hilt on the dull side. "Is this what I think it is?" Ryan asked.

"Yes. It is the beast's horn, part of it anyways. We broke off one full horn of his and then broke that into pieces for all of our kin to use in case of battle."

Ryan looked dumbstruck. Anna probably would too. Even if she was not part of this culture, she knew that was a very generous and rare gift to give. She watched Ryan's fingers trail up and down along the horn and it sent a shiver down her spine. It looked lethal.

"Thank you." Ryan was overly pleased.

"It is the least we could do, given the treatment you received. I do apologize again. It is terribly difficult on this island," the black horse said.

"Perhaps when our mission is over and done with I can speak with Zeus. I haven't had an audience with him in some time, but he may change his mind," Ryan said. "I cannot promise much, but I will try to set things straight."

All three of the horse guys bowed, and she felt like she should curtsy or something. *Whatever. It is just Ryan, right? No. This guy is Alexander the freaking Great.*

Cato had grabbed a sword from the wall and was smacking it against the bars that held them captive in the weapons room. The ringing from the noise was irritating, almost like nails on a chalkboard but Cato did not seem to mind. Damian on the other hand was on the verge of tackling Cato to the ground.

"Will you stop?" Damian massaged his temples. "It's not going to work and I don't know why you think it would."

"What am I supposed to do?" Cato breathed heavily. "Just wait to be slaughtered by gods know what?"

"Just calm down. Nothing has attacked us yet and you're freaking out." Damian was puzzled by Cato—he was always calm in these situations.

297

Cato shook his head and put his hands over his ears. *What in the hell is going on?* He was throwing a fit or something. "Need out. Need out now."

Damian tried to pry Cato's hands off of his head, but he would not budge. His breathing was increasing at an alarmingly fast pace and Damian started to panic. "Cato, breathe. Calm down."

Cato's eyes looked wild and he pushed Damian in the chest. "Are you insane? We are trapped like damn rats."

Damian held out his hand to Cato cautiously. "Give me the sword Cato." He had pressed the sword against Damian's neck.

As if just realizing what he was doing, Cato dropped the sword from Damian's throat. "Sorry."

Relived he asked, "What was that about?"

Cato shook his head. "I don't know. I think I had a panic attack or something."

"That's abnormal for you," Damian said. "Were you thinking anything?"

"I don't know. I got cold when the bars appeared and it felt like I did not have control of my body or something." Cato closed his eyes. "Is that what a panic attack feels like?"

"I guess." Damian was confused. It was pretty comfortable down here and not the least bit cold.

Damian paced around the room and waited for something, anything to happen. The creepy voice made it seem as if they were going to be attacked any minute now. Whatever is was, it was successfully building up the suspense.

After ten minutes, with nothing happening, Cato and Damian decided to sit down and play catch with a grenade. It was becoming increasingly dull just being trapped in a room full of deadly weapons and nowhere to escape. Maybe this entire thing was just a trick by whoever built this room and eventually they would be released. If only things were that easy.

"Do you think Jupiter and Zeus get along?" Cato asked randomly.

Damian shrugged, tossing the grenade back to Cato. "Probably not. The Greeks and Romans weren't exactly chums."

"They are basically the same though," Cato interjected.

"But they aren't," Damian countered. "Zeus has always seemed much more calm than Jupiter."

"I suppose you're right. He is sort of a hot head."

"All Romans are." Damian smirked.

Cato grinned and tossed the grenade back. "I would pay to see Ares fight Mars."

"As would I. It would be one hell of a show down." Damian could only imagine what it would look like. There probably wouldn't be a winner.

"Could you imagine a threesome with Venus and Aphrodite?" Cato groaned. "Now that would be something."

Damian shook his head. "You are such a disgusting creature you know that?" Cato nodded. "But if you want details, Ryan could give them to you."

Cato let out a deep groan. "Are you kidding me? That lucky bastard had them both? I thought it was just Aphrodite."

"Well, he left that part out when he told you. Aphrodite and Venus weren't thrilled to be around one another so they made him swear not to tell anyone. Of course he told me, but it was a long time ago."

"Lucky asshole." He tossed the grenade but it stopped in midair, just hovering between them.

Cato and Damian exchanged baffled looks. A chill went through his body all of a sudden, almost to the point of making him shiver. His breath suddenly became visible. "Well this isn't good."

"Roman scum," a rough voice came out of nowhere.

"This island just hates me, you know it?" Cato mumbled

Damian looked around for the man behind the voice, but there was nothing to be seen. Why must there be so many tasks before getting what they needed? This island was ridiculous and he could not wait to get off of it. At least the catacombs were somewhat bearable and only took a day or so to complete.

"I'm thankful I'm not Roman." Damian looked at Cato, who was glaring at him. "Just throwing that out there."

Cato rolled his eyes. "So, Roman hating ghosts, great."

"Ghosts?" Damian asked.

"Spirits. Whatever." Cato sighed. "More damn ghosts that make me go insane on my friends and hate me."

"That's not good." Damian looked around waiting for something to appear. Ghosts were terrible in their beliefs.

The only time the Greeks or Romans believed in spirits that did not move to the underworld, were ones that died tragically and were never given a proper burial. Those ghosts were all full of anger and unfinished business. They were dangerous.

The grenade launched from its floating position and hit Cato in the head. He rubbed the spot it hit. "Son of a bitch," Cato groaned.

"Just be thankful they don't know what it is," Damian muttered.

Apparitions started to appear all around them. Ghosts of soldiers in full uniform mainly, with gruesome wounds on their bodies. A few of them were citizens that were obviously murdered and judging by their attire, they were poor. Souls of the forgotten that had pent up anger building for thousands of years. Their eyes blazed with hatred and every one of the spirits looked as if they wanted to murder them.

"Hey everyone." Cato laughed nervously. "We mean no harm. We just want to get out of here and be on our way. Sorry for bothering you."

Damian gave him an amused look. "Smooth."

"What?" He laughed nervously. "Figured I'd try a diplomatic approach."

"I would hardly call that diplomatic, but whatever," Damian said.

"I don't see you saying anything."

"Maybe because there is nothing to say."

"Enough!" a soldier ghost yelled. "You must die."

"Why?" Cato asked. "Wouldn't you rather talk things out?"

Damian would laugh if he could, but he figured laughing would anger the ghosts even more. Cato must be stalling them so they could somehow find a way to defeat them. He only knew of certain ways to get rid of spirits from Greek beliefs and that wasn't happening. Their bodies were long gone and there was no putting them to rest.

Damian looked around for any sort of clue and noticed that the dagger Cato took matched perfectly with the ghost that was talking. *Coincidence? I think not.*

The weapons in the room must have been the weapons the ghosts had when they were killed or maybe what they were killed with. Either way, Damian figured it must have mean something important and he moved closer to Cato.

"Halt!" the ghost yelled again.

Damian stopped in his tracks but he was close enough to Cato that he could whisper, "Notice his weapon?"

Cato nodded, already grasping the dagger's hilt. "Already ahead of you." The ghost glared at Cato like he was scum. The animosity coming off the spirits was intense. Although, he probably would be angry and vengeful too given the fact this man should probably be in Elysium, Greek heaven. Soldiers almost always journeyed there and this man obviously died giving his life judging by the deep slice in his throat.

Damian looked around and counted ten ghosts. Picking one at random to fight he settled on a soldier with a stomach wound that was holding a long plain sword in his hand. Damian glanced around the walls trying to find the matching blade and finally found it.

He started to scoot over to it gradually as he held up his hands. "Look, we just want to get out of here."

"You will not leave this room alive," the ghost soldier said.

"That is hardly fair," Damian said as he moved closer to the blade.

"Nothing is fair."

"We did nothing to you." Damian took another step.

"You're very breath is reason enough."

Damian was so close. "Is that how you treated your fellow countrymen when you were alive?"

"They didn't care enough to give me a proper burial, so I could care less." Other ghosts nodded in agreement.

Finally there, Damian grabbed the long plain sword off of the wall, ran straight toward his target and plunged it into the ghost's stomach. It of course passed straight through him but it did the trick. The ghost's eyes seemed to roll behind its lids and shot up in flames until there was nothing left but a small trickle of smoke.

The rest of the flock became more agitated than before and moved in on Damian and Cato. "Well, shit," Cato groaned. "At least it worked."

"There's too many," Damian whispered.

"No, you think?" Cato rolled his eyes. "Alright, let's do this."

Damian screamed at the top of his lungs as he watched Cato charge into the ghostly battle, "Dammit, Cato!"

Chapter XXI

Ryan

"So, what was it like? Was it like the movies or really crappy?" Anna ran after him.

Ryan was getting thoroughly annoyed with Anna's badgering. This was precisely why he hated people knowing about him. Well, at least one of the reasons. This woman had no shred of common sense to realize how irritated he was.

"What was what like?" he asked sweetly, but she didn't seem to catch onto his sarcasm.

"Greece!" She exclaimed. "What did your armor look like? Oh, and were there weapons no one knows about that haven't been discovered yet? What was it like having to wear a toga all the time?"

"What is with the sudden fascination? You wanted to kill me earlier," he spat.

"I'm not over it, however, I can't change it. But it's freaking fascinating. Do you even realize how cool it is?"

Ryan imagined how peaceful it would be if he cut out her tongue. Damian would not be too happy about it though so he pressed on and did his best to ignore the giddy girl. He preferred her hatred toward him.

"You are bipolar, woman," he said.

"Probably, but who isn't these days?" She grinned up at him as she tried to keep up. "Besides, I learned a lot about you back there. It makes sense why you are so moody and what not."

"Gee thanks."

"Also, about the Damian ordeal, well I can't change it and you two are very adamant about the whole, not wanting to bang each other anymore thing," she said.

"You don't say?" He laid the sarcasm on thick.

"Yep." She ignored it. "So you had kids?"

At that point, Ryan had had enough and he slammed her against the stone wall, not too rough but enough to make his point. Her neck was firmly grasped in his hand. "Enough, Anna." His tone was far more threatening than he intended.

She did her best to nod and choked out, "Okay."

As he released her she rubbed her neck. The guilt he usually felt didn't rise up. "Why do you insist on bringing up my past, Anna? It is over and done with. Leave it there."

"Okay." Her eyes watered. "I'm just trying to understand this all still and I can't help that I am curious. It's just really interesting."

"It's never ending with you, Anna. You ask the same damn questions and keep bringing up the same shit all the time. I am sick of it. Find something else to obsess about,"

Ryan hissed.

"Jesus, okay." She rubbed her neck and Ryan finally felt bad. Hurting women was never okay in his book and she suffered enough by his hand alone.

He just wanted her to stop and he finally believed she would. "Let's go." He gently put his hand on her arm to lead her away from the wall. "Look, I am sorry about putting my hand on you like that. I know it's not okay even if I were upset."

"It's okay," she mumbled.

"It's absolutely not okay, Anna." He was having a hard time admitting he was wrong, especially to Anna who was so frustrating. "I'm sure you know I have a problem with my temper. I always have. Even as a mortal, but believe me when I say that I will try my hardest not to be rough with you. It's unforgivable."

"Really, you're good." He could see a hint of a smile tugging at the corner of her lips. "I push pretty hard when I want to know something. I'm an expert at pissing people off."

"Trust me, I don't doubt that."

She smacked him in the chest but only hit her hand on his M4 Carbine. "Dammit." She shook her hand.

"Ha, serves you right." Ryan stopped abruptly. He heard a loud hiss coming up behind them. There was no time to think so he grabbed Anna's arm and pulled her with him as he ran.

After the initial shock of breaking into a run, he let go of her when she kept up on her own. "What is it?" she breathed out.

"Something not friendly and not what we are looking for. Hide," he said.

There was one creature that popped into his head when

he heard that hissing noise and he hoped it wasn't that. The creature was a large snake, lethal beyond compare and he did not want to test his theory. As they ran down the corridor, the hissing became louder and by that knowledge, it was coming closer. They had to hide quickly.

Ryan ran past a small door and came to an abrupt stop. Anna almost flew past him but he grabbed her arm and yanked her to his side. "What?" She almost toppled to the ground.

"In here." Ryan pulled the door open.

"You can't be serious?" She eyed him as if he were crazy. It was an extremely small room, barely large enough for them both to fit in. Maybe they should find another room.

The hissing grew louder. "I sure am." He shoved Anna into the small closet and squeezed himself in to where the front of their bodies faced one another. He barely managed to close the door when the hissing seemed to be right outside of their enclosure. If it were the creature he believed it to be, it would not be able to open doors.

"This is uncomfortable," she whispered.

Her head was against his chest and there was no wiggle room around it. Unfortunately, his arms had nowhere to go except up in the air. A small shred of light came from under the door and he could barely make out any of Anna's features.

"Let's hope the damn thing moves along," he groaned.

They stood there for at least twenty minutes but the hissing wouldn't cease. The creature must smell them or something because it wouldn't leave. There was no leaving this room anytime soon and his arms were getting tired.

"Are you okay?" Anna whispered.

Ryan nodded, though he doubted she saw. "Yeah."

"You can put your arms down you know," she said quietly.

"I have no where to put them."

"You can put them over my shoulders or whatever. I don't care." He felt her body move from her shrug.

"I don't think that would be appropriate," Ryan said.

Anna let out a small laugh. "You're being ridiculous. Just do it, you big baby."

Ryan had to admit, his arms were tired and he wanted to be able to lift them tomorrow. Grudgingly, he set his arms down on her shoulders and felt his body relax. That was one less thing to worry about given there was a giant snake slithering its way around the halls.

The small light coming through the bottom of the door was shut out by something outside of it. Ryan realized he was holding his breath and released it. It had to be the basilisk. Or at least some form of the creature.

"What is it?" Anna whispered.

"A snake that can kill you by breathing on you," Ryan answered.

"How lovely."

"Yeah." He awkwardly shifted his weight from one foot to the other. "Can you reach your flashlight? I can't see a thing."

Anna

Anna's hands were pinned to her sides, but she managed to grasp hold of the flashlight that was in a lower pouch, close to the middle of her chest. "It's stuck," she groaned.

"How the hell is it stuck?" Ryan spat. God he could be such a dick with only a few words.

"I can barely reach it, Ryan," she said. "My hand doesn't bend this way naturally."

She tried to work it up from her pouch, yanking hard on it and coming up short. The string that goes around your wrist seemed stuck on something. She tugged harder on it until it finally came loose at the expense of hitting Ryan.

He slammed his hands against the wall by her head and leaned over as much as he could. The side of his head was propped against hers and she instantly knew where she hit him. She could feel his body trembling against her own.

"Ryan, I am so sorry," she squeaked.

"Shut up." She didn't take his anger personally. There was no way she could blame him for being mad.

"Like, super sorry."

His breath was quick. "I can't even reach my dick."

He groaned in despair and Anna had no idea what to do. Men needed space after getting hit in their junk and they definitely lacked in extra space in this closet. Poor guy could not even cradle himself with care.

She clicked on the flashlight and although it pointed at the ground, she could see his face in the small flicker of light if she maneuvered her head a certain way. His was leaning his head back against the wall behind him now with his eyes closed tight.

"Can I do anything?" she asked.

"Just shut up," he grumbled.

"Will do." Anna stared at his chest because it was the only thing to look at while she kept quiet.

Ryan groaned. "I feel like my balls are in my stomach. Dammit Anna, you got me good." Ryan rubbed his face before he put a hand on the wall opposite of the door. He probably didn't know what to do with himself given he couldn't reach his junk.

"Are you going to pass out?" she asked quietly. The way he was leaning against the wall opposite the door made it seem like he had a hard time standing.

"No," he grunted. Anna nearly jumped in surprise as the wall he leaned on fell down to the ground with a loud thud. "What the hell?"

Apparently the wall wasn't very well built. Anna was relieved they had a space to escape into. She was tired of being cramped up with a man she caused crotch trauma to. It was also better than being trapped with a giant hissing creature outside of their door. Now they could escape.

"Okay, this is good right?" She dropped her flashlight.

Ryan looked around the room, not moving from their little closet. "I don't know. Something about this feels familiar."

"Chill out." She squeezed her way past him to escape their little hell bubble. She felt his hand grasp her arm tightly. "What?"

Ryan shook his head. "I don't like it."

"Well, I am done being all up in your business so let's just exit into the nice big comfy room." Anna trudged out into the spacious room and gasped.

It was gorgeous and totally out of place in this hellhole of a maze. Red and purple silks were draped along the walls and a large four-poster bed with a tall canopy was sitting in the middle of the room with white silk draping around it. It was clean in here and that immediately threw up a red flag to her.

It was so romantic though. Candles were lit all around and rose pedals littered the floor. It was lovely. Beautiful. Where were the people that should be enjoying this? The candles were hardly burnt.

She turned to face Ryan whose face was in a mix of emotion as he still remained in the doorway. "I think you should get back in the closet Anna."

"No." She grinned foolishly.

Ryan held out his hand to her but she didn't move. "Please come here, Anna. I don't like this."

"What's not to like?" She waved her arms around the room. "It's like a five star hotel room."

Ryan grunted, "Get over here." He thrust his hand out to her.

She grinned playfully, although she didn't know why. "No."

"Dammit, Anna. Get over her." She finally got him to walk out of the closet to get her and his demeanor instantly transformed.

Almost like a gentleman would, he held out his hand to her and she took it willingly. Butterflies filed her stomach as he pulled her against him. "I don't know why but I need to be close to you, Anna." He nuzzled into her neck.

Her stomach did back flips. "I feel the same way."

She never realized how handsome Ryan was. His eyes were gorgeous and those pouty lips of his... what a knee buckler. She wanted those lips on hers and badly.

Ryan's hand grasped her sides until he tugged on her vest. "May I?"

Anna nodded and Ryan ripped her vest off her easily, tossing it on the ground. This was unreal. She had never thought of him in this way before but as he stood here in front of her, he was all she could think about.

With one easy motion, he removed his vest as well and begun to unstrap his weapons from his legs. It was oddly arousing watching him remove such dangerous weapons. Everything he did made her want him. He was just plain sexy.

Ryan kneeled down in front of her and ran his hands up her legs. He removed her gear as well, gently massaging her thighs as he worked. Her head rolled back at the exquisite feeling. An unwilling gasp escaped her lips when he palmed her ass. He moved so gracefully and erotically. No wonder women swooned over him.

"You're so damn beautiful," he muttered as he pushed up her shirt and kissed along her bare stomach.

Just as she was becoming accustomed to his lips on her bare skin, he picked her up as if she weighed nothing and laid her down on the bed. Regardless of the comfort below her, Anna's attention was directly on Ryan. He was sexy. His movie star good looks and wide jaw was so intoxicating that she wanted to engulf his very being.

As he sat up between her legs he pulled his shirt off and revealed a glorious sight. Goddamn his muscles were intense. The man was cut to perfection with a hard V carved in his abdomen leading down below.

"I want you," she groaned and he smiled in response. She could not wait any longer.

He leaned down over her, pressing his body into hers and without a second thought her body responded. She pulled down on his neck so she could kiss him, but his lips hovered over hers. He stared deep into her eyes for a moment with utter longing. She wondered why he wouldn't kiss her.

"Can I make love to you, Anna?" He bit his lip, which sent a quiver down her spine. She merely nodded and he seemed relieved. "Tell me what you want and I will do it."

No words came to mind—just her longing for his touch as she pushed her lips to his. He tasted wonderful. It felt so magnificent that she roughly craved more yet he was gentle with her. The last thing she would expect was this man to be gentle.

He caressed her body with such tender and smooth touches that he left goose bumps all over her. She deepened the kiss but he was ever so calm with her, as if he were savoring her mouth against his own. His aching groin had obviously diminished and was replaced with an intense longing for her. She was satisfied he wanted her so much.

Ryan pushed his body against hers and she moaned. She needed him now and for as long as she could get. Her mind became clouded as he slowly peeled off her shirt and she knew she could wait no longer.

CHAPTER XXII

Damian

"**D**AMN, HOW DID WE get out of there?" Cato heaved breaths.

Damian shrugged. "Beats me."

They had narrowly escaped from the ghost ambush and Damian sported a pretty nasty cut on his arm. Regardless of the situation, he was happy they made it out alive. It wasn't as much trouble as it seemed given the spirits were tripping over themselves with anger. How a spirit trips, he didn't know, but he was glad for it.

"Alright, I think we are just walking in circles," Cato groaned.

"I think that would technically be walking in squares, given there are no rounded corners," Damian interjected.

"You're so funny, Damian," Cato grunted. His ankle seemed to be bothering him a great deal but they had no time to rest now. He was desperate to find Anna and after seeing how massive the Centaurs were, he feared for her life.

They looked so crazed and aggravated that Damian truly believed they were in it for the kill. Why did they not take him and Cato? Perhaps this would be a hostage situation? Scenes of brutality rolled over in his mind for hours it seemed.

"What are you thinking about?" Cato asked.

"Nothing," he lied. "This place is too massive. Perhaps we should split up?"

"I really don't think us splitting up is a good idea. Then we would have to find each other as well. No good." Cato limped along.

Damian shone his flashlight on Cato. "Are you sure you're okay?"

"I'm a-okay." Cato made an okay hand signal but his face was drenched in sweat and contorting in pain.

"You're a terrible liar," said Damian.

Cato moved past him. "Come on old man. Let's stop worrying and get going. We got your crazy lover and Anna to find."

Damian ignored his comment and continued to follow behind him. He purposely did not pass him just so Cato could make his grimaces in peace. For once, Cato was the damsel in distress and he was obviously too stubborn to let it affect him.

Damian rounded a corner and pulled Cato back behind it before he could go around. "There is a big ass chicken snake looking thing."

Cato peeked around the corner. "What the hell?"

"I think that's a basilisk."

"I thought that was a giant snake?"

315

"Quit watching those wizard movies with that kid in glasses," Damian said. "I think it's sleeping."

Damian looked around the corner again and it seemed like it was actually in a deep slumber. It was huge, bigger than what he thought it would be, but perhaps the myth was distorted.

"Kill it?" Cato asked.

Damian nodded. "Go stab it."

Without a single protest, Cato sauntered around the corner and stabbed the creature in the head. A sickening crunch came from the creature's body and Damian shivered in disgust. To make matters worse, Cato begun to hack at it's head and beheaded it.

"This thing is freaky looking," Cato laughed.

"Imagine it awake." Damian shivered. "Its breath was said to kill you the instant it touched you if I remember right."

Cato's mouth dropped. "And you just let me waltz up to it like no big deal?"

"Worked, didn't it?" Damian grinned.

"Jackass," Cato muttered. "Alright, let's keep moving."

After the head of the basilisk was off, Damian noticed a sliver of light escaping the closet size door it was in front of. "There's a light coming from under the door." Damian pointed.

Cato kicked aside the head and opened the door. He peaked inside but shut it quickly. "Let's go."

"What?" Damian laughed.

Cato shook his head. "Just an empty closet. Let's go."

"Well at least grab whatever light it in there. We could use it."

"It's a ceiling light." Cato scratched his head.

Damian furred his eyebrows and made his way to the door. Cato stood in front of it making Damian very curious. "Move."

"No."

"Now."

"My ankle hurts," Cato groaned, but it was so fake Damian looked at him blankly.

Damian shoved him out of the way and opened the door. At first it seemed like a tiny hallway with a flashlight lying on the ground, until things came into perspective. "What the hell?" He felt his body burn like fire.

In a room ahead of him, there was Anna and Ryan embracing one another like lovers on a massive bed. They were both nearly naked and were passionately enthralled in one another. He reached for his gun. He was ready to kill Ryan. No stopping it. No second-guessing. He racked the slide of his gun and aimed at Ryan's back as he kissed Anna's neck.

"Whoa." Cato smacked the gun down and Damian glared at him with utter hatred. "Don't."

"Are you fucking kidding me?" Damian yelled.

Anna and Ryan finally had the nerve to sit up and look in their direction. Not a sign of shock or guilt. Smiles plastered their faces and Anna held out her hand toward him.

"Come here." She grinned.

Damian was dumbstruck. What the hell did she just ask him to do? The damn woman was cheating on him with his best friend in plan sight. She acted as if nothing was wrong with it and he held his gun up once more.

"Stop, dammit." Cato smacked the gun again. "Think

about it. Would Ryan, or Anna for that matter, really do this?"

"Ryan has done it before! All the time actually!" Damian hissed. His gun went up again.

Cato stood in front of him and blocked his targets. "Okay, I know that. But this is Anna. She is so important to you and Ryan knows that. Besides they really don't get along and Anna wanted to pretty much kill Ryan the last time we saw her."

Damian forced himself to count to ten and pinched the brim of his nose. "I don't know what to think. I just know what I am seeing."

"Damian, come join us," Anna beckoned.

He did his best to ignore her. "Okay, I see them about to have sex. So what the hell is actually going on?" Damian gripped his hair in frustration.

Cato bit his lip and faced the room. He studied it as Ryan and Anna decidedly went back to slobbering over one another. He literally felt sick to his stomach watching them.

"Well, I see a statue of Venus," Cato announced.

"Aphrodite." Damian corrected.

"Maybe a spell of some kind?" Cato suggested.

Damian hoped so. Otherwise, his best friend was going to die very slowly. "Okay, say you are right. What do we do about it?"

"Drag them out?" Cato asked.

"Get on it."

"Why me?"

"Because I want to strangle them both at the moment," Damian said. "Do you think it has something to do with the room?"

"I think so. Let's avoid going in there." Cato leaned against the wall crossing his arms. "I am not in the mood to try a threesome with those two," Damian growled. "Maybe you should go, get a little love in that heart for a second."

"Damian, Cato, come on," Anna begged as Ryan started to take off her underwear.

Damian felt his eyes get wide and Cato looked on the verge of passing out from stress. He needed to punch something and Cato was the closest one to him.

"Just try to get Anna to come over here Damian," Cato groaned. "Get her out of there and I bet this stupid love room will lose its affect."

Damian wanted to bash some heads in, but he had to try and give them the benefit of the doubt, "Fine. Switch me places."

Cato let out a sigh of relief and the traded spots in the little closet hallway. "Just, try to seduce her over here."

"Shut up," Damian spat. He closed his eyes and regained as much control as he could muster. "Anna, my love, come to me."

She looked between Ryan and Damian. Obviously torn between the two but Ryan would not relent. He wanted her attention and he did what he could to get it as he kissed down her thighs. Damian was going to have to put a little more effort into this.

"Ryan, Anna, come here and we will have some fun." Damian smiled. "Would you like that, Anna?"

She smiled and hopped off of the bed as giddy as could be. She pulled Ryan along with her to the entrance of the room but to Damian's disgust, Ryan still did not let up on kissing her neck. He bit her skin lightly leaving the faintest marks on her.

Fury was about to explode from his body.

Calm down. "Come here, love." Damian held out his hand to her and she took it blissfully without hesitation. Thank the gods.

Cato and Damian wrapped their hands around the other two's wrists while staying out of the room and yanked them into the hallway. The four of them narrowly missed landing on the basilisk's corpse. Ryan fell on top of Damian but he quickly pushed him off. He could not help his reaction as he began to pummel his fists into Ryan's skull.

His face was a mixture of shock and fear. The look on Ryan's face was welcome to Damian's angered ego and he punched him in the gut. Ryan grasped his stomach out of instinct and dropped his guard enough for Damian to land a hard blow on his cheek.

"You son of a bitch!" Damian growled.

"Get off of him," Cato struggled to pull Damian away from the now bloodied Ryan. He felt Anna's hands on him as well and his body tensed. Her touch was not welcomed.

"Damian please," Anna cried. "I don't know why we were doing that. Please Damian."

He glared at her but she looked on the verge of being sick herself. "How do you not know, Anna? His damn tongue was down your throat."

"I know. I have Ryan germs in my mouth." She looked pale. "It's gross."

Anna looked utterly disgusted and he felt a small ray of sunshine fill his heart. She did not want Ryan. That was really a first in his life that a woman preferred Damian to Ryan. Maybe they really didn't have control of their actions.

He turned to Ryan, who was pinching a bloody nose. "You bastard."

Ryan sat up against the wall with no shame about being dressed only in his black briefs. "I knew that room was evil."

"Anna, march in there and get your clothes on." She bashfully ran back into the Aphrodite room, trying her best to cover her body. "You son's of bitches better stay clear of that room."

"Damian, I am so sorry." Ryan tilted his head back while still pinching his nose. "I knew that room was familiar. Aphrodite was a little too into romance for my taste."

"And yet you still slept with her," Cato said.

Ryan shrugged. "She was gorgeous."

Anna came back out of the room, her cheeks were flushed and she still looked ill. Did the thought of Ryan really disgust her this much?

Ryan jumped up to leave Damian's death glare to gather his things from the room. Damian wanted to punch him at least one more time but he took a deep breath. He was the calm and collected one of the group. It was not their fault. *Calm yourself.*

Anna looked pitiful. "Are you okay?" Damian asked.

She laughed. "Am I okay? Are you?"

"I admit. I was about to kill you both. Thanks to Cato I didn't." Damian eyed his friend. "Then again, if I didn't insist on looking in the room you two would have went further than heavy petting."

"Please don't be upset with me." Anna looked on the verge of tears. His heart dropped seeing her cry. No matter how mad he was at the situation he knew she had no control over it.

He caressed her cheek and leaned in to kiss her. To his surprise she pulled away. "I'm not mad at you. It was just a surprise. Now let me kiss you and get those Ryan germs out of your mouth."

Thankfully, his girl grinned at him and she kissed him fiercely. "I love you, Damian."

"You too, babe."

"Okay, let's get a move on." Ryan reappeared fully dressed, but obviously apprehensive of Damian's mood. He would not even attempt to make eye contact, which Damian was glad about. He could forgive Anna for some unknown reason, but Ryan was a different story.

"Right, enough of the drama. Let's kill a damn Minotaur!" Cato clapped his hands together.

Chapter XXIII

Ryan

I F THERE WAS ONE person in the world he did not want it was Anna. She was like an annoying kid sister he could not get rid of and he had almost slept with her. He was disgusted. Revolted even, but there was nothing he could do about it.

In all honesty, he was surprised Damian did not kill him. If it were reversed he would have killed Damian in a heartbeat. Thankfully, Damian was content with just beating the hell out of him. He deserved it, even if he had no control over what he was doing.

It truly was an odd feeling though and he could not look at Anna the same. In fact, he avoided it as much as possible. Against his will, he had feelings for her and that temptation was still hiding deep inside. Hopefully he just needed to wait out whatever spell that might be lingering.

"Ugh." He shook his head trying to get the thoughts out

of his mind.

"What?" Cato asked.

They were walking side-by-side while Anna and Damian were farther up ahead. It seemed like neither one of them wanted to be near the couple right now. That, or Cato felt bad for Ryan.

Hours after the incident and Ryan still could not get the despicable thoughts out of his brain. "Just not happy about what happened."

"I don't think anyone is, but let's just never mention it again," Cato suggested.

"I think my face may need some time to recuperate," Ryan said.

Cato patted him on the back. "You sir, are a magnet for getting hurt. Just so you know."

"I've accepted that long ago."

"Good." Cato swat at the Minotaur's horn hanging around Ryan's neck. "What's this for?"

"A sure way to kill the Minotaur."

"Nice."

"Yep."

"Ryan, Cato, get up here," Damian called to them.

They both jogged to catch up and came upon another huge room. It looked like a gladiatorial arena. Dirt ground and high walls that made escape impossible and made him uneasy. Out of every life he lived, that was the most nerve wracking and scary time of his existence. It was a constant battle for his life with no sympathy or compassion.

"What the hell?" Cato grumbled.

"I don't want to go in there," Anna said. "Screw that."

"You're up, Ryan." Cato grinned.

He rolled his eyes and took a step into the arena. Cautiously looking around for another idiotic trap of some kind. He was not enjoying the reminiscent thoughts popping up in his mind.

Anna stood behind Damian at the doorway and Cato leaned against the opposite side. None of them were willing to head into the room with him. "You coming?"

Cato shook his head. "I don't want to possibly be your boy toy. No thanks."

Ryan ignored him and took more steps in. Nothing was in here. "Dead end I guess." There was no other door, just the one he came through and there was no way to climb the walls.

As he made his way back to the doorway, metal bars shot up from the ground at the door's entrance and blocked his exit. He shook the bars and saw the look of panic on his friend's faces. He knew it was impossible to budge them though it didn't stop him from trying his best. One thing was for certain, he was trapped and he did not want to find out what hell he was in for.

Behind him he heard a loud roar. His head dropped and he closed his eyes. He did not want to look.

"Ryan," Damian whispered, "get out of there now."

"What is it?" he asked, still refusing to look.

Damian inhaled deeply. "Our ticket home."

"Fabulous."

"Get the hell out of there," Cato urged. "We will find a way to fight it together."

"Good luck with that." Ryan gulped.

He turned around and saw the giant beast across the

room. It had to be at least eight feet tall with the head of bull and body of a muscular man. Foam dripped from its mouth and it was not the simple creature he imagined. This was a monster, a terrifying and muscular monster that was obviously in the mood to kill him.

As soon as Ryan turned around the monster bellowed out, obviously enraged and he had an idea as to why. The beast had just one horn and he spotted Ryan with a piece of his other one. Perhaps this was not a gift, but instead a sure way to get him killed.

"Get the fuck out of there!" Cato yelled.

Ryan turned back around to face his friends. "Damian, I am sorry for everything I've ever done to you. I don't want you to forgive me because I don't deserve it, but I want you to know that."

Damian looked as if he was going to speak so Ryan lunged away from the gate. He didn't want to hear anything, he needed to concentrate.

He took in his surroundings while never once turning his back to the Minotaur. The arena was a perfect circle. The tall walls towered over him with thousands of seats spread around the arena.

He had plenty of weapons. No doubt about that, but the one thing he knew would work on the beast was it's own horn, according to myth. It would unquestionably overpower him with ease so he needed to work his way around it.

It squat down and kept his eyes on Ryan. He stopped moving around. He had to be smart about this.

Ryan pulled the horn off from around his neck and gripped it tight. The anger in the beast's eyes was apparent and it made Ryan even more nervous. *Get a grip.*

Without warning, the beast charged toward him at full speed. Ryan ducked out of the way before it rammed him into the stone wall and spun on the ground. A large foot came stomping toward his head and Ryan rolled out of the way.

"Shoot it!" Cato yelled.

Ryan lunged toward the gate and laughed. "And break the piece of Brahma's staff? Are you crazy?"

"Move!" Damian yelled.

Ryan spin out of the way as a large fist narrowly missed his head. "Dammit!" Cato yelled.

Ryan turned around and saw Cato holding his nose. The Minotaur must have accidently hit him through the bars.

Ryan pulled out an extra dagger from his gear and now held one in each hand. As Damian distracted the beast by yelling obscenities at it, Ryan ran and jumped on the Minotaur's back. He stabbed it in the chest with his dagger and was tossed aside like a rag doll.

Before he could even process what happened he felt his body being lifted into the air and slammed down on the ground multiple times. His head spun. The arena went in and out of his sight. His body crashed to the floor one more time before he felt the weight of the beast's foot on his chest preventing him from breathing.

A booming roar filled the arena and he felt his body being lifted into the air again. He hung by his vest that was clutched in the Minotaur's large hands. His feet dangled off of the ground and it was difficult to keep his head up but they stared at one another. Its mouth foamed even more and its big brown eyes had no sign of pity in them. It wanted him dead.

It reared its head back to roar, breaking eye contact with Ryan long enough for him to thrust the horn dagger into the beast's throat. The once loud boom turned into a blood gurgling choke. It dropped Ryan instantly and he staggered to catch his balance.

The Minotaur fell to his knees, clutching at its throat, his hands quickly covered with blood. Ryan pulled the dagger out, watching the blood with interest pulsing out of the Minotaur's body. It looked up at him with its big brown eyes, but Ryan had no pity for the beast. Instead, he thrust the horn dagger into the top of the Minotaur's head with the last bit of energy he had.

"Goddamn," he groaned and fell to his knees.

He was tired and wanted to throw up. The gate must have opened because Damian caught Ryan before he fell. The room was spinning out of control.

"Are you okay?" Damian was worried. It was nice.

Ryan threw up on the dirt ground. When he was done he laid back in Damian's arms to close his eyes for just a bit of sleep.

"No resting for you," Damian declared. "You obviously have a concussion."

"No shit," Cato laughed and held onto his bloody nose. "You got banged harder than a hooker in Amsterdam."

Ryan laughed as best he could. "Yeah, that sucked."

He finally sat up on his own and stared at the Minotaur's body. Poor beast. Cursed by the god's and used as their tool. No doubt it would eventually come back to life though, like every other mythological being.

"Where did you say it was?" Cato asked as he unsheathed

his dagger.

"On his spine," Ryan muttered.

As Cato worked on cutting open the Minotaur, Ryan laid back on the dirt and stared at the stone cobble ceiling. "How are we going to get back?" he asked exasperatedly.

"I think I can help with that." A man's voice came from the seated area above the arena.

A man in hospital scrubs stood up and leaned over the edge of the wall and jumped over. Ryan cringed when he landed, but the fall did not seem to bother his limbs. Instead, the man casually sashayed over to them and put his hands on his hips. It was a feminine action that didn't seem to bother the man in the least.

"What a performance, Alexander." The man grinned, regardless of the dirty scowl Ryan could not contain. "Really, beat almost senseless and then, wham! Stabbed him in the throat. Bravo."

"And you are?" Cato asked.

"Oh, excuse me. How terribly rude of me." The tan man with pearly white teeth beamed. He looked like a fake doll of some kind. "I am Apollo, my dear Cato."

Ryan was most certainly taken by surprise. It had been years since he had actually come in contact with a God. Most of their commands were given by Ahmose, who had received it from the Council of Command—this was a rarity.

"What are you doing here?" Ryan's mouth gaped.

"A few things," Apollo said. "First, I would like to heal you."

Apollo snapped his fingers and Ryan felt his entire body feel at ease. His head was no longer spinning and any ache was virtually gone.

"Much better. So handsome without a bloody head." Apollo winked at Cato who seemed just as alarmed as Ryan was. "Second of all, I would like to offer you a way out of here. The Sirens seem to be waiting to kill you all and I think that is bad sport given you are going to save their existence."

"No offense, but why are you doing this?" Ryan asked. "The Gods are not supposed to get involved."

Apollo grit his teeth. "I do not have much power left in me, but I do have some. Father does not know I am here. It is the least I can do for your quest to save our existence. Also, I'd rather not have more of our believers dead. That would make our existence problematic as well. There are not many of you left."

"By 'father' you mean…" Damian started.

"Zeus." Apollo grinned brightly. "Although, Father spends most of his time as an airline pilot these days so he is kept rather busy."

That little tidbit didn't make Ryan happy whatsoever. They were fighting to keep the world at bay for the gods and they were playing doctor and being pilots? Was this all really worth it? *Yes.* It had to be and he needed to stop thinking as if he were a member of the Risen. They were the enemy, but after coming to the island he started to question his beliefs.

"So you are going to give us a ride home?" Cato grinned. "On your chariot or what?"

Apollo laughed a fake and disturbing chuckle. "No of course not. I will just bring you there. It saves time, don't you think?"

Apollo snapped his fingers and they appeared in Ryan's

room back at the Domus. Ryan panicked. "Did you get it, Cato?" If he didn't have the piece of Brahma's staff it would off all been for nothing.

Cato's face was pale, but he lifted up the bloody piece and tossed it to Ryan. "I didn't like that."

"I forget you human's have weak stomachs while traveling." Apollo chuckled. "You will live. For a long time in fact, so no worries."

Cato's eyes dodged over to Apollo. "Good to know."

"Eat a cracker and you will be fine." Apollo winked. "Good luck Warriors with your upcoming war. Oh, Alexander, may I have a word?"

Ryan was whisked onto his balcony by Apollo. The usual sounds of a happy city seemed eerily quiet. What was going on with Urbs?

"Alexander," Apollo started, "you know that I can tell the future correct?"

Ryan rolled his eyes at the sound of his old name. "Yes, and please call me Ryan."

"That is not your name, Alexander. Your father would disapprove."

"My father is long dead and I could care less what he thinks about my name choices."

"He is not dead, but one day you will understand," said Apollo. "Anyhow, I cannot see the exact outcome of things to arise, but I can see certain things. One of which will be very difficult for you to do."

"Such as?" Ryan asked.

"Sadly, I am forbidden to say, however I want you to understand that it is for the best. Do not dwell on the deaths of friends during this battle and you will succeed in your mission. Otherwise, you will certainly fail and the entire world as we know it will collapse into a place of pure misery."

"Amara mentioned something along those lines. About her, can you—"

"No," Apollo interrupted. "She must remain on that island."

"Why? She is the only true human on that island, besides the whole seeing the future thing," Ryan insisted. "She seems like a good person."

"Everything on that island is there for a reason, Ryan. She is there for a reason as well and will remain there because of it," Apollo answered. "I have seen what she would do with freedom and it is not good. She has become a greedy trickster and will do anything to gain her freedom. Leave her there."

Who was he to argue with a god? Though, he had made a promised and it was against his morality to break it. She was odd, but kind and Cato cared for her greatly.

"She does not give a damn about Cato." Apollo seemed to read his mind. "I promise you, freeing her will cause nothing but problems."

"I'll take your word for it." Ryan gave up for the time being.

"Good." Apollo smiled brightly once again. "I will leave you now. There is a pair of breasts that need enhanced with my name on them."

He pulled Ryan into a big hug. "Oh, okay." It was an awkward exchange.

"Take care, Alexander."

Julia

"What do you mean you don't know where they are?" Julia screamed at Emma who was fallowing behind her. "They have been gone for days and no one has heard from them."

"Do you expect me to keep track of them or something? I thought that was your job," Emma hissed. Her long blonde hair trailed behind her.

Julia stopped in her tracks. "You were Ryan's little pet. I would have thought your obsession with him would have been somewhat useful."

Emma laughed. "Do you really think I am that desperate? Ryan is done with me and I with him."

Julia crossed her arms and pointed at Ryan's door. "Open it."

"Do I look like your slave?"

"You said he wasn't in there so prove me wrong." Julia glared. "Unless you are hiding something."

Emma bit her lip. The bitch better be afraid of her. Julia had no idea where entire groups of Warriors were and it was her job to keep track of them. At the moment, she was failing and the General did not take kindly to failure.

Emma grudgingly opened Ryan's door, the sight inside made Julia immediately irate. There sat Ryan and his little posse. "You lying little bitch." She slapped Emma across the face.

Emma's eyes widened in horror. She probably did not expect such actions from her, but things changed. For some reason she felt satisfied as Emma turned and ran away from her.

Ryan stood up and crossed his room looking livid. Julia noticed he and the others were in full gear. According to Grace they ventured somewhere but she could not remember where exactly. All she knew was that she had not heard a damn thing from them and that made her suspicious.

"What the hell was that for?" Ryan spat.

Julia smirked. "Who cares? Little witch had is coming."

"I don't think she deserved to be hit. Whatever she did could have been talked about between you two," Ryan insisted.

She laughed. "You're one to talk. Always using Aden as a punching bag."

"What can I say? I like beating up the nasty little vermin you're dating." Ryan faked a smiled. "Seriously Julia, was that necessary?" She could see the worry in his eyes. Probably for his little pet.

She wanted to stab him right then and there, but she forced herself to remain calm. "Where the hell have you been? I have a mission for you and your little group of crusaders."

"Sorry but we have other things to do." Ryan crossed his arms.

"Such as?"

"Things," he repeated.

She narrowed her eyes and looked past him toward Cato. He stared at the ground and avoided her gaze as he sat on the couch. He looked pale. Anna and Damian talked between one another and occasionally looked in her direction. These little deceivers were up to something.

"I don't care what you have to do. Grace and Colette are missing and we need to rescue them," she said. "While we were in the mortal world they were caught by the Risen and

I was knocked unconscious. I couldn't find them anywhere."

Ryan's attitude seemed to change. He was obviously torn. "I'm sorry, but I can't help."

"You're kidding, right?" she growled. "What is so important that you can't help save one of your own?"

Ryan looked back at his group. "I just can't."

"Why did Anna even journey wherever you went? She isn't on your team." The question popped in her mind.

"She doesn't have a team and she wanted to help," Ryan answered. "Sorry we won't be able to assist you."

He started to close the door and she pushed it back open harshly. "This is Grace and Colette we are talking about Ryan. What is wrong with you?" Julia decided to push past Ryan and into his room. This time she received everyone's attention.

"Hey sis," Cato mumbled.

"Don't 'hey sis' me," she spat. "You all, with the exception of Anna, will push off and rescue Grace and Colette."

Damian stood up. "You are not, nor will you ever be the master of this Domus. You cannot tell us what to do."

"Since when did you grow a backbone?" She laughed. "You will. Or would you like to explain what is so important you have to do?"

"That's none of your business," Ryan said.

"I can make it my business." She smirked. "How would you like me following you nonstop?"

Ryan rolled his eyes at her and she felt a win in her favor. She knew that freeing Grace and Colette was wrong. The General had them captured, but she could not go through with it. They were her family no matter what. Risen or no Risen, they were the only people in the world that understood her. One day she hoped to make them see that light but on her own terms. Not the General's.

"Fine." Ryan gave in.

"Good." She grinned. "Ryan, Cato, and Damian get your things together. We will leave as soon as possible. Oh wait, looks like you are all ready to go."

"I'm not going anywhere without Anna." Damian glared. It was awfully brave of him to look at her in such a manner.

Julia smirked. "She is not going. This mission needs experts. No offense." She looked Anna up and down.

"No problem," Anna sneered.

Ryan gave Cato an odd look that she could not figure out.

Cato cleared his throat. "Yeah, I think I will stay here and watch things while you are gone."

"Are you serious?" She wanted to scream at them all. "We need at least three. You know that's how we do things around here."

"I have someone in mind," Ryan piped up. "If you want my help then deal with who I choose. Otherwise, fuck off."

Julia wanted to punch him. "Fine. Be ready in two hours. Whoever the person is, they better stay out of my way and actually contribute instead of hold us back."

She turned on her heel and stalked out of the room. Those stupid people will regret how terrible they just treated her. One day, she will make them all pay for their idiocy or they would all die in the process.

Chapter XXIV

Anna

"WHAT THE HELL, RYAN?" Damian asked. "We need to get the third piece of Brahma's staff. We don't have time to save anyone."

Ryan sat on his bed and pealed off his gear. "That is exactly why you three are going to head that way and I will be going with Julia." He hung his head low and Anna felt so sorry for him. Poor guy had to be around the woman he loved that seemed to have grown into the biggest bitch she had ever seen.

"How the heck are we going to do that without you?" Cato paced around Ryan's room. "You know more about it than us."

Ryan laughed. "Why would you think I would know about it? I have a basic knowledge of the place, but I have never been there Cato. You three will do fine. We will meet up back here after both our missions are complete."

Damian sat back down next to Anna on the couch and

rubbed his face. He looked tired and full of sorrow. Anna reached out and placed her arm around his shoulders. She had no idea how to help him feel better.

"Ryan, we cannot do this without you," Damian finally said.

"You have to and you will," Ryan answered. "I knew you would not leave Anna, and Cato will be your third. Julia was right about one thing—we work best in groups of three."

"I don't like this," Damian groaned.

"Neither do I. In a perfect world we would be going together, but that isn't the case. Julia suspects us and I know she isn't herself. We are all aware she may be the enemy and I will not risk what we have been working so hard to accomplish, just because you guys think you need me."

Cato laughed. "We do need you. You're our leader."

"You two have always been just as capable as me—if not more," Ryan said. "I have the fullest confidence in you all."

Anna watched the three men with interest. They were such different personalities and yet one family. She liked being a part of it, but she couldn't help feeling as if she would get in the way. They did not need her on this last mission. These last two missions she helped because she was Catholic and a woman. However, this one she was just another body and potentially someone that will just get in the way.

She was not trained for this. Everyone knew it. Experience was key when being an Immortal Warrior. Damian would not let her out of his sight and she just hoped she would not mess things up too badly for them.

"I don't like it," Damian repeated. "We are a team. It's always been us."

Ryan rolled his eyes. "I really don't see another option, Damian."

Cato nodded. "There isn't. I just know you would never fail, Ryan. I don't know what I'd do if we failed on our first solo mission."

"Well, it's about time we find out." Ryan smirked. "I truly believe you guys will be fine. If I didn't, I would have suggested one of you left with Julia instead of me."

"Can I say something?" Anna asked. The three men looked at her. "Well, it's more of a question really."

"What?" Ryan asked.

"Who's the third person?"

Julia

Those bastards. Those cocky, deceitful, sheep of the gods lied to her face about their whereabouts. Cato could never keep a secret from her and she knew everything Ryan said was a lie. Why would they keep it from her? Did they suspect anything?

She paced in frustration and threw a pillow across her room in a vain attempt of releasing some anger. Remaining calm was key and her aggravation was obvious when she spoke with them. They must not suspect a thing. It would ruin it all and at some point she needed to convince them to switch sides. It was an impossible task, but she would not give up on her brother so easily. No matter what, he was still her flesh and blood.

Who was this third person Ryan was going to bring? *Oh*

who cares? Whoever it is will probably die in the attempt to save Grace and Colette anyways. They were her targets.

Stress weighed heavily on her, as it had for many days now. Grace and Colette were branded the enemy and would not conform to the Risen's cause. She could not, for the life of her, go to them and try to convince them herself. According to Aden they were being tortured into acceptance of the future, as was Ahmose. Julia could not bear the thought, but it was not her choice. Nothing was her choice anymore.

She slipped off her black dress and kicked off her heels. There were preparations that needed to be made before she left and that didn't include revealing clothing. Aden preferred her this way, but did she?

She heard her door shut which brought her from her thoughts. Aden stood in her room, leaning against the closed door with a smirk upon his lips. "Well, hello gorgeous."

The corner of her mouth raised into a half smile. "Hello," she answered and realized she was standing in front of him wearing only her undergarments.

Part of her wanted to cover herself but she had to remind herself that he has seen her in the most private setting. It still felt odd to her, but she loved him regardless.

"Come." He held his hand out to her and she awkwardly made her way over to him. "I have something for you."

Inside, she panicked. What could it be now? He had lavished her with gifts since he brought her from the General's home and it was becoming very suffocating.

"Sit." He'd lead her to her love seat and she obeyed. "Close her eyes."

She did as she was told and heard his breathing increase.

What now Aden?

"Open," he commanded.

Julia stared at the little box in his hand. A huge diamond ring was nestled in padding of the box and gleamed in the sunlight. It was in the shape of an oval and surrounded by blue diamonds. The first thought that popped in her head was, *no.*

"I have waited quite some time to ask you this. I realize I should have wooed you before getting down on one knee with some flowers or chocolates. I couldn't wait any longer—I felt as if I were going to burst." He smiled a bright white smile. "Marry me, Julia." Aden took her left hand in his and kissed her knuckles.

Her heart dropped. Inside she screamed *no!* Instead she said, "Yes."

Aden grinned and slid the ring on her finger. He pulled her into a massive hug and lifted her into the air. "I love you."

"I love you too." She grinned. It felt wrong. Why did it feel wrong?

He tried to pull her to her bed, but she stopped in her tracks. She did not want to lay with him. She needed to get ready to betray their people for just a few moments in order to save her family.

He gave her a hurt look. "What's wrong?"

She shook her head and laughed. "I am sorry Aden, but I must get ready. I need to take a little vacation before the ritual is performed and clear my head. I need to relax before our work truly begins."

To her relief he smiled. "I understand. Just make sure you take your tonic. You know how your head hurts if you don't."

Was it going to be this easy to get away?

"I'll take plenty with me don't worry." She returned his smile. Good, he believed her. Now it was just a matter of staying off the Risen's radar and not being seen.

He hugged her once more. "You have made me the happiest man in the world. Don't take too long on your trip, my love. The General wants us by his side."

"I know." She kissed him gently on the lips. "I will only be gone for a few days, maybe less depending on how bored I get."

Aden smirked and kissed her passionately. "You are mine forever. Don't you forget it."

Ryan

Ryan changed out of his worn gear and clothes and begun to redress. Anna had of course turned the other way and he was thankful. After what happened he did not want to see her much either.

"Don't you think you should at least rest?" Damian suggested. "We have been up for a day straight."

"I don't think her highness will be okay with that." Ryan smirked. "I don't even know where we are going."

Cato shook his head in frustration. "Can't we wait until you get back?" He would not let it go.

"No. Who knows how long this will take?" Ryan sighed. "You guys are going without me. Deal with it and prepare. I want you all to get some rest and replenish yourselves though.

I have a feeling it will be a tiring trip."

He pulled on a clean black shirt and sat down on the edge of his bed to lace up his boots. Everything he wore to the island was gross and somewhat destroyed in spots. He was glad he kept spares of everything.

Damian and Cato would not stop watching him. Even the air in the room felt tense and he was almost glad to get away from his team. They depended on him too much and this would be good for them and Ryan as well.

"What?" he asked finally, sick of their stares.

Cato shook his head once again. "Nothing."

Ryan stomped down his foot after he laced it up. "Look, I'd rather go. Believe me. I don't see a way around this and I want to try and decipher whatever is going on with Julia."

That got Cato's attention. "Yeah, that's good. Do that."

Ryan nodded and turned to Damian. "Make sure you let the people of Shambhala know what you are there for. I don't want them murdering you. Judging by the myths, they don't take well to outsiders. Then again most of those stories are hearsay. No one really knows what the place is like. For all we know it could be abandoned."

Damian looked sick. He was now the leader of the group and it was a position he never really excelled at. "Okay."

Ryan strapped on his vest and looked around his walls for the best weapons for this type of mission. A few pistols and knives, couldn't forget his helmet this time. Night vision would be a must and so would silencers. Swords were probably going to be useless, but he decided to bring one anyways.

He yawned. He was exhausted. Thanks to Apollo's healing though he no longer felt pain though the need to take the pills still remained.

"Please convince her to let you rest," Damian almost pleaded.

"No can do." Ryan smirked. "Need anything else before I leave?"

"Just hide the damn piece and I think that's it." Cato said.

Ryan grabbed it from off his desk and wiped the blood off with a red rag he used to polish his weapons with. He removed the floorboard where the other piece was and took it out. As he brought the two pieces close together they acted as a magnet. Coming together, a mend was made between the breaks and looked as if they had never been separated.

With a deep breath he replaced the fuller piece back into its hiding place and stood up. "Well that was interesting."

"So it's just going to be one, long spine staff thing?" Anna finally spoke.

Ryan smirked. "No."

"But its a spine right?" she asked.

"No, at some point someone carved it to look like a spine," Ryan answered.

"Okay." She raised an eyebrow. "So what is it really?"

"A stick. But it's actually shaped more like a T."

"That is stupid," she mumbled.

"Anything else we need to discuss?" Ryan asked. He was dressed and ready to head off. Equipped with as much as he could be without losing his ability to sneak around. He was prepared to kill as many members of the Risen as possible.

Damian grimaced. "No."

Ryan stood awkwardly in front of the three people in his room. They were side by side looking at him and he did not know what he expected. Tears? Perhaps one last proposal for him to tag along? He did not know.

"Alright then. Good luck." He held out his hand to Anna, which she hesitantly took.

Cato patted him on the back. "Keep Julia safe."

Ryan agreed to and turned his attention to Damian. He held his hand out to him, but Damian pulled him into a hug. Relieved that Damian must have forgiven him for what happened in Aphrodite's room, he closed his eyes and embraced his best friend.

He felt like this was it for them and he did not want to let go. Damian wiped his nose on the back of his sleeve and stared at the floor. "Good luck, Alexander."

"And to you, Hephaestion."

Chapter XXV

Ryan

HE MADE HIS WAY to the Parlor room and found Julia waiting for him. Her hair was pulled back into a tight bun and her helmet adorned her head. She looked good in her gear. *Really good.*

Black was not his favorite color on her, but when she was dressed for success and he really enjoyed the view. "Hey."

She glared. "Hi."

What is her problem now?

Ryan strapped on his helmet and they stood in silence starring at one another. She was so angry now. Although he did not want to admit it, he knew deep down she was not herself. This was not Julia and she was not on their side. Either way, he could not force himself to do anything about it.

"Where is this third person?" Julia inquired.

Ryan let out a deep sigh. "I just stopped by their room

and they will be here shortly. They had to get ready."

"Who is it?" Julia's scowl was baffling. "I prefer you and your team given your success rate, but it seems that you all have other plans in mind."

"They are tired and need rest." It was all he could figure out to say.

Julia smiled, but the kindness did not meet her eyes. "Secrets are deadly. Remember that."

"You would do well to remember it too," said Ryan.

Once again, their staring commenced and the silence was getting extremely uncomfortable. He took the time to study her. Her eyes were rimmed in darkness as if she were about to go to a bar tonight instead of a mission. Her figure was slimming down, but her lips remained the pale pink color he always loved. It was the one sign that gave him any indication she was the same woman he had known for years.

"What?" she finally asked.

"What?" he mimicked.

"You're starring at me."

"Yes."

"Why?"

"I am trying to figure out what went wrong with you," Ryan answered honestly.

She laughed. "Nothing is wrong. I grew up."

"I was unaware that grown up meant becoming a total bitch." Ryan smiled sweetly. "Or perhaps it's because you now have experience under your belt and that requires an attitude change."

"Experience?" she asked.

"Seems you have become quite scandalous as of lately."

Anger filled inside of him as he said it. He hated that she has known another man. Ryan especially hated that the other man was Aden.

Julia peeled off her glove and held up her left hand. To his amazement he did not lose his control in that moment. On her hand sat a huge, oval diamond ring and on a particular finger that gave away it's purpose.

"You are going to marry that little fucker?" Ryan hissed. His jealousy crawled up out of his belly and into words he could not control. "Are you losing your goddamn mind, Julia?"

"Unlike you," she replaced her glove back on, "Aden shows his true feelings. He loves me and I love him. That is what people in love do. They get married."

"You haven't even been with him that long!" He contained a scream of disgust.

"What does it matter to you Ryan?" She laughed. "Every time you have married someone it was for your own personal agenda. Did they have a choice? Never. You are selfish and care for no one. Don't try and fool yourself into thinking otherwise."

"I loved you." It escaped him. "So much so, I knew you would be better without me."

She froze and he caught her eye twitch and her hands shook ever so slightly. "You are incapable of it."

"Are you okay?" he asked and took a step toward her. Her body was acting oddly and he worried for her.

She backed away. "Yes."

"You're shaking."

"So?"

"Why are you shaking?"

"I don't know," she admitted and held her hands behind her back.

He approached her and grabbed ahold of her shoulders. He looked her square in the eyes. "Julia, talk to me. What is going on with you?" She tried to pull away, but he could see her falter. He had no idea what was going on with her. "Are you having a panic attack?"

"I'm fine."

"Sorry, I'm late." A voice came from behind him.

Zee stood there ready in her gear and looked between Ryan and Julia awkwardly. Julia pulled away from Ryan and he could see the fury build in her eyes.

"Are you fucking kidding me?" she screamed at him.

Ryan's mouth dropped open. "Uh—"

"You stupid son of a bitch." Julia pushed him and pointed at Zee. "Her? That's who you picked?"

Ryan knew she would be upset, but this was a little much. "She is good and we don't have any other options."

"Oh gee, thanks." Zee crossed her arms.

"No." Julia glared at Zee and Ryan felt instant regret. He had no idea she would act so upset about Zee. It wasn't as if he was with her or had even slept with the woman.

"We are running out of time and I don't understand your distaste for her. This is about Grace and Colette so get over it."

Julia's attention snapped back to Ryan. "Whatever." She tossed a crystal in front of her and whispered their destination. "But if she slows us down I won't hesitate to cut our loses with her."

Ryan knew Zee wouldn't slow them down so he ignored

Julia's fit. They proceeded through the portal. "Washington D.C.? Really?"

"Where else would their headquarters be in the United States?" Julia asked. "It's the capital of the country."

"Technically we are in Arlington." Zee looked around and he notice Julia roll her eyes.

Snow flurries fell to the ground. It was almost morning here and they were in the middle of Arlington Cemetery. White headstones lined the ground in perfect symmetry and trees broke up the sections of the fallen. It was a place of sadness to Ryan. It reminded him of how frail human existence is and how even the bravest of individuals fall.

He was glad they were on the stone walkway instead of in the midst of the graves although he still was confused as to why they were here. This was certainly not a place to hold prisoners.

"Why are we here?" Ryan asked.

Julia looked around the area. "This is the closest we can get without being detected."

He felt the sadness of the surrounding area creep inside of his very being. "Where exactly are we trying to go?"

"The Smithsonian."

If you loved OBSCURE, Don't miss out on book three of
THE INFINITE SERIES,
INDEFINITE.

Anna

ANNA WOKE UP NEXT to Damian and smiled. He was so cute when he slept. His hair was disheveled and his mouth hung open. The only thing she didn't care for was the man's snoring. Not just baby snores either, but huge manly snores that woke her up. She was surprised he didn't wake himself with the force of his snoring either.

They were in his room, hers still didn't feel like home, and they decided to get some good sleep before they left for Shambhala. She looked out the window and it looked as if they'd slept an entire day. It was worth it though. She was exhausted after their last mission and now she felt refreshed.

She sat up on the edge of the bed and stretched her arms into the air. As she made her way to Damian's mirror she gasped in horror. She looked terrible. Her hair was a rat's nest and her clothes were winkled.

She hurriedly brushed her hair with her fingers and slapped her cheeks to bring some color to her face. Her workout clothes doubled as pajamas and she couldn't care less at this point. Damian never cared what she looked like.

"Good morning beautiful." She heard behind her.

Damian was propped up on his elbow and looked at her with such an amused gaze that she felt her cheeks blush.

"Morning."

"How did you sleep?" he asked.

She laughed and fell back onto the bed with him. "Not as well as you, sir snore-a lot."

This time he blushed and ran his hand through his hair. It's not fair how his hair went from mess to instantly fixed in just one swipe of his hand. Being a guy was so much easier.

"How about we wander around Urbs today?" He seemed bothered by her snoring nickname. "We can leave tomorrow for Shambhala."

"Do you think we should wait another day?" She was worried they would not have time for everything.

"It will be fine." Damian was not very convincing, but she took his word for it. "I just want to see what's going on with Urbs before we leave. Make sure the people are doing okay and not suffering."

Anna nodded even though she doubted things were okay. At this time of day she was already used to the sounds of a bustling city below, but now there was nothing but silence. No sounds of children playing or deals being made in the market. The smells of food were not coming through the window making her hungry. It broke her heart. She could only imagine how Damian must feel given he had made this his home a long time ago.

"Okay, I will go get dressed and meet you in the front." She smirked and ran off to her room.

She changed quickly into jeans and a tank top and sighed. Why couldn't she look as flawless as Julia everyday? Oh well, there was no time to try and put some effort in her appearance. So she threw her hair up in a ponytail and made her way to the entrance of the Domus.

Damian was leaning against one of the large columns at the top of the steps. She paused and watched him stare out at Urbs for a minute. Just by his body language she could tell he was upset and for good reason. There was no movement down below and no one in the streets from what she could see. Symbols of the Risen were plastered everywhere, even visible from here.

"Ready?" she interrupted his thoughts.

Damian turned around and she could see through his forced smile. "Come." He held out his hand to her and she took it.

They made their way down the steps and into the streets. Windows were closed and businesses were empty. It seemed like a ghost town and she did not realize she was pressing in close to Damian.

"Are you okay?" he asked and put his arm around her waist.

Truthfully, it made her uneasy to be here. "Yeah."

They turned a corner into what she called China Town and saw movement ahead. They both stopped and Damian pushed her behind him. Neither of them had weapons, which was probably a bad idea.

"This wasn't a good plan was it?" she asked. "It feels wrong being out here."

He nodded. "The city is a no man's land. I think we should go back."

Anna took a deep breath and they turned to leave. No one was in sight still and she felt relieved until she noticed a small red dot on Damian's back. She panicked, "Stop."

Damian did as she said and turned around. The little red dot was now on his chest and he noticed. "Shit."

They both looked around the roofs of the buildings and saw a man pointing a gun at them. Damian held up his hands. "What is this about?" he yelled.

The man on the roof said nothing, but a voice came from down below, "What are you doing out here?"

Anna watched as three men came into view from an alley and held various weapons in their hands. The one that spoke was in the middle, carrying a hammer and she would have thought it was funny until she saw the makeshift knife tied to the end.

He had long blond hair pulled back in a ponytail and a wound on his face that had barely started to heal. Despite everything she had been through this past week, she still felt nervous and was thankful when Damian pushed her behind him once again.

"We just came from the Domus and were checking the city out. That's it." He took a step toward them and the men held up their weapons ready for a fight. "We got back from the mortal world and noticed things have obviously changed."

"No, you think?" The man laughed. "The city is closed off. Anyone on the streets is fair game."

"What does that mean?" Damian asked.

"It means I can kill you if I please and take whatever it is you have." The man grinned wickedly.

Damian's shoulders tensed and she wished she could see his face. "You're kidding right? Why would you do that?"

"The Risen has given permission for us to do as we please with those who don't convert. Seeing as you're from the Domus, I bet you two aren't part of the club." He held up his hammer and laughed. "This is where you run."

ACKNOWLEDGEMENTS

Thanks to all the crazy people in my life. The ones I like anyways. You guys keep me sane whenever things get rough.

Also, thank you to my kids for going to bed on time so I could spend a few hours each night working on these books. You two are awesome! Momma loves you. Just quit using the bathtub as your toilet, okay?

Thank you to the amazing team of women that help me with these books. You guys put up with so much nonsense from me. I'm just full of questions aren't I?

Oh, and a big thanks goes out to my mom and dad for giving me life. That was pretty splendid of you.

I know it was in my dedication but again, thank you to our troops. As a fictional writer I romanticize war, but believe me, I am not foolish enough to believe I have even skimmed the surface of how combat really is.

A few of my friends served in the military and have helped me with this book and I want to thank you for that as well. I can't imagine it is something you guys wanted to talk about but you did it without a second thought. Love you guys.

About the Author

Nicole Corine Dyer is an author from Kansas with a Degree in Liberal Arts. After having her two children, she finally gained the courage to write her first novel, Infinite. With Obscure, book two of The Infinite Series out, she is working tirelessly on the third installment.

Her life is all about work. Day job, raising two children on her own, or writing the stories created in her mind; the hard work is never ending.

There have been ups and downs, moments of second-guessing, and endless nights staying up later then a person should. You may love it. You may hate it. There will always be a person on either side of the fence but that won't stop Nicole for putting her stories out there.

Contact Nicole
Website: www.nicolecorinedyer.com
Facebook: Author Nicole Corine Dyer
Email: nicolecorinedyer@gmail.com
Goodreads Author Nicole Corine Dyer

OTHER BOOKS

THE INFINITE SERIES
Infinite, Book 1

Made in the USA
Columbia, SC
13 August 2020

16316127R00219